TEMPTI

Rowena reached down to ease her trainer free. Charlotte responded with a little whimper, as much excitement as fear, and her hands went to the button of her jeans. She looked up, big brown eyes still wet with tears, as she rose a little to push her jeans down over the swell of her hips, and lower, exposing full-cut pink knickers decorated with white polka dots.

Rowena caught the scent of her lover's sex on the still, warm air. 'Bare,' she ordered, 'and your top too, right off.'

Charlotte was shaking visibly as she continued to strip. The panties came down, and off, exposing the full, meaty peach of her bottom. The big cheeks were quivering slightly in anticipation of the coming pain.

'Right, you wanted this, so no complaints.'

By the same author:

THE RAKE
MAIDEN
TIGER, TIGER
DEVON CREAM
PURITY
CAPTIVE
DEEP BLUE
PLEASURE TOY
VELVET SKIN
PEACHES AND CREAM
INNOCENT
SATAN'S SLUT
WENCHES, WITCHES AND STRUMPETS
DEMONIC CONGRESS
WHIPPING GIRL
CREAM TEASE
NATURAL DESIRE, STRANGE DESIGN
PRINCESS
CRUEL SHADOW
SIN'S APPRENTICE
CONCEIT AND CONSEQUENCE

TEMPTING THE GODDESS

Aishling Morgan

This book is a work of fiction.
In real life, make sure you practise safe, sane and
consensual sex.

First published in 2005 by
Nexus
Thames Wharf Studios
Rainville Road
London W6 9HA

www.eburypublishing.co.uk

Typeset by TW Typesetting, Plymouth, Devon

Printed and bound in Great Britain by Clays Ltd, St Ives PLC

ISBN 978-0-3523-4613-1

You'll notice that we have introduced a set of symbols onto our book jackets, so that you can tell at a glance what fetishes each of our brand new novels contains. Here's the key – enjoy!

cp (traditional)

cp (modern)

spanking

restraint/bondage

rope bondage/hojojutsu

latex/rubber/leather/enclosure

fem dom

willing captivity

medical

period setting

uniforms

sex rituals

Prologue

Her fingers trembling, Charlotte fumbled the buttons of her blouse open one by one. Beyond the window, the western sky was still flushed with the setting sun, a welter of gold, pink, and the red of new blood, virgin blood, the blood which would soon be trickling from her torn hymen and smeared down the length of her lover's beautiful pink cock . . .

She paused to watch the colours fade, her fingers on the last button, her blouse half open to show the full swell of the inner curves of her breasts reflected in the window pane. A curious melancholy, and a touch of fear, filled her as she watched the sun go down on her last day as a virgin, as a Maiden. When it rose again she would know how it felt to take a man's penis inside her and, if they were blessed, pregnant, in transition, from Maiden to Mother.

As the last sliver of the great red disc vanished behind the distant bulk of Dartmoor her lips were pursed tight. She was fighting down her qualms as she continued to undress, now hurriedly, and to force down the images of disapproval that came unbidden to her mind; her father, her mother, the sisters at school, Father Dawson, ranked in angry incomprehension at her denial of their life, of their God.

The images only stiffened her resolve, and as she pushed her jeans to the floor and kicked her shoes away she could feel the heat growing in her belly, the heat of desire she had so often been told to suppress, to ignore, denying her needs in favour of propriety and the cold comfort of the church. She needed what she was about to do, needed her body naked to the world, spread on an altar to her lover's cock.

It was an outrage, an outrage so profound that there would be no going back. There would be no more talk of her wilfulness, no more chances to repent, no more of Father Dawson's self-righteous little smiles. Instead he'd look on her in horror and, as she pushed off her panties to go fully nude, her mouth had curved up into a small, wicked smile ... only as new guilt filled her at the thought of Rowena.

With a last, angry glance at her watch, Rowena turned to the other girls.

'Her bitch of a mother must have kept her back!'

Andrea gave a sympathetic nod. Eve turned shy eyes to the ground. The other five, still climbing from Poppy's 4 × 4, didn't respond. Rowena waited a moment more, peering into the gathering dusk for the headlights of Charlotte's car. The lane stretched empty as far as she could see, with the bulk of Stonebarrow Hill black against the sky beyond. She shook her head.

'No, she's not coming.'

She switched on her torch, waiting until Poppy had locked the car before starting into Berne Woods where a muddy path opened between thick hedges of hawthorn and bramble. Footprints showed in the wet earth, human and dog, and a scattering of litter. The girls followed in line, speaking in excited whispers despite the loneliness of the night. Others might come, she knew, lovers seeking a quiet place to fuck, the boys' hard cocks penetrating warm, willing mouths and wet, eager pussies ...

Her mouth set in irritation as she pushed the thought from her mind. Unthinkable to let her mind dwell on men, not on Beltane, not on the night when they would be celebrating motherhood and the birth of the year. Tonight, men were irrelevant, and not to be tolerated, the rite reserved exclusively for women. Not even Nich Mordaunt had been invited to join them, for all his knowledge and understanding, or the warm feeling in her belly his presence invariably produced. It was unthinkable for any male to see what they were about to do.

The girls' whispered conversation grew quieter as they moved deeper into the wood, and stopped as they reached their destination, a ring of thirteen squat grey standing stones set in a circular clearing. Now silent save for the occasional whispered remark or instruction, they set about their tasks, gathering wood to build a fire at the centre, laying the fresh green Beltane cloths over the stones, Rowena mixing incense and the powder that would bring them up to ecstasy as they became one with the Goddess.

Mr Pedlow felt a tremor of excitement as he looked out over the irregular black mass of Berne Woods. The girls were out again, he could hear them, and catch the red flicker of their fires. His tongue flicked out to moisten his thick, pale lips, and he felt his cock twitch in his underwear. They'd be down to their bras and panties, he knew, maybe just their panties, round young breasts bouncing and quivering to the motions of their dance, cheeky bottoms snug in tight material. Maybe they'd even be nude, naughty little things that they were, bare bums, and bare, furry, cunts . . .

He put his hand to his crotch, squeezing the fat bulge of his cock and balls as he thought of what he was going to do, what he knew he could not possibly

3

stop himself from doing. Stepping back through the open French windows, he hurried up to his room. Everything was there, in readiness for the night; black boots, thick black trousers, a heavy black overcoat, binoculars, his powerful new digital SLR, his little bag of assorted creams.

Ready, his fleshy body trembling in anticipation, his cock already half stiff at the thought of all the naked or near-naked female flesh that awaited him, he made his way downstairs and out into the night. As he made his way across the field Berne Woods loomed close, and among the trees the darkness became absolute save for the occasional glimmer of firelight. Moving forward by touch alone, every footstep taken with care, he crept closer, catching first the smell of wood smoke, then the heady incense he had come to associate so strongly with the girls' antics that it quickly turned his erection to a rigid, aching bar.

Charlotte pulled the scarlet silk shift down over her head just as a gentle knock sounded at the door. The shift was a little tight, clinging across her breasts to accentuate their roundness and the stiff buds of her nipples, so that she had to fight down a trace of embarrassment as she answered. For a moment the throb of music from downstairs grew louder as the door opened, admitting Nich, the expression on his long, pale face one of gentle complicity.

'You are ready?' he asked.

Charlotte nodded. The shift covered her from neck to ankles, and yet she was acutely conscious of her nudity beneath, the swell of her breasts and bottom, but mainly the warm, urgent feeling in her sex. Her cheeks prickled in a blush as Nich's eyes moved down her body and his light, disarming smile grew to

4

something altogether more masculine. She swallowed, and let out the question she'd already asked of every more experienced friend.

'Does it hurt?'

'A little,' Nich answered, 'so I'm told. I think it's important to be ready, and that the man take it slowly.'

'I'm ready,' Charlotte assured him, 'a little scared, but ready. Only . . . only I don't suppose Horst will take it slowly . . .'

'Well, no,' Nich admitted, 'but you must understand his need to make a dramatic gesture.'

Charlotte swallowed hard, blushing hot as she fought to get out the words she wanted to say.

'I – I understand, but . . . perhaps you . . . you would help? Perhaps you would open me a little first?'

For a brief moment the dull red light of the dying sunset caught Nich's face, turning his pleased grin into a smirk of Satanic malevolence before he gave an understanding nod and took her very gently in his arms. Charlotte's body was shaking hard as she let him guide her down onto the bed, her eyes tight closed, her mouth a little open. She felt him lift her shift, and her legs, easing them wide even as the silk fell away.

With her virgin sex showing to a man for the first time in her life she could hear the voices of every nun and every priest who had ever counselled her screaming for her to stop, to keep herself pure. She bit her lip, her muscles loose as she allowed herself to be held for entry, thighs rolled up and open, her sex stretched wide, her precious maidenhead waiting. A soft rustle signalled the lifting of Nich's own robe, and suddenly his cock was touching her, firm and rounded, hot, as he pressed between her open sex lips, rubbing on her clitoris.

A sigh of ecstasy escaped Charlotte's lips at the touch, and the urge to have her body filled came stronger than ever before. Still Nich rubbed, the head of his cock moving in the slippery valley between her lips until she had begun to squirm in pleasure. Only then did he move lower, the bulk of his cock pressing to her vagina, filling out the hole, stretching her hymen taut.

She gasped, her fingers locking in the bed cover, sure he was about to take her and unable to resist. Yet he pulled back, and once more began to rub himself on her clit before again putting his cock to her hole. This time he held it, with her hymen stretched so tight she was certain she would tear, and as his knuckles began to tap against the underside of her bottom she realised he was masturbating into her.

Charlotte moaned, her head filling with guilt too strong to be denied, for her parents and those who expected her to keep herself pure, for Rowena, for her promise to Horst Sachs. She tried to twist herself away, but too late, Nich's grip holding her firmly by the leg as he milked himself into the tight hole where her hymen held her vagina closed.

Rowena put a match to the ball of scrumpled paper beneath the fire they had built and watched the flames slowly rise. It was hard to concentrate with the absence of Charlotte constantly nagging at the back of her mind, while for all the loneliness and privacy of Berne Woods it was impossible not to start at every noise from among the trees or every distant car engine. She knew she needed to render her mind pliable, to let the Goddess possess her fully, pushing out all material thoughts.

The flames were quickly catching hold, bathing the scene in yellow orange light that threw shadows of the stones and of the girls dancing across the ground and the trunks of the trees around them. As the electric torches were turned off her sense of detachment became abruptly stronger, and stronger still as she drew in a breath of the heady smell from the incense where it was already burning in a bronze chafing dish on top of a stone.

Moving to the edge of the stone circle, she took up another chafing dish, this one with a neat heap of white powder at the centre. She took a pinch, placed it on her tongue and passed the chafing dish on to Andrea. Turning back to the fire, she shut her eyes, determined not to rush, but waiting for the moment when she wanted to disrobe, and so to go nude, as she should be, the epitome of the female form, naked and unashamed, secret from the vulgar gaze of male eyes.

With his trembling so hard that he had been forced to steady his binoculars on a branch, Mr Pedlow watched the girls from his place of concealment behind a fallen tree. There were eight of them, more than ever before, although the glorious blonde with the pneumatic tits and an arse like a ripe peach was missing. There was still plenty to look at; not least the one who seemed to be in charge, Rowena, a slender, graceful young woman who carried herself with extraordinary poise. The thought of a girl's potential indignation at being watched always added a certain piquancy to the operation, but with Rowena it was magnified a hundredfold. To her, he was certain, her body would be a temple, and the thought of his gaze lingering on her most intimate secrets an unendurable outrage.

He chuckled as he adjusted his position, still careful not to make a noise, but confident in the absolute blackness of the woods from the girls' viewpoint within the circle of firelight. Rowena's poise and beauty drew his gaze, but for sheer, rude pleasure she was not the best. She lacked flesh, and more than anything it was flesh he wanted, full, plump bums and titties, gently swollen bellies, ripe, female flesh. In the absence of his perfect blonde, Charlotte, Andrea was best for flesh. She was tall, athletic, with long honey-coloured hair falling all the way to a firm, meaty bottom, tits like bumpers, and a pouting, well furred cunt. Twice he'd seen her nude.

Eve was almost as good; a little shorter, not so firm, but with a riot of jet black curls, the biggest tits of all, and a fat, wobbling bottom behind. Melanie and Louisa were closer to the average, yet young and juicy enough to arouse any man's interest, while their being sisters added a certain lewd thrill to watching them.

Two were less to his physical taste, both petite, without enough bum and tit to really get him going. It was still a delight watching them, especially Poppy, the village rich-bitch who wouldn't so much as respond to his greeting as they passed in the street. The other, Coralie, a tiny, flame-haired imp of a girl, was the least appealing, her very vitality seeming to mock him.

The eighth girl was a newcomer, tall and lithe, very slender, with long black hair, brilliant green eyes. Mr Pedlow's eyes fixed on her as he made another quick adjustment to his position, not because she was new, not because she was any more attractive than the others, but because she had begun to undress.

She did it quickly, with a disregard for her modesty that left him feeling disappointed, but only briefly. Her top came off, peeled up over her head and hung on a tree. Her bra followed, unclipped to expose small, high breasts, very firm, with her nipples pointing out and up, impudent in erection. Her shoes came off, kicked carelessly to one side. Her jeans came down, over long, elegant legs, and were hung with her top and bra. Her thumbs went into the waistband of her little pink panties and down they came, straight away, baring a firm, round bottom.

Mr Pedlow smiled. Tonight, the girls were going all the way.

From beyond the door the music crashed against Charlotte's senses, wordless heavy-metal that shook the house with every beat. Nich held her arm, firm but gentle, guiding her weak-kneed down the corridor. She could feel the wet of her juices and his own, around the mouth of her virgin sex and between her thighs. Beneath her shift her breasts felt painfully sensitive, her nipples twin points of fire, her bottom and belly prominent, feminine, ripe and ready for the plucking.

As Nich turned out the light they were plunged into absolute darkness, her eyes still struggling to adapt as the music abruptly swelled in volume and she realised he had pushed the door open. Vision came back, dark red, crimson, black, the rich dark colours of the room where the rite was to be consummated, speckled with faces lit demonic red through the thick, sweet-scented smoke.

Juliana was there, languid and uncaring in her nudity, a cup of dark wine in one hand. Rob and Troll sat together, their bearded faces full of lust and booze. Dan sat further back, nervous and guilty, trying not to stare at her breasts. Horst alone was standing, naked but for a loose wrap around his hips, his arms folded across his impressive torso, his skin glistening dull scarlet in the red light, his face set in a knowing smile.

Charlotte stumbled slightly as she stepped into the room, but Nich held her up, and she gave no resistance as his hands went low, to grip the hem of her shift. She closed her eyes as it was lifted, the throb of the music running through her as her body came bare to the gaze of the watchers, her legs, the swell of her sex, her belly, her breasts, and she was nude in front of them, nude and ready.

As she opened her eyes she caught Rob smacking his lips, and every one of them was drinking her in, both Troll and Dan with hands pressed surreptitiously to their crotches. Horst simply allowed his wrap to drop to the floor, exposing his heavy, pale genitals, his penis already beginning to swell. As Charlotte was led to the squat, cloth-covered altar at the centre of the room Juliana came up to her knees and took Horst's cock in her mouth with no more concern than had it been a sausage.

Dizzy with an ecstasy as much religious as it was physical, Rowena danced, her world a swirl of sensations, fire heat and the cool of the May night, the touch of her friends' hands, vivid light and black shadow. Her awareness had changed, coming to focus on the stone circles and the eight naked girls within, with everything outside as insubstantial as mist. She was at one with the Goddess, not a rational awareness, but a visceral certainty, entirely feminine and the perfect expression of the rite of birth and the coming of summer.

All of womanhood seemed as one, Charlotte with her in spirit if not in flesh. At the thought of the woman she wanted so badly her ecstatic trance nearly broke, and she danced with renewed frenzy to get it back, forcing all bad feeling from her mind, all that was negative and black and masculine.

* * *

10

Mr Pedlow was masturbating, his cock stiff in one tightly clenched fist. He had watched the girls strip, all eight of them, and all down to the buff. He had taken photographs too; of tops and bras being pulled up to lay bare bouncy pink titties, big and small, of jeans being eased low and skirts taken off and, best of all, of tight little panties being peeled down over ripe young bottoms. By luck, Melanie had even done it with her back to him and the firelight full on her rear, allowing a brief glimpse of a tightly puckered anus and the twin swell of shaved cunt lips. At that he had pulled his cock out, unable to hold off any longer.

Now all eight were naked, their hair twined with spring flowers, dancing among the stones in a ring, hands held, faces full of joy. He had very little idea what they were doing, except that it was some foolish pagan rite; what mattered was that they did it bare, yet tonight he realised that something was special. Not only had they all gone nude, but the heady incense was stronger and their movements more urgent than ever, more sexual too, mouths open, breasts jiggling, bottoms wiggling, in a way that made him want to fill each and every girlish orifice with fat, stiff cock.

Lying spread-eagled on the altar, Charlotte watched sidelong as Horst's cock came slowly to erection in Juliana's mouth, unable to take her eyes away for her fascination. He was long and pink, now hard and curving up from his solid belly, with Juliana just applying the finishing touches with the tip of her tongue and her lips. The head was taut with pressure, round and glossy, now wet with Juliana's spittle, but shortly to be wet with Charlotte's own juices, and her blood.

Nich had gone to the deck and, as Horst at last stepped back from Juliana, the music grew louder still, a furious, pounding beat that made Charlotte's body shake and sent shivers through her sex. Suddenly she knew she was going to come, at any moment, with or without Horst's cock inside her. The fear was gone, replaced with an urgent, triumphant desire, to have her virginity taken, so publicly, in celebration of the birth of the God; not the cold, angry God of her mentors, but a warm, fertile, pagan God, the Horned God, and as Horst stepped between her open thighs, her arms came open to receive him.

He took her up against his chest, cradling her as his cock probed between her thighs, prodding in the crease of her bottom and sliding in the wet valley of her sex lips before he found her hole. She clung on tight, in abandoned ecstasy, as once more she felt her hymen stretch to the pressure of a man's penis, stretch, and tear . . .

Charlotte screamed to the sudden, sharp pain of her penetration, falling back on the altar as Horst released her shoulders and took a firm grip on her thighs. He grunted once and the full, thick length of his erection had been jammed deep up into her body, with her torn hymen rasping on his rigid flesh as he began to fuck her.

For one moment the pain was too much, leaving her whimpering and clutching at the altar cloth even as their mingled juices trickled down between her bottom cheeks to wet it. Only when the beat of the music caught her again did the stinging give way, with Horst now fucking her in time, the others clapping and cheering as the big cock drove into her again and again, faster and faster, bringing her up to a screaming, writhing crescendo as her orgasm hit her.

She was still in climax when Horst grunted and came himself, deep inside her, the two of them together in mutual ecstasy for one long moment before he had withdrawn and stepped quickly to the side. Charlotte stayed put, thighs wide, knowing that he would want every one of his followers to see, to witness the thick fluid bubbling from her well opened hole, the white of his come marked by the red thread of her virgin blood.

Rowena's dance had grown to a wild, uncontrolled frenzy, still rhythmic, yet ever more sexual. Her hands had gone to her breasts, rubbing at the low, firm mounds to stimulate her nipples, and her hips were moving as if in urgent need of entry from behind. All her doctrines, all her concepts had fled as she fell to her knees, clutching her breasts, her bottom pushed out, in an ecstasy close to orgasm.

She had to come, then and there, in front of them all, and as her fingers went to the slippery groove of her sex they had closed around her, dancing in a ring and calling encouragement to her as she masturbated. Her body came up, her knees wide, flaunting her sex to the night as she rubbed at herself, her head full of images of open, utterly uninhibited sexual display, femininity in its essence, unrepressed, unsullied by masculine demands.

As she started to come she felt her body taken in soft arms. A mouth pressed to hers and she was kissing. Others pressed close, warm and supple, their skin wet with sweat, holding her, touching her. Mouths found her nipples, and then her sex, a firm, skilled tongue pressed straight to her clitoris and her ecstasy was perfect, raised to a level she had never achieved before, and in perfect communion with the Goddess.

Mr Pedlow had come in his hand.

One

Nich Mordaunt eased his black Triumph to a stop outside the Department of Archaeology. Crossing the grass, he ignored the occasional curious glance at his black painted fingernails or the red enamelled chaos symbols of his jewellery, and once inside made directly for the lift. He paused only in the museum that separated Dr Chaswell's room from the main corridor, glancing at his watch as he admired a beautifully wrought silver chalice taken from the ruins of a twelfth-century church. He was still looking at it when the door opened and a student emerged, smiling nervously as he passed. Nich went in, and greeted the slim, dark-haired woman who sat behind the desk with a single, affable nod and her name.

'Aileve.'

'Alice, while we're here.'

'Sorry, Alice.'

She responded with a careless gesture and adjusted her hair.

'How was your Beltane then?' he asked as he sat down.

'Fun. Yours?'

'Better than I'd anticipated. They went through with it anyway.'

'Horst Sachs and Charlotte? I thought she'd back out, or he would.'

14

'Sachs is something of a dilettante, too lazy to do any proper research, but he's serious enough in his intent. She was very nervous, but determined.'

'Rowena is much the same as Sachs, as least in so far as she only chooses those aspects of paganism that suit her personal philosophy.'

'Which is?'

'Worship of the Mother, with a slice of aggressive feminism and one or two details of her own thrown in.'

'That much I'd worked out. Nothing more exotic?'

'Not really, no. I'd hoped for more anyway and, in fact, if I hadn't given her a bit of encouragement it would have been very tame indeed. Still, she's on the right track, and deserves encouragement.'

'Unlike Ariesian.'

Dr Chaswell pursed her lips. 'Ariesian, yes. I've been thinking about Ariesian, especially this new house of his. Elune is furious.'

'Well she might be. What is she going to do?'

'Nothing.'

Dr Chaswell settled back in her chair, to cup her small, high breasts through her blouse, Nich watching appreciatively as she brought her nipples to erection.

'Do you think they should be bigger, more like Juliana's perhaps?'

Nich laughed and went on.

'But do tell all. What did you do to Rowena?'

'I can't. You are a male, inherently negative, and as such can never be admitted to the female mystery.'

Nich merely grinned.

'Really, there's not that much to tell,' Dr Chaswell went on. 'Eight of us met at Berne Woods, near Charmouth . . .'

'The stone circle?'

'Yes, do you know it?'

'Of course.'

'They set out green cloths to symbolise spring, lit a fire, burned incense and took some sort of powder, both presumably containing drugs of some kind. We danced, in a circle, naked, making ourselves dizzy and reaching really quite a nice high. At the peak Rowena began to masturbate, and we closed around her. I think that would have been it, but I was getting bored and I quite wanted to enjoy her.'

'So you did?'

'Yes. I kissed her, and she responded well, so I licked her to help her come. It wasn't expected, because most of them were embarrassed about it afterwards. I think they'll do it again though, perhaps with a little prompting.'

'Hmm, interesting. Was she obsessive about not having any men around, or is that just an excuse to let them overcome their inhibitions about stripping off?'

'She's quite obsessive, so is Andrea. Eve's just shy. The others would prefer a male element, I think, but only if it was somebody they could trust.'

Nich nodded and Dr Chaswell paused to arrange some papers on her desk before speaking again.

'How about you?'

'Perhaps more authentic,' Nich responded, 'at least in so far as Charlotte gave up her virginity, but otherwise very ordinary stuff. Other than Sachs they're really just overgrown kids out for a laugh. There was red lighting, a lot of pot, loud music, which admittedly seemed to help Charlotte to come, but no element of competition among the males . . . well, not officially.'

'No? What did you do, Nich?'

'Let's just say that if Charlotte is pregnant, Horst Sachs will not necessarily be the father.'

* * *

Rowena's mouth was set in grim determination as she walked up the narrow lane. It was a route she'd taken a hundred times before, as Charlotte's friend since childhood, and it was still a struggle not to think of Mr and Mrs Dowling as towering, authoritative figures, he stern and humourless, she haughty and forever ready with a judgement. Yet it had to be done. Charlotte was no longer a child, and she had the right to come and go as she pleased, without reference to her parents.

At the gate Rowena paused, taking a moment to reaffirm who she was, no longer the schoolgirl with a bad attitude, but a grown woman, strong minded and independent. She went in. Mrs Dowling was seated on an ornate iron chair at the centre of the lawn, a cup of tea and a plate of biscuits at her elbow, a copy of *Fox and Hound* held negligently in one hand. She looked up as Rowena approached, and smiled.

'Hello, Rowena dear. If you are looking for Charlotte, I'm afraid she's still out.'

'Still out?' Rowena echoed, taken aback. 'She didn't stay in last night then?'

'Oh, no. She went out, with that charming Sachs boy, to see some film in Exeter apparently.'

'And she stayed over, with Horst Sachs?' Rowena asked, trying to keep the mounting horror from her voice.

'Yes,' Mrs Dowling replied. 'It seemed sensible.'

Rowena bit down her instinctive reply, not wishing to point out that Horst's parents were in Austria, and that if their son was charming then it was the sort of charm usually associated with snakes. Drawing in her breath, she forced herself to smile politely as Mrs Dowling went on.

'She should be back presently. Would you like a cup of tea?'

'No, thank you,' Rowena answered. 'It was nothing important. I'll give her a call.'

Mrs Dowling responded with a complacent smile and Rowena moved away. Full of doubt and anger, it was all she could do not to break into a run until she was out of sight of the house. If Horst Sachs had lured Charlotte out on Beltane eve it could only be for one possible reason, and if she had every faith in her friend's chastity, she had an equal and opposite amount in that of Horst Sachs. She tried Charlotte's mobile, but it was switched off. Cursing under her breath, she made for her parents' house and a car.

Horst Sachs had been after Charlotte for years. He'd even been the one to suggest paganism to them, at the time simply a choice to allow her to defy the school. It was something Rowena had struggled to forget, but the moment was clear in her mind – she and Charlotte, at fifteen, sulky and rebellious after a confirmation class. They had been at the limit of the school grounds, smoking smuggled cigarettes and drinking a bottle of communion wine stolen from the sisters. Horst had been riding, smart in a well cut hunting jacket and jodhpurs, his blond hair windswept and dishevelled.

Even Rowena had found it hard not to deny the attraction of his look, or his words. He had urged them to be strong, to refuse confirmation and hold their ground. She'd done it, scandalising the school as the first pupil in two hundred years to formally reject Christianity in general and Catholicism in particular. Through all the talks with the sisters, with Father Dawson, with her parents, she had held firm. Charlotte had not, giving in after just the third interview, but it hadn't changed her outlook, not deep down, and she had come to worship Rowena.

Then there has been that wonderful moment, two years later, when she and Charlotte had become lovers, another memory etched clearly into her mind, but not one she wished to forget, just the opposite. The autumn breeze rustling the pines by Hayes Farm as Charlotte struggled to keep up with the other runners. Holding back to be with her friend, indifferent to the house points she would lose. Charlotte clinging to her, panting, wet with sweat, heavy breasts rising and falling under her sports top. Finally giving in to the feelings that had been building in her for so long. Fear of rejection as she gently kissed her friend. Joy as Charlotte responded, their mouths opening together in a long kiss. Giggling as they ran into the woods. Fumbling, clumsy in their urgency to get at each other. Their tops lifted, silent in mutual admiration as they stroked and teased each others' breasts . . .

Her chain of thought broke as she reached her house. Nobody was about, and she took the Punto, driving quickly down to the A35 and towards Honiton. By the time Rowena reached Rockbeare she had worked herself into a state of near fury. From the first Horst Sachs' arrogant, self-confident masculinity had put her back up, and her defences. Charlotte had claimed to feel the same, and yet Rowena had always sensed an uncertainty, while there was no mistaking the way Horst looked at them. He wanted them both and, when he'd found out the two girls were lovers, had even dared to suggest the three of them go to bed together, a suggestion that had left Rowena speechless with indignation.

After parking the car outside the gate, she continued on foot, half dreading what she might find, half hoping, so that there could be no denial. The view from the Sachs' house was almost identical to that from the dormitory windows at St Cecilia's, a great sweep of checkerboard fields with Dartmoor rising in the distance. The sense of nostalgia was immediate, and strong. It was all too easy to remember herself as a girl, staring out across the same panorama, wishing she could be somewhere out there, anywhere, but free of the stifling restrictions imposed on her by the sisters. The first day she'd cried, and now it was hard to hold back the tears as she marched up to the house, peering in at the living room window through half-open curtains.

The sight that met her eyes instantly brought her anger to the boil. There had been a party, obviously, and no ordinary party. Every wall of the room was draped in hangings of a deep crimson. Red bulbs replaced the ordinary lights, some of them still on. Beer cans, bottles and glasses littered every surface. A bronze tripod supported a chafing dish full of ash, with a cube of greasy brown cannabis resin and an open penknife lying to one side. At the centre of the room a low table had been covered with a red cloth, a cloth that bore a stain, cross-shaped, just in the way an excited girl might leave a stain on a bed sheet.

Choking back tears of rage, Rowena ran to the door, to pound on the heavy brass knocker. Finally it was answered, by Sachs himself, bleary-eyed, with a scarlet dressing gown half-wrapped around his muscular body and his blond hair a dishevelled mop. As he saw Rowena his expression of annoyance turned to a quiet, knowing smile.

'Where is she, you bastard!' she demanded. 'What have you done to her!?'

'Nothing she didn't want,' he answered casually.

'You fucking pig!'

Rowena's hand lashed out, but Horst moved quickly back, laughing as she stumbled.

'Temper, temper! There's no call for that, Rowena.

After all, you know I'd have been happy to have you too.'

She caught the implication immediately, that he'd taken Charlotte's virginity, and would have been happy to take her own as well, an outrage which rendered her incapable of speech, but only for a moment.

'What have you done?' she repeated, pushing past him into the house. 'You've had her, haven't you, you utter bastard! Where is she? Charlotte! Charlotte!'

'You're too late,' Sachs remarked with a yawn. 'She left about half an hour ago. Coffee?'

'Fuck off!'

'Suit yourself. I'm going to have one anyway.'

He moved to the kitchen and Rowena followed, tight-lipped with anger.

'So what happened, Horst? And don't lie to me, because I've seen your shoddy little attempt at a Beltane ritual.'

Horst didn't reply, his attention fixed on an elaborate coffee machine as he adjusted it. Rowena waited, fighting to bring her temper under control, until at last he responded.

'Yes, I suppose shoddy isn't an unfair description, although it would have been a great deal better had you come along, and brought a few of the girls. We did have Juliana, at least. She sucked my cock.'

'Juliana? So Nich was here?'

'Yes. They acted as my acolytes although, as you say, there's only so much you can do with an ordinary house and –'

'Will you answer me, Horst! What did you do with Charlotte?'

'What do you expect? I fucked her.'

'No. She wouldn't. You're lying, you utter bastard!'

21

Horst merely shrugged. Rowena opened her mouth to make a fresh denial, but closed it, thinking of the cross-shaped stain on the altar cloth, coloured dark with dried blood. Juliana was no virgin. As Horst casually drew himself a mug of black coffee she was too angry to speak.

'Are you sure you won't have a coffee?' he enquired.

Rowena found her voice.

'She was going to be my handmaiden, and you violated her! You little shit, you . . .'

'Hardly violated,' Horst answered. 'She was more than willing.'

'No. It's not possible. She would never give herself to a man, never! You must have drugged her –'

'Far from it. She came to me of her own accord, Rowena, and you know it.'

'No, not my Charlotte, I don't believe it!'

'Ask her yourself then.'

'I will! And if . . . if . . .'

'Face it, Rowena, you lost, I won. Now, in recognition of my supremacy, why don't you get down on your knees and wrap that pretty, painted mouth around my cock? After all, it is the time of year for taking seed into your body.'

Rowena found herself unable to answer, her mouth working in outrage but no words coming. At last she turned for the door, with Sachs' mocking laughter ringing in her ears as she left.

Mr Pedlow's face was set in a satisfied smirk as he examined the results of his night's work. The new camera had performed remarkably well, although by the end his batteries had been running low. Given the dim and uncertain firelight, the pictures were impressively clear, and deliciously rude.

In the best of them, those girls with their faces to the camera were clearly recognisable, something he was sure would provide excellent leverage should they ever catch him at it. All eight showed clearly in one picture or another, and in six of those eight cases he knew their parents and could be certain that the discovery of how their daughters danced naked in the woods would come not only as a surprise, but a serious shock.

The exceptions were Coralie, who sold fossils, gemstones and crystals in Charmouth and seemed to be entirely independent, and the new girl, who he was fairly sure was not local at all. That was a shame, because it suggested she might not come again, and she was a dirty bitch, going down on Rowena, to lick cunt.

Sadly, he had not had a clear view of the final, ecstatic moments of the night. Rowena's back had been to him, while other girls and one of the standing stones had obscured his view. Yet he'd clearly seen the black-haired girl go down between Rowena's thighs, while Andrea and Melanie had been suckling. Just the thought was enough to send a shiver right through him, and to set his cock stiff once again.

Some of the earlier photos were rude though, very rude. The girls had stripped with little or no concern for their modesty, blissfully unaware of his prying eyes. He had managed to capture most of the glorious Andrea's strip, front and back, with the light full on her. Using the motor drive, he'd even managed to capture the instant when her big tits bounced free of her sports bra, and the one with her bent to remove her knickers from her foot hinted at the split fig of her cunt.

He'd done less well with Eve, who'd been between him and the firelight, but there were some breathtaking shots of her huge breasts bouncing as she danced, making him wish he could squeeze the fat globes around his cock and fuck in her cleavage. Melanie and Louisa had stayed close together, as always, side by side as they undressed. That had made it hard to get a good shot, but there was one excellent picture of Melanie easing her panties down off her bottom with her sister already nude in the background.

Poppy had provided the rudest shot of all, caught in the act of taking her panties off, with her slim buttocks far enough apart to show the full glory of her neat pink cunt and the tight, dun brown dimple of her anal star. Only with Coralie had he failed to get a decent picture, although there were plenty of her dancing.

All morning he'd been studying them, with a carefully arranged montage of pretty faces and firm young bodies arranged on his screen, until he'd come in his hand twice and his cock had begun to get sore. Only then had he begun to study each picture in more detail, enjoying the intrusive thrill of inspecting the girls' most intimate parts close up.

Now, with Poppy's heavily pixillated cunt magnified to occupy the entire screen, he peered close, trying to work out whether or not she was virgin. She was certainly tight, her neat little lips a perfect purse of girl flesh, and probably inviolate. Yet for all the power and technology of both camera and computer it was impossible to be certain. What he needed was a closer view, more intrusive still, something that would allow him to inspect every tiny bump on their nipples, every bulge and fold of their soft little cunts, every crevice of their tight, virgin bumholes, so close he'd be able to tell whether or not they'd wiped properly . . .

* * *

Charlotte sat with her chin in her hands, looking out across the sea but with her eyes barely focused. Her mind was awash with guilt, for what she'd done, and what she hadn't. Surrendering her virginity at a Beltane rite had been the result of months of soul searching, and if Horst Sachs had encouraged her, then it had been what she truly wanted as well, what she truly needed.

Ever since her introduction to the old religion her ideas had been focused on the celebration of female fertility. She had absorbed ideas both ancient and modern, of the annual cycle of birth and death and rebirth, with all of life flowing from the womb of the Goddess. She had studied every piece of evidence for fertility rites, from pre-historic times to the rise of Christianity, every lingering pagan ritual surviving in the celebration of the Goddess, the May Queen, anything.

All of it had come together to form an overpowering urge to play that role, to be the chosen one, becoming a woman on Beltane night. Only Rowena had held her back, insisting that the stories of girls losing their virginity in celebration of the coming of summer were a patriarchal distortion of the true meaning of the festival. To Rowena the Goddess was paramount, and for any woman to submit herself to a man, sacrilege.

Against Rowena had been Horst Sachs, with his passionate avowal of the role of the Horned God. His strong, slightly cruel masculinity drew her like a magnet despite her very real feelings for Rowena, and yet the year before she had resisted her needs. Instead of accepting Horst's invitation she had gone with Rowena, to dance among the standing stones of Berne Circle in their first Beltane rite. The experience, while intense, had not been completely fulfilling.

Then had come Nich Mordaunt, with his open delight in her rebellion and support for her ideas. He had met Horst at a festival near Tawmouth in Devon, and quickly become an influence. Nich seemed to know everything, seldom admitting uncertainty and presenting his arguments with absolute confidence. To listen to Nich speak of the cycle of the year, of the way the early Christians had absorbed and twisted the old festivals, of how alien the God of her parents and teachers was to Britain, all of it had fascinated her, and also resolved her last doubts about her beliefs.

He had also reinforced her need for the sacrifice of her own virginity, so strongly that she'd not only determined to do it, but begun to have doubts as to whether Horst or Nich should be her lover. His insistence that in the original rites the prize had always gone to the most virile man, or the cleverest, had meshed perfectly with her own desires, leading her to ensure that when the time came, she had taken both their seed.

Even Nich's influence might not have been sufficient, but he had introduced her in turn to his friend Juliana, and to the archaeologist, Dr Alice Chaswell, both pagans, both absolutely confident in their beliefs, both black haired and green eyed, clearly sisters. When the final moment came, and she had stood in indecision, expected by both Rowena and Horst, it had been Alice who came to her, who persuaded her to follow her heart.

Now it was done, with a vengeance, her hymen torn, her womb flooded with two men's sperm. She had expected ecstasy, and got it, not only from the glorious orgasm she'd achieved on the altar, but afterwards, with a feeling of fulfilment beyond anything she had imagined. Ever since she had woken in

Horst's bed that morning she had been filled with an urge to shout her joy to the sky, and yet her delight had been punctuated by bouts of acute melancholy when the possible consequences of her actions managed to intrude.

Strongest was her dread of the inevitable confrontation with Rowena. Possibly Rowena would belt her, the way she had after catching Charlotte and Emily Smith together in the showers. That Charlotte felt she could take, for all the pain, even that she deserved it. What she knew she could not take was the possibility of outright rejection.

It had even occurred to her to lie, to claim that Horst had taken her against her will, or drugged her. Yet it was pointless. There had been too many witnesses, all of who would vouch that she had been willing, while Nich's testimony alone would be enough to show up a lie. She had not even been drunk.

Less strong emotionally, but even more important, was the possibility that she was carrying Horst's child, or Nich's. So much of her need had focused on her being left pregnant at the end of the ritual that using contraception had been unthinkable. She had longed to be made pregnant, for all that the consequences hardly bore thinking about, and Beltane had fallen at the very peak of her fertility.

Her mouth set in a rebellious scowl as she considered the confession she'd have to make to her parents if she was pregnant. Not that she'd tell the whole truth, concealing just how lewd she'd been, because she knew full well how much her lewdness would matter, especially to her mother. Nor would that be the end of it. There would be further interviews, with Father Dawson and perhaps other priests, doctors, social workers, and no doubt all sorts of other prying busybodies.

She drew a heavy sigh, only to smile once more as the sheer joy of what she'd done welled up inside her. Perhaps now that she'd done it she could find the strength inside herself that she'd always lacked? Perhaps she could defy her critics, as Rowena had defied the sisters and even Father Dawson over confirmation? Perhaps she could be as strong as Rowena, as strong even as Juliana, or Alice, who walked the world as if she owned it?

Her smile became a wry grimace at the realisation that she could never, ever be like Alice, nor even Rowena. She would cower down and mumble apologies and attempts at explanation, as always, trying to please everybody and only ending up making most of them angry, which seemed to be her fate. Yet for all that, she had, for once, made her own decision and stuck with it. She had given her virginity in celebration of the Goddess, and nothing and nobody could take that away.

Glancing up towards the top of Stonebarrow, Rowena hesitated, but for no more than a moment. Charlotte had gone home only briefly, to drop the car off, then left, saying she needed some fresh air. That almost certainly meant the wild ground along the ridge of Stonebarrow, a place both of them had gone when they needed a little solitude, for years and, more recently, to make love or just lie naked in each other's arms where they had so many secret places.

There had been rows too, and there was about to be another one. It was never easy to be angry with Charlotte, whose meek acceptance of guilt had always been enough to defuse the wrath of all but the most sadistic or self-righteous people. One or two of the sisters had seemed to take an active pleasure in Charlotte's ready submission, and Rowena herself had once taken a belt to her friend's bottom. It had left her feeling better, with Charlotte's sin absolved, and briefly made her wonder whether Father Dawson was right when he said the anti-Christian urges within her came from the Devil. Whatever happened, Rowena knew in her heart that, for all her sense of betrayal and disgust, she would not be able to end their relationship, nor did she want to.

She walked fast, up the lane to where the woods began, pausing twice at the entrance to half-over-grown tracks to look for signs that somebody had gone down them. One had a spider's web across it, still wet with dew, the other was heavily constricted by bright green nettles. She moved on, now sure where Charlotte would be, beyond the makeshift fence that closed off an old path where it had been broken by a landslip.

A faded red notice warned her of danger, but she ignored it, scrambling over and down the exposed slope of golden sand to the little ledge of under-growth where she and Charlotte had so often sat to talk and kiss and gaze out over the sea. Sure enough, Charlotte was there, her tumble of blonde curls unmistakable over a bright red top. Obviously Char-lotte had meant to be found. Rowena stopped, just feet away, as her friend turned to look up from big brown eyes already wet with tears.

'I – I'm sorry, Ro, truly sorry . . .'

Rowena swallowed the huge lump in her throat, the torrent of angry words she'd been planning dying before they'd begun. In their place came a single question.

'Why?'

Charlotte's face had begun to work with emotion, but she didn't answer, instead turning and rising a little, onto her knees with her head hung, kneeling in pathetic submission, as if too weak even to talk back. Again Rowena tried to bring out her flood of angry accusations, and again held it back, cursing herself for what did come out.

'I still want you.'

Charlotte looked up, and there were tears in her eyes.

'Thank you, Ro ... I love you.'

Rowena closed her eyes, close to tears herself and yet boiling with frustration at her inability to express her fury for what Charlotte had done. Finally it was her friend who spoke.

'Perhaps ... perhaps you should punish me, if – if you think you should?'

Rowena opened her eyes, looking down. Charlotte's face was streaked with tears, her mouth curved down in miserable contrition, but for a moment one corner flickered, as if she was going to smile. Rowena shook her head, her temper finally coming to the boil.

'No, Lottie, you don't get away with it that easily. Why did you do it, why? And with Horst Sachs of all people!'

Charlotte's tears started again, harder than before and mixed with heavy sobs. Rowena held her ground, her arms folded, determined not to back down, for all her need to take her girlfriend in her arms for a cuddle, before spanking the silly bitch's great wobbling bottom to a glowing crimson ...

'Well?' Rowena demanded. 'Answer me!'

'You know!' Charlotte wailed. 'I had to ... to take a man into me on Beltane night! I told you, Ro, I told you, but you wouldn't accept it! I'm sorry, but I had to, and ... and who else but Horst!?'

'Who else!? Nobody else, that's who, Lottie, you little slut! I thought you understood, Lottie, I – oh, Mother, when I think of that bastard putting his dirty cock inside you –'

She burst into tears, finally unable to contain her emotions. Charlotte rose, putting her arms out for a cuddle, but Rowena pushed her away, sobbing bitterly as her friend sank back into a kneeling position, more contrite than ever, finally speaking in a mumble.

'Never again, I promise, Ro. Forgive me, and I'll be yours for ever.'

Rowena shook her head, although she knew she was going to accept the offer. After a while she swallowed and wiped her eyes, then looked down at Charlotte.

'Never again, you swear?'

'Yes. I swear. I'll never let him have me again.'

Rowena forced a smile, ignoring the possible doubt of Charlotte's meaning.

'What am I going to do with you, Lottie?'

Charlotte responded with a wry smile, then spoke.

'Can I – can I hold you, or am I still in the doghouse?'

'You're still in the doghouse,' Rowena answered, against her instinct.

'Oh,' Charlotte answered, hung her head lower still and after a long pause raised it. 'Cuddle? Please?'

'Lottie, you've – you've betrayed me. You've betrayed us!'

'I know. I'm sorry, really, deeply sorry. Maybe you should beat me?'

'No.'

'Why not?'

'Why not!? Because then you'd think it's all okay, and it's not! That's why not!'

'I'd like you to, and I think you'd like to.'

Rowena drew in her breath, knowing it was true, and that if she gave in it would be Charlotte who had won, not her. It had been the same before, Charlotte's guilt erased and Rowena feeling angry and confused. Charlotte spoke again.

'Come on, Ro, spank me, hard, and then it will all be better.'

'No it won't. It won't undo what's done, will it?'

'No, but it will make you feel a little better, won't it?'

Rowena shook her head, but the urge to do it was strong, too strong, and with her mouth set in a tight line as much in regret for her own weakness as in anger, she reached down to ease her trainer free. Charlotte responded with a little whimper, as much excitement as fear, and her hands went to the button of her jeans. She looked up, big brown eyes still wet with tears, as she rose a little to push her jeans down over the swell of her hips, and lower, exposing full-cut pink knickers decorated with white polka dots. Rowena caught the scent of her lover's sex on the still, warm air and she was lost.

'Bare,' she ordered, 'and your top too, right off.'

Charlotte responded with a single, nervous nod, leaving her jeans at half-mast around her bottom as her hands went to her crop top, which already showed a good slice of gently curved, creamy midriff. Rowena watched as the little garment came up, Charlotte biting her lips as she exposed a full-cupped pink bra, slightly too small, so that slices of chubby girl-flesh bulged from the sides and spilt out over the top. Putting her top down on the grass, Charlotte looked up doubtfully.

'Everything?'

'Everything, Lottie.'

'Yes, but what if somebody came?'

'Then they would see you having your bottom spanked, in the nude, because that's the way I want you.'

She didn't mean it, the thought of Charlotte being seen naked by any man adding an instinctive pang to her jealousy and her anger. It wasn't going to happen. Time and again they'd been in the same place and never seen anybody, yet it was impossible not to feel nervous as Charlotte shyly unclipped her bra and pulled the cups free. At the sight of her lover's full, pale breasts Rowena felt her belly clench, and she tightened her grip on her shoe.

Charlotte was shaking visibly as she continued to strip, pulling off her shoes and socks, fumbling her jeans down and away, hesitating only when it came to her panties. Her thumbs went into the waistband, her body lifted, ready to pull them down, but she had stopped, once more looking up at Rowena.

'Don't play games with me, Charlotte, it doesn't work,' Rowena stated. 'Just get them off.'

It was a lie. Charlotte's show of hesitancy and embarrassment had increased her sexual feelings further still, a helpless reaction that made her want to apply the trainer even harder.

The panties came down, and off, exposing the full, meaty peach of Charlotte's bottom. As meek and accepting as ever, she lay face down in the grass, her hips slightly lifted to offer the pale, cheeky globe for spanking. Rowena stepped forward, straddling her lover, then sinking into a squat on Charlotte's back, to pin her down in the warm grass.

Rowena found it impossible not to smile as she hefted her trainer above Charlotte's defenceless bottom. The big cheeks were quivering slightly in anticipation of the coming pain, and she could feel the urgency of Charlotte's breathing. She drew in her breath.

'Right, you wanted this, so no complaints.'

Charlotte's answer was an unhappy whimper, followed by a squeal of shock and pain as the trainer landed on her bottom with a meaty smack. Rowena took no notice, applying a second and a third stroke, aimed hard at the crest of Charlotte's bottom, to set the big cheeks wobbling and spreading. The instant Charlotte found her voice she was pleading for mercy between squeals, squirming her body and kicking her legs.

The pained struggles only encouraged Rowena, who spanked harder still, until Charlotte had been sent into a writhing, helpless tantrum, thrashing her body from side to side and beating her fists on the ground, squalling her head off and begging without a thought for dignity, kicking her legs and bucking her hips to spread her cheeks and fill the warm spring air with the scent of her sex.

Only when the whole fat ball of Charlotte's bottom had been turned a rich red did Rowena stop and dismount. Charlotte turned to her immediately, clinging close, her body shivering and wracked with sobs as she nuzzled her tear-stained face against Rowena's chest. For a moment Rowena let it happen, stroking Charlotte's hair, before she spoke.

'Uh, uh, not yet, Lottie.'

Charlotte looked up in surprise and would have spoken, but her words came out in a squeak as her ankles were caught. Realising what was about to happen to her as she was turned onto her back, she began to struggle, and plead.

'No, not that, no – please, Ro . . .'

Rowena took no notice whatsoever. Charlotte's legs were hauled up and her sex was showing, the moist pink folds wet with excitement, the hole open. Eyes closed tight, sobbing bitterly, Charlotte allowed the inspection of her sex. Her chest was heaving, her fingers locking and unlocking in the grass, her nipples rock-hard points, with a trickle of white fluid running from her open hole.

'You utter slut!' Rowena sneered, and brought the trainer hard down on the pouting tuck of Charlotte's bottom cheeks.

The spanking began again, and Charlotte was squealing and wriggling immediately, no more reserved than before. Yet her squeals had taken on a new tone, and there was no mistaking the swollen condition of her sex, nor how wet she was. Again Rowena stopped, still angry, but flushed with pleasure too and, for all the knowledge that she was being manipulated, still determined to take her feelings out as best she could.

Charlotte sprawled on the grass as her ankles were released, her arms open for a cuddle. Rowena shook her head, her fingers already tugging at her jeans, to pull the fly wide. As Charlotte saw she gave a single, muted sigh, but stayed as she was, watching from moist eyes as Rowena quickly pushed down her jeans and knickers. Bare, Rowena quickly moved to straddle Charlotte's head.

Pausing only to allow the spanked girl to take in exactly what was about to be done to her, Rowena sat her bare bottom firmly in Charlotte's face. It was something she'd longed to do, but which had always seemed too degrading for her lover. That was no longer true. Charlotte had betrayed her, and having a bare bottom sat in her face was the least she deserved. Sitting upright, so that she was perched full on Charlotte's face, pussy to mouth and bottom hole to nose, she gave a single, curt order.

'Lick.'

Charlotte didn't need telling. Her whole body was shivering as she did it, but her tongue was on Rowena's sex, lapping urgently. Rowena's anger faded as her pleasure rose, and yet an important part of that pleasure resided in knowing that Charlotte's

35

bottom was smarting from punishment, also the feel of the soft, slightly squashed nose tip against her bottom hole.

When Charlotte's thighs came up and open Rowena laughed, in sheer joy for her lover's helpless response to punishment and humiliation. Charlotte's hands went down, to stroke at the tuck of her smacked bottom and at her sex, masturbating in utter submission, and Rowena laughed louder still. The licking became abruptly more urgent and Rowena went quiet, her eyes closed in bliss as her pleasure began to rise towards orgasm. Charlotte began to squirm, her nose wriggling in the moist dimple of Rowena's bottom hole, and they were coming, together, in a mutual ecstasy that held for a long, long time, until Rowena finally allowed herself to slump to the ground.

They crawled together, cuddling close in silence, save for a single, heartfelt sigh from Rowena. She had known it would be impossible to reject Charlotte, yet even as her lover snuggled close to her side she felt she'd been tricked. She did feel better for what they had done, and yet while she had given in to her love for Charlotte, it did nothing to erase the stain of her betrayal.

Two

First placing Horst's pint of lager on the table, then his own glass of dark ale, Nich Mordaunt seated himself. Rain in the night had left the east Devon landscape verdant green, and despite the brittle sunlight there was still a crisp touch to the air. Nobody else had come out to the beer garden, while aside from his bike there were only two vehicles in the car park.

'Good, wasn't it?' Horst said, his tone inviting praise.

'Excellent,' Nich assured him. 'Charlotte was magnificent. Yet I do feel we could make improvements.'

'Such as?'

'The location, the audience, the ritual . . .'

'Oh. Not so good then?'

'As I said, excellent, in the circumstances. We live in a country that's been firmly under the dead hand of Christianity for over a thousand years, and where what little paganism that does flourish is still strongly influenced by Christian morals. Yet you put together a Beltane celebration that included the giving up of a maiden's virginity. That's impressive.'

'Probably the first time in a millennium, maybe a millennium and a half,' Horst replied, smiling.

'Not quite,' Nich admitted, 'but nevertheless, a remarkable achievement.'

'Juliana?' Horst queried.

Nich ignored the question, taking a swallow of beer before he continued.

'Now you need to capitalise on your achievement. Let's think about the congregation for a start.'

'Troll and Rob and Dan are the only guys I know who could handle it. We don't want people who're going to freak and run off to the police, or sell out to the papers.'

'No, *we* don't,' Nich admitted, 'at least, not while we're holding rites in your parents' house.'

'Where then? I mean, you know Rowena and her lot are going to get caught in the end, don't you?'

'Perhaps,' Nich admitted, 'but if you're going to take your beliefs seriously, you can't allow yourself to be restricted by laws built on Christian morals. Which is why the police now immediately stamp on any event I do, publicly at least.'

Horst made a face, his uncertainty clear, but Nich carried on regardless.

'What you need is a worthwhile venue, a decent congregation and a more authentic ritual. The last I can supply, for the others, I suggest we turn to Ariesian.'

'Fuck that! The man's a total sell-out!'

'Absolutely, who better to gather you a congregation, to find you a venue, to cover your expenses.'

'Yes, but he's not the real thing, is he? With him it's all flowers and nuts and . . . although apparently he's a real bastard. I met one girl who'd been to bed with him and she said he was a major pig. She wouldn't say exactly what he did.'

'I've heard the same, and you're right about his public image.'

'Sure. You said it yourself, he's taken all the worst aspects from Gardiner and Wheatley and co and dressed them up to pander to a salacious press without risking –'

'– the law or offending political correctness,' Nich finished. 'Exactly.'

'I don't get it.'

'He's a populist,' Nich explained, 'and like all populists he tries to please all of the people all of the time. Therefore he is inevitably mediocre. Yet he's also a good self-publicist and manager. He has the eyes of the pagan community, but his rituals are insipid, his God emasculated, his Goddess a travesty. A good many of the people who attend his events must realise that.'

'Sure. So you think we should try and pinch his congregation?'

'The cream of his congregation, yes. We need only circulate rumours of what you did on Beltane night and people will flock to you. In due time you'll have a core of supporters, and the focus will shift from him to you.'

Horst frowned, more uncertain than ever.

'I'd have to be out.'

'Eventually, yes,' Nich admitted, 'but that is a problem you'll have to face sooner or later. Your father is retiring, isn't he? To Austria?'

'If they find the right house, yes.'

'And the house at Rockbeare will become yours by deed of gift?'

'Yes, but I wouldn't get a penny otherwise if they found out, even about Beltane.'

'Come, come,' Nich urged, grinning. 'Are they likely to? Besides, do you have any idea what Ariesian makes from donations, TV, magazine articles?'

Horst nodded and pursed his lips in thought.

'Do it,' Nich urged. 'Attend his solstice rite. He probably knows about you already, and would no doubt love to accept you as an acolyte. The rumours will already be spreading among the crowds.'

Nich had allowed his grin to grow to its malevolent best, and Horst responded in kind. Both raised their glasses, knocking them gently together before drinking.

'By the time Samhain comes around,' Nich went on, 'you'll be able to lay on a truly authentic celebration. I'd be proud to be Master of Ceremonies, naturally, if you'll have me? You should be fine as long as my name doesn't appear on the posters.'

'Of course, who else? What would you suggest?'

Nich pondered for a moment before he spoke again.

'Sacrifice is the Celtic tradition, to represent the death of the Horned God, ideally in a wicker man. Indeed, Ariesian might be an excellent candidate, but it would be difficult to further advance our cause while shut up in Broadmoor.'

Horst had been peering closely, evidently unsure if Nich was joking, then gave a small, slightly nervous laugh.

'A ram might be more feasible,' Nich admitted. 'We could even have a barbecue afterwards.'

'Wouldn't that be rather trivialising the rite?' Horst asked, his tone suggesting he was still unsure whether or not Nich was joking.

'Not at all,' Nich assured him. 'Taking the body of the God into oneself is entirely apt. Even the Christians do it, after a fashion.'

Horst gave a thoughtful nod.

'What else? We need something sexual.'

'No difficulty there,' Nich stated. 'Although we may need to keep it to an inner circle. In fact, your ritual would have been more appropriate for Samhain than Beltane.'

'It would? I thought Samhain was about death.'

'Only in the sense that death, after a fashion, must necessarily come before rebirth.'

'Hang on. Beltane is the spring festival, about the birth of the year, Samhain the autumn festival, the last harvest, about the death of the year. You said as much yourself.'

'In the circumstances I was hardly going to contradict Charlotte's beliefs,' Nich admitted, 'not when her compliance was so essential to the rite. If you think about it, birth may be the result of sex, but not immediately. According to the original traditions it is at Samhain that the Mother takes the seed of the Horned God, who then dies, and is reborn at Beltane.'

'That's not what you said at all!'

'Never mind that. Rituals varied across the centuries, between cultures and between tribes. What we did was essentially an expression of Charlotte's personal belief system, but no less valid for that.'

'But I designed it. I persuaded her.'

'You allowed her to make her own ideas solid. The earliest, pre-Celtic system is simple. There should be a feast on the last night of the old year, with honey, nuts, fruit, fresh-killed meat and all the good things of the autumn. Dried pieces of fly agaric were also traditional. A girl should be chosen, a virgin, and the most attractive, in the sense of her expressing fertility . . . like Charlotte in fact. She should go to the altar, or the centre of a stone circle. The men should then compete to take her, so that the most virile impregnates her, thus ensuring the rebirth of the Horned God from the womb of the Mother. In some Celtic cultures the man would then be sacrificed.'

'I see. But I thought the priest was the one . . .'

'In a few cultures, yes, not usually.'

Horst paused, looking doubtful.

'How can you be so sure of yourself?'

Nich merely shrugged.

'Where would we find another virgin, anyway?' Horst asked. 'Let alone one like Charlotte.'

'The supply of virgins is not an easy matter, true,' Nich admitted, 'but there must be other girls whose beliefs have grown along the same lines as Charlotte's.'

Horst made a sceptical face.

Mr Pedlow had chanced to be coming out of the Post Office when Charlotte Dowling and Rowena Shields had walked past. Pretending to count his change, he had paused to admire the magnificent globe of Charlotte's bottom, at that moment snug in tight blue jeans worn so low they showed the top of a pair of pastel pink knickers.

As he'd watched her meaty cheeks rise and fall to the motion of her walk he'd realised that there was something odd. She'd seemed a little uncomfortable and, as the two girls moved away down the street, she had twice touched herself, as if to nurse a bruise. Despite the delicious possibilities offered by the thought of her with a bruised bottom, his first thought was that she'd taken a fall from a horse.

A couple of days later his normal morning survey of the neighbourhood through his binoculars had revealed Poppy Melcombe's bright red 4×4 arriving at Charlotte's house. It was a hot day, and Charlotte had emerged with a beach towel, presenting an opportunity too good to miss. Taking his binoculars, his camera, his large and colourful guide to British birds and a two-square-metre sheet of camouflage netting, he had himself driven down to Charmouth and climbed up onto the rough ground where Stonebarrow rose above the beach.

As he had hoped, Charlotte and Poppy had been there, also Rowena, the three girls sunbathing in their favourite spot, not far from the café. All three were in bikinis, providing quite the finest display of female flesh on the beach despite obstinately keeping their tops on. In Charlotte's case it hadn't made much difference – her opulent breasts spilled out from a hopelessly small, bright red bikini top – but it had not been her breasts that drew his attention.

If her breasts were threatening to burst out of her top, then with her bottom it was too late. Most of her abundant flesh had already escaped. The seat of her bikini had worked deep between her cheeks, to show off enough puppy fat for a litter of Saint Bernards with some to spare. He could also see that she was bruised, on both cheeks, and with suspicious regularity, raising the possibility that she had in fact been punished.

The thought of Charlotte being given a bare bottom spanking set his heart hammering so fast he was forced to close his eyes until he'd recovered himself, and just to watch her on the beach had been enough to make him want to pull out his cock and masturbate to orgasm. His position had been far too public, and he'd held back, contenting himself with taking a string of photographs. Back at the house he'd downloaded them and, after bringing himself to a long-overdue climax, had made a careful study of each.

There was no escaping it. Charlotte had been spanked, hard, and probably on the bare bottom. No other explanation fitted. Immediately he began to concoct fantasies over how it might have happened. It hardly seemed likely that she was punished by her parents, although the idea of her held kicking and squealing over her father's knee held immense appeal, her mother's still more so. A kinky boyfriend seemed far more likely, if less satisfying, and yet he was fairly sure she wasn't going out with anybody.

Certainly she wasn't regularly seen with any boy, to the extent that he had begun to wonder if her naked cavortings in Berne Woods didn't extend to full-blown lesbianism in private. Certainly she seemed suspiciously intimate with Rowena Shields, and the two girls had been at school together, St Cecilia's near Rockbeare, a private school run by nuns. He had read quite enough dirty stories in his time to know what girls got up to at that sort of establishment, while if Rowena was prepared to do it with her other friends, why not Charlotte?

That was the most sensible, and the most satisfying conclusion, that Rowena had spanked Charlotte, a conclusion that sent him into a second round of masturbation more frenzied than the first. Only as he was about to come did he realise that there was a still juicier option. Possibly Charlotte's spanking related to her absence from Berne Woods the other night. Possibly she'd infringed some rule of the group and so incurred a punishment. Possibly the other girls had passed Charlotte around, over their knees one by one with her divine bottom stuck high in the air, stark naked, chubby cunt lips on view from the rear, to be spanked while she begged for mercy and squealed like a stuck pig . . .

It was definitely something that needed to be investigated.

Charlotte lay back on her bed, her mind a jumble of emotions. Her period was due in days, but neither her body, nor her mind, felt right. It was impossible to define exactly what was different, and she could only describe it as a sense of ripening.

The prospect of being pregnant both terrified and delighted her. It was hard to keep her mind from the consequences, especially her parents' inevitable reaction. They would be furious, and their first thought would be to discover who was responsible. Not that it would be hard to guess. Plenty of boys, and men, had shown interest in her, but every single one, save Nich, had seemed impossibly banal beside Horst Sachs.

She would be unable to deny it, and once she had admitted he was responsible a chain of events would be set in motion as inevitable as the turn of the seasons. Father Dawson would be consulted and, after a few euphemistic and righteous comments on the impossibility of abortion, he would suggest marriage. Her parents would seize on the idea, blissfully unaware of Horst's darker side and viewing him simply as a suitable match, the only son of a wealthy family, a wealthy Catholic family.

Once the chain of events had been set in motion, she knew that she herself would be powerless to stop them. Horst himself might refuse, or not. Rowena would fight it, but unless they simply ran away together there would be little she could achieve. Running held a romantic appeal, but the drawbacks were obvious. They would have to work, and neither had much in the way of qualifications or useful skills. The thought of leaving home, and Dorset, produced an instant pang of melancholy, and she pushed it all from her mind, preferring, as always, to leave the decision to other people.

Her hand went to the gentle swell of her belly, trying to sense a difference in the feel of her flesh, for all that she knew it was absurd so soon after she had been filled. Yet even if it was only her imagination, there did seem to be a difference, a firmness, a roundness. Just touching produced a blissful sense of fulfilment and set her thoughts running on what she'd done, her virginity taken on Beltane night, and the possibility that she had been left pregnant.

The sense of satisfaction was immense, and the sense of loss painful. For all the stinging pain of her torn hymen, the feeling of having a cock inside her had been glorious, and not something she wanted to give up. The sensation of being open, of accepting a man between her thighs, had also been wonderful. She wanted both again, and in different ways, to hold a man on top of her as he eased his cock in, to kneel with her bottom lifted and her sex offered for penetration, to hold herself wide, to show everything . . .

If she was pregnant, there would be no further risk. She could do as she pleased, except that she had promised Rowena she wouldn't.

Or had she? She'd promised she wouldn't let Horst near her, yes, but Horst was not the only man in the world. There was Nich . . .

Nich had been gentle, very careful and considerate. His cock had been better than Horst's too, larger, smooth and pale, making her want to hold it, to suck it. The way he'd rubbed it between her pussy lips had been wonderful, bringing her close to orgasm, and the thought of actually being brought off that way was enough to send a shiver right through her. The moment Horst had taken her virginity, with her coming on his cock, had been supreme, and yet if she did it again, she was sure Nich would prove the more exciting lover.

Not that it was going to happen. She'd promised Rowena, but there was no harm in thinking about it. Her hand went lower, to pop the button of her jeans and push further down to the front of her knickers.

The plump, furry mound of her sex felt warm and sensitive, making her want to go lower still. Lifting her bottom from the bed, she pushed her jeans and knickers down to her ankles and let her thighs come wide with a low sigh. Her body was half bare, vulnerable. Her legs were open, ready to accept a man. Her pussy was showing, ready to be filled.

She quickly pulled up her top and bra, baring her breasts and taking one in hand, to play with an already stiff nipple as she began to stroke her pussy. Already she was wet, the soft crevice between her lips slippery with juice. She eased a finger in, feeling the torn rim of her hymen, no longer painful. She'd been fucked, she was probably pregnant, and it felt wonderful.

After a moment of fingering herself she began to tease her clitoris, remembering how it had felt to have Nich rub his cock on the same little bump, with her still virgin, yet spread wide. She wished he'd fucked her properly, along with Horst, sharing her virginity. Perhaps the others should have had her too, one by one, in an all-consuming rite of passion, nothing held back in celebration of her body.

That would have been right, if they'd taken her, cock after cock after cock pushed up into her newly penetrated pussy hole, the perfect celebration, woman and man, with no thought for petty jealousies. She'd have been left filled with sperm, right to the top of her head, her womb swollen with it, and beyond any possible doubt pregnant . . .

She came on the word, her teeth gritted hard to stop herself screaming. For one glorious moment nothing mattered at all save for her ecstasy, focused on having her belly filled to the brim with hot male come, to impregnate her. Her muscles had gone tight, her bottom lifting from the bed, her fingers working furiously in the sopping crease of her sex as she rode her orgasm, stopping only when she could bear it no more.

As her body went slowly limp the bad feelings came back, not least that she had promised never again to indulge in the delightful experience she'd just come over, never again . . .

Never again? It was impossible.

Rowena folded her legs underneath herself as Poppy's 4 × 4 came to a halt in the drive. The situation with Charlotte was resolved, in so far as they'd settled down to their old pattern of life, open friendship punctuated by moments of passion when they could be alone together. Her friends knew, and eventually there would come the moment she was obliged to come out as a lesbian to her parents, but it was not something she was in a rush to do.

Poppy got out of the car, followed by Coralie, and, slightly to Rowena's surprise and embarrassment, Dr Alice Chaswell. For all the pleasure it had given her at the time, it was still a little hard to come to terms with the way Alice had gone down on her in front of the others, and with her own reaction. She knew it shouldn't matter, that once she had been lifted to the strange ecstasy of their rites that contact between them should be natural, completely unfettered. Yet she was still struggling to overcome the tenets of her upbringing, both in regarding sex as sinful and dirty, and that if she was to have sex at all, it should be with a single partner, a male partner.

If Alice felt any such qualms they did not show. She greeted Rowena, Charlotte, Eve and Melanie with an all-encompassing smile and curled herself up on the lawn beside them. Poppy and Coralie also sat down and, after a brief exchange of greetings and kisses, Rowena spoke.

'The first thing you should all know is that Lottie won't be going to see Horst Sachs again. That's over, so let's put it behind us.'

Nobody commented, and she went on in a lighter tone.

'So what's next? Does anyone have any suggestions for solstice?'

Poppy spoke up, her tone more than a little defensive.

'I think we should go to Stonehenge.'

'To Ariesian's gathering?' Rowena responded.

'Why not?' Poppy queried.

'Because he's such a fake, not to mention being a male!' Rowena answered her. 'To follow the old religion you cannot have a priest, you know that. I could never subordinate myself to him, and that includes paying to go to his gathering!'

'So don't pay,' Poppy answered her. 'Nip over the fence. I'm going to.'

'Come on, Ro,' Melanie urged, 'it's the event of the year!'

'I have to be there,' Coralie put in. 'I'm doing a stall.'

Rowena sighed.

'Okay, you know I only lead by consent. So three of you want to go? I'd prefer us to do something on our own, and I don't want to quarrel. Would you three accept a vote?'

Poppy shrugged. Melanie nodded. Coralie spoke after a moment.

'I suppose I could find somebody else, if I had to.'

'Thank you,' Rowena responded. 'Lottie, Eve?'

'I'd rather be with you,' Charlotte stated, with no more than a touch of reluctance.

Eve nodded shyly.

'Three each way,' Rowena said, 'and we know Andrea wouldn't want to go.'

'We know Louisa would,' Poppy pointed out.

'Four each,' Rowena admitted. 'Alice, what do you think?'

'I agree with you about Ariesian,' Alice answered, 'but I think we should go. After all, how are we supposed to challenge his view of Paganism if we're not there?'

'By providing an alternative,' Rowena pointed out.

'Absolutely,' Alice agreed, 'but there are too few of us to make that work. I say we should go, and hold our own rite there, an exclusively female rite. That way we make our point, and perhaps draw in more people.'

'Brilliant!' Poppy responded instantly. 'I'm up for that.'

Rowena hesitated only an instant.

'You're right, Alice. Thank you. Let's do it.'

'What if Horst is there?' Charlotte asked.

'Ignore him,' Poppy advised.

'He's bound to come up to me!'

'Then tell him to get lost.'

'I can't do that! I don't think I could even face him!'

'I'll have to tell him he's not wanted, I suppose,' Rowena sighed.

Poppy answered her.

'Don't worry, Ro, I'll do it.'

Mr Pedlow put his binoculars away, earnestly wishing he'd been able to hear what the girls were saying. All in all it had been an intensely frustrating afternoon. Knowing that Mr and Mrs Shields were in Exeter, and as it was a beautiful day, it had not seemed too much to hope that Rowena would spend some time sunbathing in her garden, perhaps topless, just possibly nude.

His position in the woods was ideal for observing her house, and even allowed him to check up on the Dowlings at the same time. He'd been delighted to see Charlotte making her way down the lane, and more delighted still when the other girls had arrived. It seemed entirely possible that they would strip off, at least partially, maybe even play some dirty little game together, something that involved gradual disrobing, touching each other, even spanked bottoms ...

Nothing had happened. They had merely talked and, other than the occasional trill of girlish laughter or a voice raised to make a point, he hadn't even been able to hear, let alone make out the details of their conversation. Not one of them had so much as taken her top off, let alone peeled nude as he had hoped, or done any of the delightfully rude little things he liked to watch.

Finally he gave up and went to watch girls on the beach instead, who could at least be relied on to be wearing bathing costumes. He felt cheated, and was more determined than ever to set up something in the way of improved surveillance. Exactly what was a different matter, never mind how to go about it, but once he'd got home and had a leisurely wank over his pictures of the girls stripping for their ritual he logged on to the internet and began to search for equipment, preferably to be supplied by discreet mail order.

Horst Sachs was grinning as he pushed the paddock gate closed. The large black sheep he had just chivvied inside spent a moment running aimlessly about and then settled down to graze placidly on the lush grass. He was feeling thoroughly pleased with himself, not only because he'd managed to buy the animal for just fifteen pounds in Honiton within a few days of Nich making the suggestion, but because he knew the purchase would meet with the approval of his father, something which had been largely absent from his life since his early teens.

Since leaving university the pressure from his parents to get a job, or at the least do something to make his way in the world, had been incessant. His private answer was that as their only son, he stood to inherit quite enough to keep him in moderate comfort for life, and that his ambition was to become a leading pagan figure, going down in history alongside Crowley, Gardiner, and others who had openly rebelled against Christianity. It was not something he could admit to, yet.

An interest in sheep breeding was, very much so. Despite having made his fortune as a money broker and seldom if ever got his hands dirty save in the metaphorical sense, his father had a boundless enthusiasm for the country life. In its time the house at Rockbeare had been a smallholding, and they still owned three acres of pasture, all but the paddock leased out to local farmers.

Previously, Horst had shared his father's taste only when it came to horses, riding being something that gave the thrill of danger he craved and also time to be alone and think. Hunting was also enjoyable, albeit done in a manner rather too civilised and bloodless for his tastes, as well as the opportunities riding provided for passing by St Cecilia's and other interesting places.

Both horses had come over to investigate the new arrival, although the ram showed little interest in return. Horst watched for a while, admiring his purchase's thick black-brown coat, solid, curling horns, and what he was doing his best to convince himself was a malevolent gleam in the eye. At length the sound of a car's engine distracted him and he turned to see Poppy Melcombe's unmistakable red 4 × 4 pass the gate at the far side of the paddock.

Quickly running his hands through the spiky brush of his corn blond hair and undoing a second button on his shirt, he composed himself in a position of careless elegance against the paddock gate. He listened as Poppy drew up beyond the house, her tyres crunching on the gravel, and as she slammed the car door, only then calling out. She responded, and quickly appeared, walking briskly across the lawn, her petite figure outlined through a loose summer dress that left no doubt whatsoever that her breasts were bare underneath, or that she was wearing full-cut white knickers. Determined to be cool, and not to stare, he flashed her a smile.

'Hi,' she greeted him, 'I was hoping you'd be in. What is that? No, don't answer that, I know what it is . . . he rather. But why?'

The ram had turned his rear towards them, presenting a pair of large testicles encased in a drop-shaped scrotum of heavily wrinkled, jet black flesh. Horst could see no reason to lie, just the opposite.

'Good, isn't he? He's a cross between a Cheviot and a Welsh Mountain black, fifteen quid at Honiton. He's due to be the sacrifice for my Samhain rite.'

'You're joking! No, you're not, are you. Fuck me!'

'If you insist.'

She gave him a single, distinctly warm glance, then went on.

'Never mind the ram. Rowena is well pissed off with you.'

'That's only to be expected, but I did suggest we all work together.'

'No chance, not with Ro. Anyway, Lottie doesn't want anything to do with you, which is what I came to say.'

Horst felt an immediate tightening of his stomach, but held his voice steady as he replied.

'I expected that, sort of.'

Poppy didn't answer, leaving a slightly embarrassed silence, with Horst wishing the ram would turn around. He could smell her scent, faint but alluring and undoubtedly expensive. Unlike Charlotte, there was a confidence and vitality about her that always made it hard to know what to say, and yet her appeal was undeniable. Finally she spoke.

'What's he called?'

'I wasn't going to name him,' Horst answered her, and stopped, not wanting to admit that he might find it difficult to plunge a knife into an animal he'd made a pet.

'You should,' Poppy insisted. 'He looks very evil doesn't he?'

'I thought that.'

'Lucifer then, or Mephistopheles, or Beelzebub?'

He laughed.

'Don't let Rowena hear you saying that sort of thing! She'll flip.'

Poppy laughed in turn.

'Believe me, I've had it all, how the Christian church has twisted pagan beliefs to make the Horned God a devil. Why should you care though?'

'I don't. I've given up trying with her.'

'I know. When she came round, after you'd had Lottie, you asked her to suck your cock, didn't you?'

She was looking right at him, and Horst swallowed, taken aback by her frankness.

'Yes,' he admitted, and laughed. 'Not that I actually expected her to do it.'

'Not Ro, no, not ever. I'd have done it.'

He swallowed again, harder. For a moment he was sure she was mocking him, but her expression was perfectly serious, her lips slightly parted, and painted, scarlet.

'What was it you said, something about her lippy?'

'Why don't you get down on your knees and wrap that pretty, painted mouth around my cock?'

'Gladly.'

Horst let out his breath as she dropped into a squat, her head level with his crotch. Her fingers went straight to the fly of his work jeans, to ease down the zip with her pretty, elfin face set in an expression of expectant delight. She burrowed her hand into the opening, to pull down the front of his briefs and release his cock. He gasped as she took it in hand, and closed his eyes in pleasure. With her fingers folded gently around his already stiffening shaft, she began to masturbate him, purring gently to herself as she watched his cock grow.

They could be seen, from any car that passed in the lane, and from the windows of two houses, both distant, but not that distant. Poppy didn't seem to care, stroking his cock with attentive pleasure as he stiffened to erection, while he could no more bring himself to stop her than fly. After a while she popped him into her mouth, and his pleasure doubled at the warm, wet sensation.

She was making little satisfied noises in her throat as she sucked, obviously enjoying herself enormously. Soon his cock was rock hard, and her eyes were shut in bliss as she moved her mouth up and down the shaft, now smeared with scarlet lipstick. He put a hand out, steadying himself against the paddock fence, wanting to take the exquisite experience further, knowing he would soon come in her mouth, but not wanting to break the moment. Poppy solved the problem, pulling back.

'I'm not going to let you fuck me.'

Even as she spoke she was pulling up her dress, and it came right off, baring her little breasts, her torso, her slender legs, so that as she went back to work on his cock she was in nothing but her sandals and fresh white panties, a stark contrast to his dirty shirt and mud-spattered work jeans.

He didn't argue, but began to stroke her dense black curls as she worked on his cock, sucking, licking, teasing with the tip of her tongue, until he felt sure that he would explode in her face at any instant. Again she stopped, this time to get him properly showing, humming happily to herself as she unfastened his belt and the button of his jeans.

All of it got tugged down, to his knees, leaving his erection standing proud between the sides of his shirt as she went back to sucking, now also stroking his balls. He was looking, watching her pretty face as she slid her mouth up and down on his cock shaft, her eyes closed in bliss, her little tits jiggling to the motion of her sucking. Suddenly it was too much. He felt his cock jerk, and Poppy gave a delighted squeal as her mouth filled with hot, thick come.

He grabbed his cock as she pulled back, laughing, to milk what was left of his spunk into her face and over her chest. She took it, rocked back on her hands, smiling as his come pattered down into her cleavage and over the low swell of her belly. Only when he'd quite finished did she move, standing to give him a look of mock disapproval.

'You're a bit of a mess, sorry,' he ventured.

'Don't be,' she answered. 'That was nice. I love it when a man gets really carried away.'

'I can get a great deal more carried away than that,' he told her.

'Not with me,' she stated firmly. 'I'm a virgin, and I'm staying that way.'

Three

Charlotte was pregnant. The day her period should have started had passed, and another, and a third, all the while with her hope and fear growing stronger together. After a week had passed she was certain. She'd always been regular, and it seemed close to blasphemy to ever have imagined she would not conceive. How else could it possibly be, taken as a virgin on a Beltane altar? Of course she was pregnant.

For days her moods swung wildly, from depression and self-pity to an erotic ecstasy that would leave her spread-eagled on her bed with one hand on her belly and as much of the other as she could get pushed up her pussy hole, masturbating with the ball of her thumb. As she did it her head would be filled with images of cock; Horst's, Nich's, imaginary ones of ever increasing size, until she was imagining herself being fucked by the Horned God himself.

One sultry afternoon at the beginning of June found her alone, her father at work, her mother shopping in Exeter. Rowena and Poppy were at the beach, but she hadn't wanted to go. Her cycle of misery and exaltation had reached its high point, and as she lay naked on her bed she was gently stroking her belly with her fingertips, her eyes lightly closed, aware of very little but her body. In her imagination she was in Berne Woods, at the circle, nude and waiting for the God to come and fill her with a monstrous cock as hard as wood.

It was an enticing image, but as her thighs came up and open to show off her pussy she stopped, thinking of how much more exciting it would be to actually go up to the woods and do it there. The idea scared her, first at the thought of how hideously embarrassing it would be to get caught masturbating, then at the possible consequences if she was caught. Yet with the fear came a strong thrill, while she knew the actual chances of getting caught were remote.

Berne Woods belonged to an old man, a magistrate and as near as anyone came to being the local squire. To the best of her knowledge he never enjoyed his property at all. She could even take a small detour to see if his car was outside his house. It had to be done, if only to magnify the thrill in her belly. Telling herself that she probably wouldn't masturbate, but just pretend and then do it at home, she slipped on a pair of panties and a bra, then took the bra off. Having her breasts bare felt good, fecund and pleasantly naughty, while nobody need know.

After slipping on a light summer dress of pale blue cotton and a pair of sandals, she left the house. Her stomach was fluttering as she walked, with her mind moving between guilt and pleasure, self-reproach for wanting to be so dirty, and determination to absolutely revel in it. As she climbed a stile her dress snagged briefly on a badly struck nail, filling her head with new images, of losing her dress and being obliged to walk in just her panties, which made her need stronger still.

As she approached the old man's house she told herself she'd only do it if his car wasn't there, sure it would be and that common sense would therefore win. It wasn't, taking away her last excuse not to do what she wanted so badly. As she walked on she was biting her lip, her fingers knotting together in her excitement and uncertainty. She'd said she'd do it if the car wasn't there, so now she had to, no backing out.

She was still telling herself she was being silly as she started into Berne Woods. As always there was a scattering of litter where the cars parked – cans and bottles, the torn pages of a dirty magazine, a used condom – filling her with disgust but setting her mind firmly on the idea of cock. Some man had been erect there, maybe just the night before, pleasuring his girlfriend, his cock hard and urgent in her hand, her mouth, her pussy . . .

Charlotte's last doubts faded as she pushed deeper into the wood. She was going to do it, she had to. Once she'd passed the ancient and faded PRIVATE sign there was no more litter, and the thin mud from the previous night's rain showed no marks at all. Nobody had come there, and nobody was likely to. Perhaps she could go nude, as she wanted to, as she really needed to be . . .

In sudden decision she reached down, to pull her dress up and off, over her head, to leave her breasts naked, walking in just her panties and sandals, as she had imagined. It set her heart pounding, and redoubled her fear, but she stayed topless, telling herself that if any man did see her she'd give him a piece of her mind, calling him a Peeping Tom and a dirty bastard. It wasn't true. She knew she didn't have the courage, and besides, she was the dirty one.

The circle stood as ever, thirteen squat grey sentinels, the little clearing oddly silent, with that same peculiar atmosphere, at once sensual and arcane, it had held for as long as she'd known about it, long before she had associated it with worship. As she stepped within the ring even to be wearing panties suddenly became deeply inappropriate. It was no place for the false modesty of a sour, patriarchal religion, but for joy in her nakedness.

She stripped quickly, her fingers shaking hard as she peeled down her knickers and hung them on a bush with her dress. With her sandals kicked free, she was naked, not a stitch of clothing to cover her. It felt glorious, and she went to stand in the middle of the circle, her hands behind her head, stretching in the warm air, acutely conscious of the size and weight of her breasts, of the odd feeling in her pregnant belly, of the urgent need of her sex.

Sinking slowly to her knees, she wondered how it would be best to be taken. On her back, thighs wide and open to the air seemed most appropriate, and she lay down, her eyes closed, imagining how it would be. She was ready, naked and aroused at a sacred site. If a man came there would be no question that she was ready to be mounted. It wouldn't be any man, but one of those few who understood, in whom she could sense the power of the Horned God, or why not the God himself? In her head the symbol could become the reality.

Slipping her hand down to her sex, she began to masturbate, gently, teasing the lips of her pussy and the mouth of her vagina to see how open she was. The answer was that she was running juice, wide and ready, enough to accommodate the great, thick trunk of a penis. Her mind turned to images of the Green Man, another aspect of the same deity, sinister, terrifying even, in the quiet of the wood, ready to fill any unsuspecting maiden with his great log of a cock.

It was perfect, wonderful, imagining herself caught unawares, being naughty with herself, masturbating naked in the woods, and just taken, her pussy fucked, deep and hard, gallon after gallon of hot, thick spunk ejaculated into her body, filling her until it burst from her straining hole. She'd be held by the hips, utterly helpless, the great woody penis thrust hard up her, in and out, until she was screaming in an abandoned ecstasy over which she had no control whatsoever . . .

She stopped, right on the edge of orgasm, panting gently as her fantasies burnt in her head. It was hard to resolve her need to give herself with her desire to be taken regardless. Perhaps she could be let loose in the woods, chased down and taken by the victor, with no control over who had her, an idea which came from her studies of old rituals. Better, she could seek to give herself to Horst . . . no, Nich, only to discover that he was not as he seemed.

Suddenly it was perfect. She flipped herself over onto her knees, sticking her bottom up, now too excited to even think of being caught. It was the right position, the one she'd be caught in. Nich would take her to the circle, watch her strip and lay herself down at the centre, ready and open. Only when she opened her eyes the Green Man would be towering over her, twelve feet tall, his face knotted wood, his hair straggling ivy, his cock a projecting bough impossibly large for her sex.

She would run, screaming, off through the trees, but it would do her no good. A root would rise to trip her and down she'd go, onto her knees in the mud, bottom up, just as she was. Fingers like thick, supple twigs would lock in the soft flesh of her hips and waist, taking her in an unbreakable grip. The massive penis would find her hole, and in it would go, stretching her to an impossible limit, filling her whole body until it seemed to be coming out of her gaping mouth, and pumping gallon upon gallon of spunk

61

into her belly, with no possibility that she wouldn't end up pregnant . . .

Charlotte came, screaming out her ecstasy at the top of her voice, completely unable to control herself. Her muscles were contracting painfully hard, her whole body locked in orgasm, her pussy and bottom tightening over and over, her belly and breasts quivering in reaction, her feet hammering on the ground. She hit a second peak, and a third, imagining how utterly helpless she would feel, when a crow of laughter sounded from behind her.

She jerked around, clutching at her chest and her sex, a fresh scream ready to break from her lips, and not of ecstasy, to find Rowena standing at the edge of the clearing, smiling, her eyes bright with mischief. Filled with as much relief as embarrassment, Charlotte managed a weak smile, only for the embarrassment to grow stronger as she realised that the shock had made her wet herself a little. Rowena spoke, her voice still full of laughter.

'You might have waited for me, you dirty bitch!'

Charlotte shook her head, unable to speak for the hammering of her heart and her desperate need for air. Rowena went on.

'I've been watching you, Lottie, since you got on your knees.'

'Do – do you . . .' Charlotte managed, recognising her lover's tone, 'do you want me to do it for you?'

'Of course,' Rowena replied. 'What were you thinking of, licking me?'

Charlotte smiled, not wanting to lie, or upset Rowena.

'I need it, I tell you,' Rowena said. 'After watching you like that, I don't think I've ever needed it so badly. Come to me.'

Charlotte obeyed, coming willingly into Rowena's arms and allowing herself to be cuddled, kissed, touched, ever more intimately. She'd melted in moments, helping Rowena to pull off the beach dress she was wearing, and the bright yellow bikini beneath. Naked, they cuddled together, kissing and stroking each other's bodies, Rowena taking the lead, until she was on top of Charlotte, both licking at the other's pussy.

With Rowena's pert, naked bottom in her face, Charlotte gave in completely to her feelings, licking eagerly. When Rowena abruptly sat up she didn't slow at all, even though her face was smothered in bottom and her nose pressed to her lover's anus. She could hear Rowena's soft moans, and licked all the harder, thinking of the position she was in as punishment for her disloyal thoughts. It seemed entirely appropriate to have a bottom put in her face and, as Rowena went through a long, shuddering orgasm, Charlotte was wondering how she could possibly have wanted any other pleasure than with the two of them together. Even when Rowena had finished she stayed perched as she was for a while, before dismounting to lie down on the grass, resting her head on Charlotte's tummy.

'So why here?' she asked, sounding a little hurt. 'You know I'd have wanted to come with you.'

'I'm sorry,' Charlotte answered automatically. 'I – I don't know really. How did you find me?'

'I saw you leave the house. Poppy was flirting with some men on the beach, so I came away, to see you. You've been in an odd mood lately, Lottie. What's the matter?'

Charlotte hesitated, biting her lip, then answered. 'I'm pregnant.'

Mr Pedlow sat back, his cock slowly deflating in his hand. It had been good, very good, although there were still one or two bugs to be ironed out. The motion alarm converted from a porch light, which had previously alerted him to one deer, two foxes, a selection of birds and any number of rabbits, had for once caught something worth seeing: Charlotte Dowling, in nothing but a pair of big white panties and little strappy sandals.

Her subsequent behaviour had been more than he had hoped for in his wildest dreams. First stripping nude, then stretching her gorgeous naked body in the dappled sunlight, then lying down, and not to sunbathe, nor read, nor simply to enjoy the cool air on her naked body, but to masturbate her dirty little cunt.

By the time she'd changed position he'd been close to orgasm, his eyes glued to his monitor screen as he tugged fervently on the hardest erection he could remember achieving in years. The sight of her glorious bottom, turned up with the cheeks spread to show the puckered, pinky-brown ring of her anus and plump, wet lips of her fat little cunt had been too much. He'd come before she had.

Then there had been Rowena, the sight of the two girls together enough to set his fists clenching and his feet drumming on the floor in a delight in his voyeurism as immature as it was crude. By the time Rowena had sat in Charlotte's face his cock had been hard again, and for the first time in what seemed an age he'd managed to orgasm twice in a row, albeit releasing only a miserable dribble of spunk.

Once he'd got his breath back, as the girls lay together and talked, he'd begun to consider improving the system. He'd set the three cameras high, where they were unlikely to be seen or disturbed by animals, but he now realised that the angle deprived him of the full potential for cunt. He'd need them set low, which raised problems of concealment, while ideally he wanted more than three, to make certain he got the full benefit of every angle of the girls' bodies. Then there was the alarm, which had to be made less sensitive, or positioned so that only a human would set it off. Lastly there was the sound, with bird calls and even the noise of the wind inclined to obscure the girls' voices and sighs of ecstasy.

He was attempting to adjust the sound when he caught Charlotte's confession. The girls continued to talk, with increasing urgency, Rowena's voice rising in anger. Mr Pedlow wasn't interested. He was considering the implications of Charlotte being pregnant. It meant she'd fucked, and her a good Roman Catholic girl for all her bizarre antics in the woods. No doubt the culprit was the muscular blond young man he'd seen about the village once or twice, either with Charlotte or one or another of her friends.

Yes, it was easy imagining her giving in to him. He was the sort of man who always got the girls, the bastard. He'd probably pushed her into it, talking his way round her and showing off his physique, and yet that was no excuse for Charlotte to let her knickers down, none at all. She'd been naughty, very naughty. So naughty in fact that she deserved her panties taken down and her fat little bottom spanked until it was bright pink . . .

Just knowing about it made him feel very smug indeed. He derived a great deal of pleasure from the thought of her agonising embarrassment if she were ever to discover that he'd seen every tiny secret detail of her lovely young body, not to mention what she did to herself and with Rowena. Knowing that she was pregnant was nearly as good, an intimate detail of her life she'd evidently only just revealed to her closest friend. Then again, a pregnant girl was unlikely to be able to hide it for very long. Her parents were sure to find out soon enough, so if Charlotte Dowling was pregnant it could only mean one thing – a wedding.

A sense of pique replaced his smugness. If there was to be a wedding in the district, especially one involving the Dowlings, then he ought to be invited. They were neighbours, after all, and had known each other for years. Not to invite him was a blatant snub . . .

His irritation faded at the realisation that the invitations probably hadn't been sent out. It made sense, although with Charlotte pregnant the family presumably wouldn't be wasting any time. Doubtless his invitation would arrive any day, but it would be as well to make sure . . .

Twin security cameras swivelled to face the car as Poppy drew the 4×4 to a halt in front of the high stone arch. A massive gate closed the arch off, bright steel in contrast to the rich yellow of the stone. Nich peered between the seats to read the elaborately carved legend on the arch – RAMSPOUND – set above a sequence of astrological symbols with Aries at the peak. Beyond, a tarmac driveway curved between tall, well clipped hedges of Leyland Cypress. Beyond, all that could be seen of the house were two pointed roofs of new red tile.

'Come on, Ariesian,' Poppy said after a moment. 'Open the fucking gate then!'

'Hang on,' Nich stated. 'Let me out.'

Horst climbed from the front passenger seat, allowing Nich to descend. Poppy and Alice remained in the car. Together the men walked towards the gates, where an intercom was set into the stone of the arch. Nich pressed the buzzer and after a brief pause a silky, female voice answered, in English, but with an oriental inflection.

'Yes? How may I help you?'

Nich answered.

'We have an appointment with Ariesian, for two o'clock.'

'Very well, I shall see if my Lord is expecting you.'

The intercom clicked off. Horst turned Nich a puzzled frown.

'My Lord?'

Nich shrugged.

Nothing happened. Poppy sounded the horn. Still nothing happened. The cameras moved again, with a soft whirr as they focused in, first on Nich and Horst, then on the car and its occupants. Finally the gates swung open. Poppy started through, Nich and Horst following on foot, down the drive to where it curved between the dense hedges, opening out to a broad carriage sweep facing a wide, single-storey house built in new yellow brick with a steeply sloped roof of red tile. It was big, the façade a good forty metres wide, and deep, with the two towers visible from outside rising as wings.

'His own design, I'm told,' Horst remarked.

'Yes,' Nich responded. 'I think he got the idea from Tesco. Did you know it's built on a sacred site?'

'I'd heard something.'

'A wood circle, Wilsford Henge. Alice was involved with the excavation. She tried to fight the planning permission too, but as there was only the double circle of post holes left, and it had been partially erased by a later building, she lost. The house is built directly over it, so that the altar would have been at the exact centre.'

'Does he have an altar there?'

'Let's see.'

An arch identical to the one they'd come through occupied the exact centre of the front, with the same set of carvings. Nich stepped towards it, only to stop as a girl appeared from one side. She was Chinese, slight, exquisitely pretty, and dressed only in a minuscule emerald green bikini and matching heels. Her lustrous black hair hung to her thighs, and her eyes and lips had been made up with the same vivid green, offset with black. She gave a little bow, indicating that they should follow her.

Her bikini was little more than a thong, and Nich allowed his eyes to follow the sweet rotation of her rump as the four of them were led around the side of the house and in through a second door. They passed through a kitchen, immaculately tidy, as if it had never been used, and out to what appeared to be a cloister, with ram's head pillars supporting the roof of a perfectly square paved area, enclosing not an altar, but a huge swimming pool.

Ariesian was seated on a sun lounger a little way around the pool, his jet black bouffant hair and deeply tanned face unmistakable from his numerous TV appearances. Another Chinese girl sat beside him on an ordinary chair, almost identical to the first except in that her bikini and make-up were blue. Beside her was a Champagne bucket with a bottle of Dom Perignon half submerged in ice, and a single glass. Nich nodded politely as Ariesian lifted his shades, speaking.

'Nich Mordaunt. To what do I owe the pleasure?'

His eyes had moved to the two girls, taking in Poppy's black miniskirt and crop top, with the jewel in her belly button piercing twinkling in the bright sunlight, and Alice's tight black jeans and top. He spoke again as Nich made to reply.

'It's a hot day. Why don't you girls jump in the pool while we men talk?'

'I don't have a costume,' Poppy answered, blushing ever so slightly.

Alice simply gave an appreciative nod and began to undress, Ariesian watching her as Nich began to speak.

'I'll come straight to the point. I think we should co-operate this solstice.'

Ariesian laughed, never taking his eyes from Alice as she pushed her jeans and knickers down her legs as one.

'Don't think I don't know what your situation is, Nich. After that stunt you pulled on Dartmoor the police are going to come down on you like a ton of bricks the moment you so much as put a poster up.'

'That's true,' Nich admitted, 'but you know my name will pull a crowd –'

'– and get me closed down. I can't afford to take stupid risks, Nich. This is big business now, not some tinpot little affair. If you knew how much I'll be earning just on magazine and TV rights . . .'

Nich raised his hand.

'I'm not suggesting I appear on the programme, and I don't want any money. I prefer to see myself in a supporting role.'

'I don't have male acolytes. You should know that.'

'Hardly an acolyte,' Nich answered him and paused to draw breath.

Alice, now stark naked, slipped herself into the pool with barely a splash. Poppy had also begun to undress, with a good deal less self-confidence, and a little smirk appeared briefly on Ariesian's face as she hesitated with her thumbs in the waistband of her panties, began to pull them down, hesitated again, thought better of it and jumped in with them still on. Ariesian gave an amused chuckle as Nich went on.

'This is my friend and associate, Horst Sachs, who you may have heard of?'

'No.'

'He's been building up a following in east Devon and Dorset, quite successfully. Now as you know, my aim is to return to the oldest, purest forms of Pagan worship, with all the contamination of both Christianity and modernism removed. A lot of people agree, and we feel it would be to your advantage to allow us to present our case.'

'To my advantage? Why?'

'To be frank,' Nich stated, 'many people are saying that you are a populist, and that you will compromise your beliefs in order to placate the authorities. Some are even beginning to think you're a fraud, and in it purely for the money. If you provide Horst and me with a pavilion –'

'By all means. Pavilions are twelve pounds a square foot. Would twenty by forty suit you?'

'For our mutual benefit, as I was saying,' Nich went on, 'and therefore at no charge –'

'No charge? You really have no idea, do you, Nich? I still have to hire the pavilion, not to mention my other overheads. I'd like to be altruistic, believe me, but I simply can't afford it.'

Nich glanced around at the opulent vulgarity of the house, then to where Alice was floating lazily on her back at the centre of the pool. Ariesian's eyes also moved to Alice, and his mouth curved up into a smile as Nich continued.

'Our feelings are that your gain in credibility by our presence will easily offset your costs, and besides, we can't afford your rates.'

'It's nearly ten grand,' Horst pointed out.

Ariesian merely shrugged.

'A space then,' Nich suggested, 'perhaps marked off by ropes?'

They fell to discussing the details, Nich offering a

series of suggestions, on each of which Ariesian either set a price or dismissed out of hand. Horst watched the girls swim, putting in only the occasional remark, but with increasing heat as it became evident that Ariesian was mocking them.

Finally Ariesian laughed.

'Face it, Nich, you're washed up. You can come, I'm not banning you or anything. It's twenty-five quid a ticket. Yi will sort it on your way out. Now you two girls, you I'll let in for free, in return for a little dance. In fact, why don't you stay and discuss it?'

Horst turned quickly to the pool, but Poppy was already striking out for the side. Reaching it, she pulled herself up, her slight body running water, her knickers now completely transparent, to show the thick bush of her pubic hair in front. Ariesian's eyes followed her as she went to take a towel from a rack, the neat curves of her bottom showing through the clinging cotton. Alice had stayed in the pool, apparently oblivious to what was going on, until Ariesian spoke again.

'Now there's a girl with sense. I think she's staying.'

Alice's eyes came open, their brilliant green colour clear even across half the width of the swimming pool.

'I'll stay a while, if you don't mind, Nich? Perhaps I can persuade Ariesian to think again.'

'I'm sure you can,' Ariesian chuckled.

Alice closed her eyes again. Ariesian adjusted his shades to cover his own, then clicked his fingers to the Chinese girl at his side, who began to work on the foil of the Champagne bottle. Dismissed, Nich gave a precise bow to Ariesian and turned on his heel. The Chinese girl, Yi, her face set in the same sweet smile, indicated that they should follow her. Horst hesitated, glancing from Nich to Alice, then Poppy, who was frantically trying to dry herself and gather up her discarded clothes at the same time. Ariesian watched.

The girl stayed floating at the centre of the pool, her eyes closed. Only when Ariesian spoke again did she trouble to look at him.

'So, what exactly is it you want, Juliana?'

'I'm Alice,' she replied. 'Juliana is my sister.'

'So you're not Mordaunt's girlfriend?'

'Perhaps I was.'

She struck out for the side of the pool, to pull herself from the water with a single, easy motion. In the background he caught the sound of Poppy's car as the engine started. He watched Alice as she went to fetch a towel, his eyes never leaving her body, not troubling to conceal his knowing smirk. As she took the towel he spoke again.

'You're going to convince me to give your boyfriend a break, are you? He does know what you're going to have to do, doesn't he?'

It was hard to keep the laughter from his voice. Alice didn't answer, drying her body with the same casual indifference to her nudity she had shown before. He went on, relishing his own words and the images they conjured up.

'You know what they say in the porn industry? Blowjob or no job. Well, it's the same around here, although I suspect you've realised that, eh, a clever girl like you? I bet you have. Only this time, I want the whole enchilada. I want to fuck you, Alice, and I want Nich to know I've fucked you.'

He'd expected her to react, sure that the suggestion of a cock being put to her cunt in payment for a favour would puncture even her cool. It didn't, and as she bent to dry her toes he found himself presented with the full moon of her rear view, her long legs rising to slim bottom cheeks, with the shaved lips of her cunt peeping out from between her thighs and her bottom hole on show. For a moment he wondered if she was deliberately mocking him, perhaps taunting him with her body with the intention of denying him at the last moment. He determined not to rise to the bait, but went on, sure he could eventually provoke a reaction from her.

'You have a pretty cunt, Alice. I see you shave. I like girls who shave. Nice arsehole too: tight. So, let's bargain, yeah? What does Nich expect? You suck my cock and he gets a pavilion I could hire for ten grand? Hey, you're good, but you're not that good! This is the deal. A nice, slow blowjob is worth fifty quid, so Nich and his mate get in for free. Three hundred an hour, I reckon you're worth, so if we fuck he can have his own stall, but you stay the night, and you do as you're told. If he wants that pavilion, I get you for a week, and the first thing I'm going to do is grease that tight little arsehole of yours and slide my big fat willy right up your tube.'

He laughed, expecting her to round on him in anger. Xiu Mei was blushing, but Alice barely reacted, simply lifting each of her heavy breasts in turn to dry underneath and then holding the towel up.

'Should I put this back on the rack?'

'Um ... er ... no,' Ariesian managed, thrown completely off balance. 'It goes in the wash. Xiu Mei, take it.'

The Chinese girl gave an obedient bob and rose to take the wet towel from Alice, who began to wind another one around her long wet hair. She spoke as she sat down on the vacant chair.

'You've got the wrong end of the stick, Ariesian. I didn't stay so that I could bargain for Nich. I stayed because I wanted to.'

'Oh yes?' he asked, still doubtful.

'Yes,' she assured him. 'You're right. Nich is washed up, and I – well, I suppose I'm just the sort of girl who likes to be with a winner.'

She was close enough to touch, her naked body within reach, and his cock was stiffening in his bathing shorts. Yet he held back, sure that the moment he made a move she would dance away, laughing, as her sister had once done at a festival where he'd approached her. Fighting to keep his cool, he answered her.

'So you want to be with me? Is that what you're saying?'

'Yes.'

'What if I don't believe you?'

She slid from the chair, onto her knees. He watched, still full of doubt as she crawled slowly around the sun lounger, the movements of her naked body as elegant as any cat, her green eyes never leaving his face. As she reached the far side she came up onto her knees again, her body across his, pulled down the front of his shorts and very casually took his cock in her mouth.

Ariesian could only stare at first, watching Alice's beautiful face with the thick stump of his penis deep in her mouth. She'd closed her eyes, working on him with every evidence of enjoyment, and as his penis began to swell the last of his doubts dissolved. He'd been wrong all along. She wasn't the little tease he'd supposed. Just the opposite. She was a whore, giving herself to whoever could provide her with the most.

It wasn't going to stop her getting her fucking, but even as he began to grow erect in her mouth he knew exactly what he was going to do: use her thoroughly, until he'd sated his appetite, and then get rid of her. He smiled at the prospect, a few months of excellent sex followed by the perfect revenge, rejecting her as her sister had rejected him, but only once she'd been well and truly used.

He took hold of his cock and balls, ringing himself so that he could masturbate into her mouth as he imagined all the things he wanted do to her; spunk in her face, make her eat it from his cock, maybe even the floor, make her dress like the bitch whore she was, fuck her in front of other men, bugger her, maybe bugger her and make her suck his dirty penis clean . . .

The thought was too good to let him hold back. He began to tug hard at his cock. Like the experienced slut she was, she began to suck the end, ready for his spunk. He imagined how it would look, his cock steaming from the hot, slimy cavity of her rectum, the head in her mouth, the utter disgust on her face. The spunk erupted and he'd come, full in her mouth. Alice swallowed the first explosion before opening her pretty mouth to let him milk what was left onto her already slimy tongue.

Mr Pedlow moved ponderously down the High Street, his eyes bulging slightly as his vision caressed a particularly well filled pair of jeans. He didn't know the girl, but she had a nice bottom and that was what mattered, so as she turned to go into a shop he favoured her with a smile, wishing it could be a pat on her well turned rump instead.

Twice during the week he had passed Mrs Dowling in the street, each time exchanging polite greetings, but no more. Nor had he received an invitation. Yet he was sure the news would be around the district.

Unless he was greatly mistaken there was a fresh buzz among local gossips, and more than once he had passed groups of women whose conversation had stopped abruptly and continued in low tones as soon as he was safely beyond them.

His sense of pique, always sensitive to the smallest slight, real or imagined, had grown as he became increasingly sure that Charlotte would be getting married and that he was being deliberately excluded from the guest list. It was too much, when everyone of the slightest consequence for miles around was sure to be invited. In fact, the idea of him not being invited was so preposterous that he was still telling himself that either the Dowlings were for some reason delaying the announcement, or that his invitation had been mislaid.

In any event, it was clearly time for him to drop a hint, and as Mrs Dowling herself emerged from a shop some little way down the street he was presented the perfect opportunity. Beaming broadly, he increased his pace, addressing her as soon as he was close enough to be heard.

'Good afternoon, Mrs Dowling, and may I be among the first to congratulate you on the joyous news.'

Four

'Go behind the screen and pop this on, if you would.'

Charlotte's face creased up in consternation as she accepted the object from Dr Martins. It was a hospital gown, theoretically to cover her modesty, but even without putting it on she could tell it would be practically useless. Not only did it look as if it had been designed for a dwarf, but one of the ties at the side had come away. Nevertheless, she went behind the screen as instructed, determined not to make a fuss.

As she undressed, peeling off her clothes with ever increasing embarrassment, a nurse came into the room and stayed, adding to Charlotte's already overwhelming chagrin. Removing her panties took an effort of will and set her lower lips trembling, a reaction that grew worse as she pulled the gown on. It was even worse than she'd imagined, too short to cover her bottom, so that a good half of her chubby cheeks showed behind and the fur of her sex at the front. At the best of times the upper part would scarcely have covered her breasts, but with one tie missing she had a choice of leaving both bulging out so badly it looked obscene, or doing up the remaining tie and risking having one breast slip out completely.

'Are you quite okay there, Charlotte?' Dr Martins called out, only increasing her frustration as she struggled to make the decision.

'Yes, Doctor, sorry,' she answered hastily, her face red with blushes as she did the offending tie up.

She stepped out, Dr Martins giving no more than a brief glance and pointing at an examination chair with his pen. The nurse was still there, poking among the contents of a flat tray. In an agony of embarrassment, Charlotte made for the chair, lowering herself into it. Dr Martins turned to her.

'Feet up,' he instructed her, his voice showing a trace of impatience. 'Don't worry, you haven't anything I've not seen before, many, many times.'

Charlotte didn't answer. She couldn't, her embarrassment reaching a new peak as she lifted her legs and placed her feet in the stirrups, to spread her sex wide for his inspection. He stepped close, frowning in what could only be disapproval. Charlotte closed her eyes and bit back a sob, then winced as a wooden spatula touched the side of her vagina, holding the hole open so that he could inspect her torn hymen.

Still peering into her vagina, Dr Martins gave a little click of his tongue, then spoke.

'Yes, I see. Clearly.'

'I did say!' Charlotte moaned, her reserve finally breaking completely.

'You'd be surprised how often you girls lie about these things,' he answered, and finally removed the spatula. 'Right, if you could fill this.'

She opened her eyes, to find the nurse holding out a urine bottle. Dr Martins turned his back. The nurse didn't, but watched in what Charlotte was convinced was amusement. If she'd thought her embarrassment was bad before, it was as nothing compared to her feelings as she pressed the cold glass of the bottle mouth to her sex. At first the pee wouldn't come, for all that her bladder had felt weak since waking up that morning, but at last she managed to start her pee, only to find it wouldn't stop.

'You might have gone behind the screen,' Dr Martins remarked with ill-concealed disgust as he turned again. 'That's plenty, thank you.'

Charlotte's response was a bitter sob. Her pee was still gushing out into the bottle, so much she was sure it would overflow, soaking her pussy, the chair, the floor . . .

It didn't, but stopped a couple of inches from the top. She handed the warm bottle to the nurse, who took it in rubber-clad hands and went to a side bench. Charlotte was left, acutely conscious of her spread thighs and her wet, open sex. Dr Martins went to join the nurse and she was ignored, splay-legged in her embarrassment, for what seemed an age. Finally, with another click of his tongue, Dr Martins turned around.

'Yes, it's positive. That means you're pregnant, Charlotte.'

'I know, I told you that!' Charlotte wailed.

'It's best to get a professional opinion. You may get dressed now.'

'Thank you,' Charlotte answered.

As she swung her legs down from the chair her left breast fell out of her robe.

Two hours later she was bundling herself into Poppy's car, dragging her bag behind her. Even as the door closed a great weight seemed to have been lifted from her shoulders. For a while at least she would be able to shut out the awfulness of the previous few days. The arguments were bad enough, and the endless interrogations, given despite the fact that she'd admitted first to being pregnant and then that Horst Sachs was the father within minutes of her mother's first furious demand. Worse still was the constant air of reproach, the house filled with a sullen silence broken only by flares of anger, demands for her to explain herself, bitter monologues.

Things had gone from bad to worse. The family had been alerted to her disgrace in a series of tense, whispered phone calls, none of which she was privy to. Mr and Mrs Sachs had been contacted in Austria and were returning to England, while she herself had been dragged to Rockbeare by her father so that he could confront Horst in her presence.

The question of marriage had yet to be raised, but she knew it was coming, and when. A meeting had been arranged for her with Father Dawson. It was a meeting she was dreading, as she could already see his condescending little smile and hear his voice, mild yet firm, and infinitely patient, as if it were only her all too evident stupidity that prevented her understanding him immediately.

She had at least been allowed to go to the festival with the others, although with the distinct implication that as she had already ruined herself it really made no difference what she did. This attitude was a symptom of the rather public martyrdom that was part of her mother's reaction to the news – a part Charlotte suspected brought her a secret enjoyment.

Despite the knowledge of what she faced, her relief at being alone with the girls was immense. They alone were fully sympathetic, Poppy turning to wink at her from the driving seat, both Melanie and Louisa throwing her concerned glances as she squeezed up on the seat.

Rowena glanced around as the engine rumbled to life.

'Do you know how they found out?'

'No! Yes . . . not really. Old Mr Pedlow came up to Mummy to congratulate her on my wedding!'

'What wedding? How the hell did he know anyway!?'

'Search me! I didn't tell him!'

'Somebody must have done, and it wasn't me.'

Charlotte made a face and quickly changed the subject.

'How are the others getting there?'

'Eve's going in Coralie's van,' Poppy answered. 'Andrea's with Nich and Juliana. Hey, did you hear? Alice has gone off with Ariesian!'

'You're joking!' Charlotte answered her.

'No I'm not. I went up with them, when Nich was trying to get a deal for some space at the festival, and she stayed. She hasn't come back either, and Horst says she's moved in with him.'

'No! How's Nich taking it?'

'Pretty calmly, or at least it seems that way, but I bet he's furious inside.'

'I bet. What a bitch!'

Alice lay stretched out on a sun lounger by the pool at Ramspound. Her only garments were a PVC bra top that held her full breasts up and left the large pink zip that closed it thrust forward as if on offer to be pulled down, and a matching pair of shorts, cut to leave most of her bottom spilling out at the rear and so tight that the shape of her sex showed in detail at the front, with another large pink zip half open to expose the first gentle rise of her bare pubic mound. Beside the lounger stood a pair of shiny black heels.

Behind her reflective shades her eyes were closed, and her thoughts were far detached from her surroundings: of a man holding up a cross, his shouted words loud above the crackle of flames as the timber frame of a half-built church burned, then lost as it collapsed in an explosion of sparks and ash. Ariesian's voice broke into her reverie.

'Time for one more, Babe.'

Alice rose without hesitation, slipping into her heels and letting her hips sway gently as she crossed to where he stood. He was in a white bathrobe, and he let it drop as she reached him, revealing his naked, heavily tanned body beneath, his once-toned muscles now beginning to show the slackness of age. She let him take her hand and lead her inside, to a great square bedroom symmetrically arranged with an arched doorway in each of the four walls and a huge four-poster bed at the centre.

He paused, sending her forward with a pat on her bottom. Kicking off her heels, she climbed up onto the bed, crawling, the water-filled mattress rippling beneath her. As she reached the centre she turned, to find that he'd gone to one of the four identical chairs in the corners of the room and was sitting with his hands in his lap, idly toying with the thick stump of his cock and his heavy balls.

'Show me what you've got,' he ordered.

Alice smiled and knelt up, her knees set wide, to take her big breasts in her hands. He gave a satisfied nod as she began to mould and squeeze them, showing off her cleavage, running her fingers over the little bumps her already stiff nipples made in the PVC, moving to let them loll forward and shaking her body to make them shiver and bounce in the little bra top. Already his cock was beginning to stiffen, and she licked her lips at the sight as she once more knelt high, and put her fingers to the fat pink zip that held her breasts in.

He had begun to pull harder at his cock as Alice eased her zip down, very slowly, showing off inch after inch of deep pink cleavage, until at last it could take the strain no more and sprang open, releasing her breasts, high and firm for all their size. Holding the sides of her bra top open, she pushed her chest out to show them off. Ariesian swallowed hard.

'Fuck me, Babe, but I'll swear those joy bags of yours get bigger every time I see them!'

Alice blew him a kiss and bounced her naked breasts in her hands, showing off just how big and firm they really were. His cock was nearly hard, the meaty foreskin rolling back with each tug to show the head within. She quickly shrugged off her bra top and began to pose, first with her hands behind her head and her breasts thrust well out, then forward on all fours to let them hang, heavy and round beneath her chest. As she rose again a teasing curtain of jet black hair remained to cover them, with just the ripe red buds of her nipples poking through.

She gave a little shimmy, making them quiver, before slowly drawing the curtains of her hair apart to show them off in their full magnificence. Ariesian's face had begun to go red, and his cock was rock hard, the veins standing out on the short, thick shaft and the head a glossy purple with pressure. Alice smiled and gave her breasts another jiggle. He sighed and spoke.

'You gorgeous little slut! Now turn around, and let's see you peel those shorts off your sweet arse, nice and slow.'

Alice giggled as one hand moved lower, to take the second zip firmly between finger and thumb. Her other hand went to her mouth, pressing the tip of a single finger to her lips in a gesture of mock uncertainty even as she peeled the zip fully down. Ariesian made a little choking noise in his throat and curled what he could get of his hand around his cock shaft, wanking as she began to turn.

She did it slowly, making sure he had plenty of time to drink in the new angle on her breasts and the curve of her hip, all the while with her back dipped in to keep her bottom well pushed out. Her knees stayed wide too, to keep the already overstretched seat of her shorts as tight as possible over her bottom. With her back right to him, the pose left her rear pushed out as a round, meaty ball, half clad in shiny black, half bare, cheeky girl flesh.

Ariesian paused to blow his breath out as Alice looked back over her shoulder and pushed her thumbs into the waistband of her shorts. Realising she was waiting for an order, he nodded, and the shorts began to come down, slowly, exposing the smooth, pale flesh of her lower back, the soft V where her bottom cheeks began to open out, the deep cleft between them, and at last the full spread of her bottom, pushed out in rude display.

Her cheeks were well parted, and she knew her anus was showing as well as the neatly turned fig of her sex with her hole moist and open at the centre. It was too much for him, and before she could take her shorts off to complete her strip he was scrabbling onto the bed, cock in hand, mumbling obscene endearments.

'Get it up then, Babe, right up . . . show me, show me your sweet little cunt . . . yes, that's right . . . oh, you little whore, you gorgeous little whore!'

Alice had gone down on all fours, then on her face, her bottom stuck high as she reached back to spread her sex. She felt his cock touch her leg, then between her cheeks, rubbing in her slit as he grunted and mumbled, his words no longer coherent. Reaching back, she took the thick stem of his cock and fed it into herself, sighing deeply as her hole filled. He sighed in turn, and began to fuck her, his hands locked in the flesh of her hips, his belly slapping on her upturned bottom.

Alice took it panting and gasping, at first with her face right down, then on all fours with her breasts jumping and slapping together to his thrusts until he took them in hand, groping at them as he fucked her and called her his darling, his baby and his whore. She wondered if he'd carry out the threat he'd made again and again and bugger her, and how it would feel to have his thick penis forced into her anal ring instead of slid up her pussy but, as before, he failed to control himself.

With a last grunt he filled her hole with come, making Alice gasp as his cock was rammed in as far as it would go. He held himself deep in, pawing at her bottom and mumbling to himself, gave a last few firm shoves into her slippery hole and pulled free, to leave her with his come running down between the lips of her sex. She reached back, eager to masturbate, only to receive a firm slap across her bottom.

'No time for that, Babe. We'd better get moving.'

Nich considered the fence around Ariesian's Stonehenge Solstice Festival site. It was higher than he'd expected, while large men with Alsatian dogs patrolled at regular intervals. It had also been run across open downland, making it impossible to approach under concealment except where it ran along the edges of the roads. Nor did he particularly want to go in, as the sight before him inspired only melancholy.

The stones themselves were fenced off as always, and the area deserted save for a small group of druids standing among the sarsens. For all their solemn air they seemed more than a little forlorn when set beside the huge and colourful throng beyond the fences, although the stones themselves retained a quiet dignity beside the structure Ariesian had erected a bare two hundred yards distant.

It rose a good thirty feet into the air, a replica of the henge as it might have been when complete, only three times the size and rather obviously constructed of grey canvas and painted plywood on metal frames. An avenue had been fenced off, leading north-east in mimicry of the original, only not to the river Avon, but to a large caravan decorated with an enormous plastic ram. At the centre, a model of the altar stone rose above the heads of the crowds, with the rings rising higher still.

The crowd pressed close around the false stones. On top of each of the great trilithons stood a human figure, female and dressed in a short white tunic of some fine material that floated around them as they danced. Even at a distance it was plain that the girls had nothing but thongs beneath their tunics, the hems lifting to their motion to show off triangles of white material to the front, and the bare globes of muscular yet rounded bottoms at the rear. Among them was Alice.

Nich shook his head in wonder.

The car park had been full long before they arrived, and the gates across the A303 closed. Police had directed them to an overflow car park in a field, where they gathered and walked across to where they could see over the site. Although the site itself was crowded, a good many, like them, had halted outside.

Glancing around, Nich gave a thoughtful nod.

Before long there would be as many out as in, while near the gates there seemed to be more than a little discontent among those refused admission. Two young men were walking towards him, both in sweat shirts emblazoned with the names of rock bands. Neither looked happy; their voices were raised and one was making angry gesticulations. As they approached they parted company, and Nich stepped into the path of the nearest.

'What's the matter? Are they turning people away?'

The initial response was a hostile glance, quickly changing to recognition.

'You're Nich Mordaunt, aren't you? I saw you at Stanton Rocks, fucking ace that was!'

Nich merely grinned as the youth went on.

'Forty quid on the gate, they want this year, the bastards!'

'I thought it was twenty-five?'

'Twenty-five in advance, yeah. Forty on the gate, and there's dogs and that with the pigs.'

Nich gave a sympathetic nod. Behind him, Rowena, Charlotte and Andrea stood together, with the other girls talking to Horst and his friends. Only Coralie and Eve had gone in. The youth had stayed put, looking interested.

'Are you going to do something?'

'Just possibly. Do you see the blond man over there, talking to the dark, petite girl?'

'Sure.'

'That is Horst Sachs, who this year celebrated Beltane together with the beautiful golden-haired girl with her two friends, there. Suffice to say that she is now carrying a child. That is how a pagan festival should be celebrated.'

The youth's eyes had gone to Horst, then Charlotte, where they stayed, his jaw falling slowly open. Charlotte was in a loose, pale blue dress which showed her opulent curves to full advantage, clinging to the outlines of her breasts in particular. Horst looked no less impressive from a feminine perspective, and an idea began to form in Nich's mind.

'Spread the word,' he instructed the youth. 'I'll be making an announcement presently, from the barrow up there.'

The youth nodded and moved off. Nich moved

towards the others. The lone barrow up the slope from Stonehenge was fenced off, but only with barbed wire. Nich glanced at his watch, calculating his chances. They seemed good, with the police concentrated on the roads and car park, just a few at the gate, in the compound and near the stones themselves. Horst was talking to Poppy; both were smiling and full of life.

'Time to act,' Nich announced. 'Come with me.'

'What are we going to do?' Horst asked, following as Nich moved towards Rowena and her group.

Nich ignored him, speaking to Rowena and Charlotte as well when he did reply. 'I think we're all agreed that something should be done to burst Ariesian's bubble?'

Rowena gave a doubtful nod and Nich quickly went on.

'Then let's put our differences aside. When Ariesian comes out I'm going to announce Horst, from that barrow up there, and I think Charlotte should be –'

'No way!' Rowena answered him. 'Not ever, Nich, not –'

Nich raised his hands.

'What choice do we have? Horst and Lottie make the perfect embodiment –'

'No,' Rowena answered firmly.

'Nich's right,' Horst put in. 'You're just being envious, Ro, and –'

'Envious!?' Rowena spat. 'You fucking pig! You lure my girlfriend off and –'

'Calm down, please,' Juliana put in, stepping forward. 'Think how Ariesian would laugh at you two. So if you're not prepared to let Lottie go up with Horst, Rowena, what are you prepared to do?'

'I'll go up with her,' Rowena answered. 'Nich can announce us.'

'There has to be a male and female principle,' Horst objected.

Rowena responded, and Andrea, Horst quickly adding his voice again, then Juliana, and for a moment they were all speaking together and none listening. Nich shook his head and threw a nervous glance in the direction of the false henge, then swore.

Ariesian had stepped from the caravan. He was dressed in a simple white robe, falling to the ground, and, Nich suspected, concealing built up shoes. In one hand he held a staff of rough oak, but with the top curved in the manner of a Bishop's crozier, around which mistletoe had been tangled. He also wore a crown of mistletoe, set on top of the massive, curling ram's horns that seemed to grow from either side of his head. A cloak led back from his shoulders, clasped in front with a massive golden ram's head broach, and supported behind him by the two Chinese girls, both clad in the same abbreviated white tunics as his dancers.

'Be quiet, all of you!' Nich commanded. 'We have to do something now, or never.'

The expression on Rowena's face was enough to make it absolutely clear she would not give way, but Ariesian had already begun the slow walk along the avenue. A few people had also begun to gather near the barrow, or were watching him and those with him. Poppy spoke up.

'You're being silly, Ro. I'll go up if Lottie won't.'

Melanie had been about to speak too, and Nich snatched at the chance.

'Great idea. Horst can have handmaidens. In fact, we'll outdo Ariesian. Melanie, Louisa, Juliana?'

Juliana nodded and Melanie made to reply, only for Rowena to speak first.

'No, absolutely not! I'm not having women

portrayed as subservient! The female principle should be dominant, always!'

'Then let Charlotte come up,' Nich urged, Juliana and Poppy quickly adding their voices. 'I'll stand between them if you like, but –'

'Okay!' Rowena snapped. 'Do it. Go on, Lottie, but don't you dare touch her, you bastard!'

Horst didn't respond, because Nich was already pulling him towards the barrow. Charlotte hesitated only a moment before following with the others. Down the slope, Ariesian was nearing the false stones, walking on a carpet of white rose petals strewn by girls in sandals and tunics. Nich ran faster, tugging Horst behind him, until he reached the fence that closed off the barrow.

'Strip, quickly,' Nich ordered, pushing down the top strand of the wire and swinging a leg across.

'Strip?' Horst queried. 'What, all the way?'

'You'd look a right idiot in just your underpants!' Nich answered him. 'Come on. No, climb over first, or you'll do yourself an injury.'

Horst nodded, looking more than a little doubtful as he clambered over the fence and began to pull off his clothes. The crowd was beginning to gather around them, blocking off Nich's view of the henge, and incidentally concealing Horst as he undressed. Charlotte had crossed the fence, but stood irresolute and blushing as she watched Horst strip. Rowena's face was like thunder. With no time for further argument, Nich scrambled to the top of the barrow.

Across the down Ariesian had reached the centre of the false henge and was being helped up onto the huge model of the altar stone. Drawing in his breath, Nich pointed across the heads of the crowd and let out a scream at the top of his voice.

'Look! Is this the avatar of the Horned God? Is this the representation of fertility, a frail old man who needs to be helped on his way? No! I say he is a cheat, and a sacrilegious cheat at that! Each year a new man should be chosen to represent the God, we know that, do we not!? This is not Ariesian, and could never be. Instead, I will give you our avatar, and not some doddering old degenerate who seeks only to line his pockets at your expense!'

As he finished, Nich shook his fist at the distant figure in the ram's horn headdress. Ariesian was too far away to hear, the intervening crowd too noisy. It didn't matter. Plenty of people had heard, and were turning to look at him, a wave of interest that spread out from the barrow, across the crowd outside the compound and within. Unfortunately the crowd of pagans weren't the only ones taking notice. Both security and a few policemen had seen, and were already talking together or into their communicators. Quickly, Nich reached his hands down, grasping Horst's and Charlotte's as they came up beside him.

'Here!' he yelled. 'Here are the chosen for this turn of the cycle, as golden as the corn, as fertile as the earth itself!'

Charlotte was fully clothed, although with the wind blowing her lightweight dress against her full curves it was no more than a minor detail. Horst was naked, and stood proud with his chin lifted as a delighted roar went up from the crowd. On the altar stone Ariesian was attempting to perform his ritual, but just about every eye in the vast crowd had turned to the three figures on the barrow, along with a majority of the TV cameras. A gust of wind caught them, blowing Charlotte's golden curls into a glorious sunlit halo and making her dress swirl around her legs, as

Nich held his pose, despite the yellow-jacketed figures already pushing towards him through the crowd.

'Shouldn't we go?' Horst urged in a frantic whisper.

'Just a second more,' Nich answered as the first of the security guards reached the edge of the crowd surrounding the barrow. 'Okay, over the far side.'

He made an urgent signal to Juliana, who had gathered up Horst's clothes. At the edge of the crowd two security men were trying to force their way in, pushing and pulling. One huge, bearded man pushed back and a security guard was sent sprawling. The first of the policemen to come up tried to intervene, overreacting by drawing his baton to strike out at the big man. Shouts of protest went up. Somebody threw a beer can, still full, the yellow liquid arching through the air to splash into the face of a security man.

More police and more security men began to come up, and yet more were converging from every corner of the down as Nich tumbled quickly over the wire, with Horst already scrambling frantically into his trousers. Charlotte was quickly hustled away by Rowena, already in Andrea's coat with her hair concealed beneath a thick woolly hat. Horst swore as he snagged his leg on the wire, but joined Nich, dashing for the nearest grove of trees with several dozen others. Behind them Ariesian's Solstice Festival began to dissolve into riot.

'Bastard!' Ariesian spat, throwing himself down on his sun lounger. 'I swear I'll kill the little shit!'

Alice responded with a consoling smile, which he ignored, instead snarling at Yi, who stood to the side with her brown eyes wide and full of concern.

'What do you think you're staring at? Get me some Champagne.'

He kicked out as she passed, the tip of his shoe catching her bottom, to make her stumble and leave a muddy stain on the seat of her tunic. She scrambled away, at a run, Xiu Mei following. Alice knelt down beside the sun lounger.

'Let me suck you. It'll make you feel better.'

His response was a grunt, but he lifted his robe and pushed down the boxer shorts beneath, exposing his fat, stubby cock. She immediately leant close, to take it in her mouth, sucking and working her tongue with such skill that pleasure had quickly begun to jostle with the burning anger inside him.

The festival had been ruined, and entirely because of Mordaunt and his idiot friends. His solstice speech had gone unheard, his ceremony had been cut short, no collection had been taken up and merchandising was down to a quarter of what it had been the year before. There was still a profit, but not close to what it should have been, while the Chief Constable had already demanded to see him and he knew it would take all his influence to stop the event being banned the next year.

It was very hard indeed to turn his mind away from the disaster, even with his cock rapidly growing in Alice's mouth. She at least had given him some satisfaction, dancing in full view of Mordaunt. It was only a shame he'd been unable to make her do it nude. Again he cursed, this time at the agreement with the police that ensured there would be no nudity at his festivals. It was a shame, because otherwise he'd have made Alice strip, and not in a way that might be interpreted as a celebration of the female body, but something smutty, something lewd, in her little PVC outfit, or fishnets and a tight leather skirt, like the whore she was . . .

Yet if he hadn't had her nude then, at least he could now.

'Get your gear off,' he ordered.

Alice obeyed without hesitation, pulling back from his cock to quickly peel her tunic off over her head and push her thong down and off. She was going to take the white heels he'd chosen for her off as well, but he shook his head and she kept them on. Again her lipstick-red mouth came wide and she had taken his now half-stiff cock in, sucking eagerly with her big breasts swinging to the motion.

Yi appeared with the Champagne, a bottle of Dom Perignon already in an ice bucket. With a single nervous glance to where the naked Alice was sucking cock, she put the bucket down and covered it with a cloth, leaving just the neck of the bottle sticking out. She made to go, but Ariesian snapped his fingers, pointing to the pool side.

'Stay here, and call your sister. I want you two to watch this.'

Ariesian had been watching Alice's face as he spoke, hoping for a show of shame. There was nothing, as if she hadn't heard, her eyes closed as she worked on his cock. Yi's response was very different: pink-faced embarrassment as she bobbed her head and retreated to signal her sister. She was soon back though, as he'd known she would be, Xiu Mei also, both watching from a doorway.

Feeling distinctly better, and very pleased with himself, he began to wonder just how far he could push Alice. Something about her made him cautious; perhaps the lean strength of her body, the casual confidence with which she carried herself, her extraordinary imperturbability. Yet so far she had behaved like an utter slut, and a submissive one at that, doing just as she was told without ever complaining.

He reached down to take her by the hair, twisting his fist into the glossy black strands. She merely began to suck more eagerly, bobbing her head up and down on his now erect cock. He twisted harder, to force her head down, right onto his erection, until he could feel the knob pushing into her throat and her cheeks had begun to bulge. Still she made no protest.

Taking hold of the base of his cock, he began to move her head up and down, fucking her throat, with his hand twisted viciously hard in her hair. She made no effort to stop him, for all that her throat was twitching as she began to gag on his penis. It had to hurt, and he wondered if she actually enjoyed the pain, or if she was merely so desperate to be with him that she would do anything he wanted. Whichever it was, hurting her was providing him with immense satisfaction, because it was still impossible not to think of her as Nich Mordaunt's ex-girlfriend. He pulled her head up by the hair, leaving his spit-wet cock joined to her mouth by a single thick strand of saliva for a moment before he twisted his hand to force her to look into his eyes.

'Tell me, did Nich ever fuck you up your arse?'

She shook her head, finally betraying a touch of nervousness. Ariesian laughed.

'Xiu Mei!' he called. 'Fetch some hand cream. I'm going to fuck this little tart's arsehole for her.'

Xiu Mei ran into the house and Ariesian pushed Alice's head back onto his cock. She went straight back to sucking. He chuckled, still unsure why she was so pliable, but keen to take advantage. There seemed to be nothing he could do to make her rebel, tempting him to push her further still. In the end she'd break, and that was when he'd throw her out, well used, hopefully to crawl back to Mordaunt while he moved on to fresh meat.

It was always the same. No woman had ever been enough to satisfy him for long, while most of them started to throw their weight around after a while. Alice might, or might not, but he knew that once he'd had full use of her sexually he'd want to move on. For the moment, there was a long way to go, and the next stage of her journey was to see how well she could accommodate his cock in her rectum.

Xiu Mei was soon back, her hand trembling and her eyes downcast as she handed him the tube of cream. He had Alice's head held well down, her lips spread over the base of his cock, his knob jammed down her throat. Her face was beginning to go red, and mucus had started to bubble from her nose as she fought to breathe, bringing a new cruelty to mind. He pulled her head up, leaving her gasping.

'Keep it open,' he ordered, holding her firmly by the hair so that her mouth was towards him.

She obeyed, and he was finding it impossible not to grin as he put the tube of hand cream half into her open mouth and squeezed. The expression of alarm on her face as she realised what was to be done to her was a delight to see, also the disgust as the cream squashed out in a long white worm, piling onto her tongue. He squeezed out as much as he could, laughing at her distress and delighted to have finally got a reaction out of her. Only when no more cream would come did he drop the tube and jam his now achingly erect cock back into her open mouth.

He felt the cold cream squash out over his knob as he drove it down her throat once more and sighed in pleasure. It felt glorious, cool and slippery around his knob, and he spent a moment fucking in her windpipe before once more pulling her off. She was gasping again, her mouth a white cavity with bits of pink showing here and there, his cock the same, slippery with cold cream and ready for her bottom.

'You can lube your arsehole up if any more

cream'll come out,' he offered as he swung his legs off the lounger, 'or use what's in your mouth.'

Alice nodded weakly and put a finger in her mouth to pull out some cream. She was red in the face, her skin prickling with sweat, her expression showed exhaustion and disgust. Yet as he stood up she took his place on the lounger, only face down with her thighs cocked out to either side, spreading the muscular little globe of her bottom, with her anus stretched taut between her cheeks.

'That's right, you little tart, show it off,' Ariesian drawled, delighted, but still astonished by her compliance.

He took his cock, rubbing the slimy shaft and grinning in satisfaction as Alice reached back between her bottom cheeks. Across the pool Xiu Mei's hand went to her mouth in shock and Yi cowered back until only her face could be seen, watching as Alice put one long finger to her anus, smeared cream around the hole, and then pushed it deep up. Ariesian was chuckling as he watched Alice finger her bottom. She looked wonderfully tight, her ring stretched even on a single finger, and as she pulled it free her hole closed immediately, squeezing out a short fat worm of cream.

'I'm ready,' she sighed.

She was shaking as she took a firm grip on the sun lounger, her spread bottom cheeks twitching in anticipation, her ring pulsing slowly, with the thick cream now running down to soil the little bar of flesh between anus and vagina, then the hole itself. Ariesian got behind her, revelling in the sight of the tiny bottom hole he was about to use. She looked tight, and if Nich hadn't buggered her, then perhaps nobody had? Squatting across her body, he put his cock between her cheeks, rubbing it on her slimy hole as he spoke.

'So you're virgin up the bum, are you?'

Alice gave a single, nervous nod. He could feel the anxious twitching of her sphincter against his cock, a delicious sensation, tempting him to bugger her then and there, even just to pop it in to say he'd had her and then spunk in her open hole. He held back, determined to get the most out of taking her anal virginity, pushing just a little harder to make her squeak in alarm as her ring began to spread out over his knob.

'Fuck, but you're tight!' he gasped. 'Yeah, you're virgin all right, I can tell. Amazing nobody's ever had you, with that dirty little wiggle and the shape of your arse. Amazing. No boy ever had the guts, eh? Didn't dare, did they? Well, I do . . .'

He broke off. Alice was gasping and clutching the lounger, but despite the cream and the insertion of her finger she was impossibly tight. It hurt his cock, but he was determined, and pushed again, his words coming out in a snarl as she grunted in pain.

'Slacken up, you silly bitch, or it'll only hurt more!'

Alice gave a soft whimper, and abruptly her anus grew softer and less taut. Ariesian adjusted his position a little, so that he could see. Looking down in savage satisfaction, he watched her bottom hole push in, until her ring had begun to open around his helmet. She was whimpering, and her cheeks were twitching in shocked reaction, but he pushed all the harder, watching as her anus struggled to take the load he was pushing in, and suddenly gave.

She squealed in shock and pain as his cock head popped in up her ring, but he didn't give her time to recover, eager to feel the sensitive flesh of his foreskin go in. Her legs had begun to kick in futile remonstrance as he continued to push, her hole spreading to the fat bulk of his cock, a ring of glistening pink flesh so taut he was sure she'd split. She began to shake her head, her whimpering changed to heartfelt sobs as her bumhole pushed in to the strain. He grunted as he gave one last push, then he was in, her hole agape, the full, fat bulk of his penis wedged into her slippery rectum.

Alice calmed down a little bit as he began to bugger her, merely gasping and clutching at the sun lounger as her straining bottom hole pulled in and out to the motion of his cock. He took her by the hips, keeping her well spread to allow him to watch, and enjoyed her pained reaction almost as much as the feel of having his erection moving in the hot, slimy cavity of her gut. It was going to be impossible to hold off for long, he knew, his pleasure already rising towards orgasm.

Giving in, he began to pump harder, making Alice gasp more urgently still, until a mixture of spittle and cold cream had begun to bubble from her mouth. His teeth gritted in savage joy as he rode towards climax, watching her twitching body and thinking of how he'd leave her, buggered and sore with cold cream oozing from her anus just as it was seeping from her mouth, only mixed with spunk too.

It wouldn't be the last time either. He'd bugger her repeatedly, until it was as easy to get his cock up her arse as in her cunt. He'd make her wear a plug in her arse, to keep her stretched, and use bigger ones as she grew slowly looser, and when he'd finished with her he would send her back to Mordaunt with her ring so slack she had to wear her plug all the time, a huge one. He'd make her put a cucumber up and eat it . . .

He was on the edge of orgasm, but stopped, remembering what he'd promised himself the first time he'd had her. Grunting, he pulled himself out, his cock flicking up as it left her gaping anus, to stand rock solid from his belly, bubbles of pre-come already emerging from the slimy tip. Snatching her hair, he pulled her sharply around, cock to mouth.

For one utterly glorious instant he saw the expression on her face, her eyes fixed on his steaming erection as she realised what he was about to make her do, and then it was too late. His cock was in her mouth, and her face screwed up tight as he came, spunk exploding down her throat as he jammed it deep. She'd begun to choke immediately, a mixture of come and mucus erupting from her nose as her throat went into spasms on his cock.

He held it deep, ignoring her struggles, until he was quite finished, and even then keeping it in. To his astonishment she didn't seem to mind, but stopped thrashing as soon as she could breathe, and as she sucked him clean his last vestiges of caution, and respect, disappeared. When he finally pulled back she was left with a trickle of mess running down her chin and more hanging from her nose, making him laugh as he stood away.

'You really are a little whore, aren't you?'

Alice gave a weak nod, still gasping for breath as she slumped down, too far gone even to try and cover herself, her anus still agape behind. Now feeling thoroughly pleased with himself, Ariesian took the bottle from the ice bucket, twisting the tab of the wire cage open through the foil and discarding both before putting his hand to the cork. It was stiff, and he had to bunch his muscles to shift it, only for the pressure to suddenly give. The cork shot free, high into the air, followed by a froth of bubbles, much of which splashed down onto Alice's upturned bottom. He laughed, and on a sudden, sadistic impulse he put his thumb over the end of the bottle and shook it hard.

She saw, but didn't realise what he was about to do until he had pressed the bottle neck to her anus. With that she gasped, and tried to squirm away, but he quickly snatched an arm, twisting it into the small of her back, and let go, jamming the bottle neck up her well lubricated hole with the same motion. She gasped, squirming in his grip, her bottom wriggling frantically as Champagne squirted in up her rectum. He was laughing, and shaking the bottle, making more go up as her bumhole pulsed on the slippery bottle neck, only to slip free as she gave a violent lurch.

Her Champagne enema instantly erupted from her anus, squirting out in a long, high arc of dirty froth that splashed down into the swimming pool. More came as he jumped quickly back, a second long spurt all over the pool side, the lounger and one of her legs, and more, bubbling out to run down over her cunt and into the open, excited hole.

Ariesian was laughing so hard he had to put his hands on his knees as he watched her evacuate. Tears were streaming from his eyes, and only as he wiped them did he realise that she had lifted her bottom, not to get her belly out of the sticky pool beneath her, but to masturbate, with her hand pushed down between her spread thighs and her fingers working urgently on her sex.

He could only gape in astonishment, unable to comprehend how any woman could take pleasure in being so utterly used, and yet there was no mistaking what she was doing, nor the ecstasy on her face. Already she was beginning to come, her muscular bottom cheeks tightening over and over, her anus bubbling brownish froth, her mouth wide and still dribbling a dirty mixture of spunk, mucus and cold cream from one corner. He remembered something he'd read, about women who wanted to be totally controlled, and at last he understood. To her he was a worthy Master, unlike Mordaunt, a true Master, strong and assertive, capable of bringing her to an ecstasy she could never achieve with a lesser man.

As she went through a shivering, gasping orgasm he simply watched, the half-empty bottle of Champagne held loosely in one hand, his mouth set in a cruel grin. Even by the time she'd started to come down he decided he would probably keep her on a little longer than most, at least until he had utterly spoiled her for anybody else. For the moment, she was going to have to clean the swimming pool, nude, and under the guidance of Yi and Xiu Mei.

Five

Staring glumly from the car window, Charlotte watched the Devon scenery pass, her eyes only half focused, indifferent to the late bluebells and primroses that made the hedges bright with colour. Only as they drew near to Rockbeare did her attention shift, and then only with an all too familiar pang of despondency as they turned the last corner before her old school. For a moment there was only the high wall of flaking yellow stone to be seen, until they reached the gate. Beyond was the familiar façade of St Cecilia's, with its air of damp and gloom that never quite seemed to dissipate even on the brightest days. Now, with a dull overcast, the feel of rain in the air and the huge cedars shaking to a fresh breeze, it seemed darker and more oppressive than ever. Only one detail had changed: the addition of a security camera. But as her sense of misery grew deeper still the cloud broke in the distance, briefly illuminating one of the Dartmoor tors in brilliant, sparkling gold.

She forced a smile, telling herself it was a sign to urge her to courage, but knowing full well that what little she had would soon break down in front of Father Dawson. Her father parked the car in the space opposite the gates and got out, walking in silence alongside the wall to where it rose to become the east face of the priest's house. Father Dawson was expecting them, and stood just inside the window of his study, his small, round face creased into a smile, his hands clasped together as if in consternation.

As they waited for the door to open she was trying to tell herself that the solution was to stand proud, to tell him everything, that she had rejected the Christian God, that she had willingly surrendered her virginity in a Pagan ritual, and had wanted to become pregnant more than anything else in the world. His reaction was sure to be utter horror, perhaps rejection, even excommunication. As she had been taught just yards away, the commonest reasons for excommunication were apostasy, heresy, and schism.

She was certainly guilty of apostasy, and of heresy with a vengeance, if not schism. Rowena would have walked in and boldly stated her case, but Rowena was the girl who had refused confirmation at a Catholic girls' school and held her ground. She thought of how delighted the girls would be, and Horst, and Nich, causing her mouth to once again flicker into a smile just in time for Father Dawson to open the door.

He also was smiling, the same indulgent smirk she remembered so vividly from her days at St Cecilia's. His manner hadn't changed either, as he reached out to shepherd her in with a hand placed gently on her waist.

'Mr Dowling, and Lottie. Do come in. How are you? How are you indeed? The drawing room would, I think, be best. Less formal, I do think. Now, a little tea, or shall we get straight down to business? Will you be joining us, Mr Dowling, as it's at least a thought that I might be better speaking to Lottie alone?'

Her father hesitated, but gave a single, stern nod and withdrew the way he had come. Charlotte allowed herself to be ushered into the drawing room and waited until Father Dawson had taken his seat, the same chair he had occupied so many times before, just as she was standing in the same position. Suddenly she felt as if she were twelve again and about to be asked to recite some piece of doctrine she'd failed to take in.

'Do sit down, do sit down,' he urged, indicating the other armchair. 'And so, I understand that celebrations are in order!'

'Er . . .'

'Indeed, indeed, I quite understand. The situation is unfortunate, but I can assure you that the church has a great deal of experience in coping with such matters. You will of course be wishing to marry young Horst?'

Charlotte hesitated, knowing it was her moment to stand tall and announce what she had done. It was impossible, with his bright, beady eyes fixed on her, his indulgent smile broader than ever, his head undoubtedly full of a thousand reasons why any deviation from his suggested path was simple foolishness. She found her head starting to bob in automatic agreement, but somehow managed to force out at least an approximation of what she wanted to say.

'I – I feel I am . . . that is, that I may be – may be losing my faith.'

He chuckled, with one small noise expressing all the absurdity of her statement.

'Oh dear, oh dear! We can't have that, can we?'

Charlotte made a wry face. Against his easy condescension all her Pagan ideals suddenly seemed absurd, no more than the imaginings of a wilful child, her surrender to Horst both silly and dirty. Only shame at her lack of courage enabled her to go on at all.

'No, really, Father, I've – I've begun to doubt. I don't understand –'

'Nor do I!' he laughed, interrupting before she could bring her thoughts into focus. 'The ways of God are ineffable, far beyond the comprehension of mere mortal man, and you scarcely more than a child!'

He shook his head, still smiling, clearly astonished and amused at her precocity.

'No, it's not that, I mean . . . I mean, how can there be no female aspect to the deity? Or is there? Isn't Mother Mary just an aspect of the Goddess? If so, how can we say that the female principle is subordinate to the male? Isn't the resurrection just a distorted version of the cycle of the year? Isn't the idea of a single, male God . . .'

It had come out in a rush, and Father Dawson's merry laughter had stopped halfway through, his face taking on a tinge of plum. She stopped, expecting an explosion of anger which never came.

Father Dawson laughed, but if he had contained his anger, there was a hard edge to his voice as he spoke again.

'Now tell me, Lottie, what brought all this nonsense on? Has somebody been putting ideas into your head?'

He had moved forward on his chair, for once serious as he peered at her from rheumy eyes.

'Does all this have anything to do with a man named Nich Mordaunt? Slim, red hair, frankly strange?'

He nodded. Charlotte's expression had already betrayed the answer. Father Dawson drew his breath in and began to speak again, with fresh urgency.

106

'This is something I am not going to explain, Lottie, and which in any case I very much doubt you would understand, but Nich Mordaunt is not the sort of person a girl like you should be associating with, nor any other girl for that matter.'

'He doesn't seem that way,' she protested, unable to meet the priest's eyes but determined to at least offer some defence of her friend. 'He's actually rather gentle, and he always listens, which is more than –'

'Lottie, my child,' he interrupted. 'Mordaunt is – is like a viper in the bosom of the church. I am sorry to use such strong words to one so tender, but it is the simple truth. He preaches every sort of lie you could care to imagine, and a great many I sincerely hope will never sully your mind. Now, I'm sure we will have all this nonsense cleared up in no time at all, but meanwhile, just in case, there is a colleague of mine I'd like you to see, Father Phillip Somner.'

Rowena walked slowly, Charlotte's hand held tightly in her own, as they made their way into Berne Woods. Neither spoke, each alone with her thoughts, until they reached the familiar clearing with its ring of stones. Rowena sat down on one of the broadest. Charlotte remained standing, her hands held in front of her, fidgeting.

'We could just run away?' Charlotte said suddenly. 'Perhaps up to London?'

'No,' Rowena answered firmly. 'I've never run from anything, and I'm not running from this. Tell this Father Somner to go to hell, his own hell.'

'I can't!'

'Then I'll do it for you.'

'No, Ro, please, you know that would only make it worse. He'd tell Father Dawson, and he'd tell Mum and Dad, and –'

107

'So what!? You're old enough to do as you please, Charlotte.'

Charlotte merely hung her head, looking unhappy. Rowena got up, to take Charlotte in her arms, holding her for a long moment before once more seating herself.

'Did Dawson make you take confession?' she asked.

Charlotte nodded.

'What did you tell him?'

'I lied. Other than – than with Horst, and I just said we got drunk one day at his house.'

'What did he give you?'

'A month of fasting and prayer, you know what he's like. He even rang my Mum to discuss it. I'm not allowed anything except water and some stupid diet with no meat or fish, or anything tasty. I don't feel absolved, not at all. Not the way I did after you spanked me on the cliffs.'

Rowena smiled, not wanting to admit the experience had left her feeling manipulated. Charlotte returned the smile, now with a familiar glint in her eye as she spoke.

'Would you – would you like to do that again?'

'What for?'

'Maybe . . . at the solstice festival?'

'I'm not cross with you about that. Poppy maybe, I'd put her across my knee and gladly. Anyway, Nich was right, in the end, we had to do something to prick Ariesian's bubble.'

'Maybe . . .' Charlotte mused, 'maybe for not standing up to Father Dawson? Or accepting Christian confession?'

Rowena made to reply, intending to comfort her lover, but paused, changing her tack.

'We all protect our beliefs as best we can, Lottie,

and I could never punish you for that, but if you'd like to be spanked, just come across my knee.'

'Please, Ro, yes. But I want to be spanked for something.'

Rowena nodded, unsure if she fully understood. Sitting fully upright, she patted her lap.

'Come on then, over you go, I suppose I'd better deal with you, if only because I don't think you got enough before, not for what you did. Besides, if you're to be punished, it should be done here, don't you think, so that you can repent of your submission to a mere man in front of the Goddess?'

Charlotte nodded, smiling shyly as she stepped forward to lay herself gently across Rowena's knee, her feet braced wide and her hands set well apart in the grass. Rowena's hands went to the hem of Charlotte's dress, lifting it up to expose a pair of big, polka dot knickers, this time yellow on white. She took them down without fuss, laying bare the full, trembling globe of Charlotte's bottom. The big cheeks were raised and a little parted, allowing Rowena to smell her lover's excitement as she adjusted the panties to knee level. Placing a hand on one plump bottom cheek, she began to spank.

As she applied the slaps to Charlotte's bottom, Rowena couldn't help but feel as before, that she was being manipulated, and that the true benefit of the spanking would go to the victim. Yet it felt good, and this time there was no anger, only satisfaction as the chubby globes lifted so willingly for punishment began to take on colour. Charlotte was taking it quite well too, kicking a little, and responding to each smack with a little gasp or sob, but not really making a fuss.

Only when Rowena's hand began to sting did a sense of irritation begin to well up inside her.

Charlotte's bottom was a rich, even pink, and the smell of pussy hung thick in the air. It was a punishment, and supposed to hurt, whatever the consequences. She stopped, briefly adjusted her position to allow herself to pull her slender leather belt from her jeans and set to work once more, only now with each stroke bringing the far more pleasing smack of leather on girl flesh and a squeak of very real pain.

In no time Charlotte had begun to squall, kicking her legs and shaking her head in her pain, yet making no effort to escape. With her own pleasure rising, Rowena paused again, to pull her lover's dress up and off, then to heave the big bra up, to leave Charlotte's heavy breasts swinging and bouncing to the slaps as her beating continued.

Mr Pedlow settled back with immense satisfaction. The system was now working perfectly, with sound and vision both relaying him the scene in the stone circle to a quality as good as he might have expected from an amateur video – an extremely dirty amateur video. He had turned the volume up, the better to enjoy the smack of leather on girlish bottom flesh, while the view was truly marvellous.

Two windows on his giant monitor screen showed the views from different cameras. One was low and to Charlotte's front, showing her face framed in tumbled blonde curls and set in mixed pain and ecstasy as her arousal grew and the punishment got harder. It also showed her breasts, both fat globes bouncing and quivering between her disarranged bra and Rowena's leg, with her nipples stiff in erection.

The other view was better still, from behind, and just a touch off centre. Almost the whole of Charlotte's body showed, shivering gold hair and jiggling boobs, kicking legs and wobbling bottom cheeks, but best of all, a wet, ready cunt and a tightly dimpled anus that had begun to twitch in reaction. It was a glorious sight, and his eyes were riveted to the screen as he clenched his rock-hard cock in his hand. Yet he held back from coming, sure that once Charlotte had been thoroughly spanked she would get Rowena's bottom in her face, perhaps even be made to lick it. It was too good an opportunity to miss.

Sure enough, when the punishment finally stopped, with Charlotte standing to rub at the blazing red ball of her bottom, Rowena wasted very little time. First she took Charlotte in her arms, hugging and kissing, also stroking her lover's whipped bottom. Before long Charlotte was being eased gently down onto the grass at the centre of the circle, and Mr Pedlow was forced to make frantic adjustments to his system in order to bring the right cameras into play.

By the time he did, Charlotte was on her back, stark naked but for the pretty polka dot panties tangled around her ankles and a pair of sandals. She had begun to masturbate, stroking her cunt as Rowena got into position. It was some position, straddled across Charlotte's head with her jeans and panties pushed down to show off her firm little bottom, right above her lover's face.

As Rowena reached back to pull her bottom cheeks apart Mr Pedlow had to let go of his cock to stop himself coming on the spot. She was showing everything, her cunt open and wet, her anus stretched taut. With trembling fingers he operated the remote zoom, hoping to get so close he'd be able to see if Rowena had wiped properly, and praying she hadn't.

It worked. The focus swam for just an instant before the entire twenty-one inch screen filled with a close-up of Rowena's anus, every little crease and bulge of flesh obscenely swollen, the skin moist and flecked with tiny rolls of pale blue loo paper. His mouth came wide and his muscles locked painfully tight as he grabbed his cock. A wet, pink object that could only possibly be the tip of Charlotte's tongue appeared on the screen, hesitant, then poked into the exact centre of Rowena's pouting anus.

Charlotte was in perfect ecstasy. Her tongue was up Rowena's bottom, probing deep as they masturbated together. Her own bottom was hot with spanking, a glorious feeling, physical ecstasy mixed with a sense of absolution infinitely stronger and finer than anything provided by any mere priest. This was how it should be, an honest, physical punishment in the application of a firm hand to her naked bottom, followed by pleasuring the woman who had beaten her, and all the better because her priestess was also her lover.

Her ecstasy as she started to come was as high and fine as anything she had experienced before. The heat of her smacked bottom seemed to pull her whole being into focus on her clitoris, while the taste and feel of Rowena's bottom hole had her squirming in utter, delighted submission. When her muscles locked she drove her tongue in as deep as it would go, revelling in the rubbery feel of her lover's anal ring as she came, bucking and writhing on the ground, clutching at her aching sex, unable to breath.

It took ages to come down, and long before she had Rowena had shifted position, now queened neatly on Charlotte's face, pussy to mouth and bumhole to nose. Charlotte was licking busily the instant she'd caught her breath, eager to make Rowena come. Nor did it take long; Rowena quickly began to wriggle, smothering Charlotte once more. With her nose tip rubbing in the spit-wet cavity of

Rowena's bottom hole and her tongue lapping just as fast as it could, Charlotte put everything into giving pleasure, only hoping it came close to her own ecstasy as her lover came in her face.

Rowena gave a pleased sigh as she climbed off. Charlotte wiped her mouth, wanting to giggle in sheer delight for what they'd done. For all that it was something intensely private, it was amusing to think of how Father Dawson would have reacted had he known, let alone had he seen. Certainly it was very difficult to imagine him retaining his infuriating air of smug superiority.

Mr Pedlow's fervent masturbation came to an abrupt halt as a fountain of spunk erupted from his cock.

Leaning on the paddock gate, Horst admired the ram he had purchased with a mixture of pride and apprehension. Well fed, and still growing, the animal had put on weight, and most of it muscle. His horns were also better developed, thick and heavily ridged, curling out from his skull in the style of his Welsh Mountain parentage. There was also a new truculence in his manner, and Horst had taken to dumping his oil cake into the trough from outside the field rather than go in through the gate. Sacrificing him was clearly not going to be a simple matter.

He'd been listening to the distinctive sound of Nich's motorbike as it approached up the lane and drew to a stop, so raised one hand in casual salute as he heard his friend's voice from behind him. Nich joined him at the gate, his leather jacket open over a plain black sweat shirt, his red hair fixed back into a short ponytail.

'Very impressive,' Nich remarked, extending a stick to tickle the beast behind one ear.

'I've called him Machiavelli,' Horst stated, 'I thought the name was appropriate. Mac for short. By the way, does the name Father Phillip Somner mean anything to you?'

'Yes,' Nich admitted. 'He's a priest, obviously. Pretty ghastly, very much the muscular Christian, he is, into early morning runs and cold showers. He's appeared on one or two TV debates, with Ariesian, and with me once. He's based near Basingstoke. Why?'

'Charlotte has to go and see him.'

'Oh dear, poor Charlotte. Not that he's of any consequence. As far as he's concerned, the resurgence of Paganism is simply a childish revolt against the spiritual authority of the church, the Roman Catholic Church, that is. He regards other Christian sects as the products of equally childish revolts across the years. Still, he considers himself an authority on the subject. Did she defy Dawson then?'

'Not really, no. Apparently she tried, and he got her to admit she knew you.'

'Ah, that would explain a lot. Somner considers himself the first port of call for repentant pagans. In his view there are three sorts of people: the righteous, like himself, intelligent and inherently good; the common herd, good in principle but dim and easily led astray; and the unrighteous, like myself, intelligent but inherently evil. I imagine he'll give her a long lecture, explaining how I'm the tool of Beelzebub, although doubtless in less fine language. Once he's sure he's returned her to the straight and narrow that'll be the end of it. He'll give her penance to do though, something mildly demeaning, like unpaid cleaning work. He does that a lot, but I've never been able to work out if he's a sadist or a miser. Could be both, I suppose.'

Nich continued to tickle the ram, which seemed to appreciate the attention.

'What if she really does change her mind?' Horst queried.

'She won't, not Charlotte. Okay, she seems meek. In fact, she *is* meek, but only in the sense that she'll always try and defuse a situation by agreeing with whatever's being said at the time. After all, if she was that gullible she'd never have rejected Christianity in the first place, would she?'

'I suppose not,' Horst admitted.

'There won't be a problem,' Nich went on. 'She'll simply nod her head and agree with everything he says. He'll be well pleased with himself, give her absolution and some damn fool penance, and off she'll go, straight back to Rowena. Now that is another problem altogether.'

'Rowena?'

'Exactly. Rowena is difficult. She has no concept of compromise, and, to be fair, she is obviously very much in love with Charlotte. Her heart's in the right place though, and we need her onside.'

'Why?'

'Because she has influence, especially with Charlotte.'

'There are other girls. Poppy for instance.'

'Poppy's a delight, it's true. Are you two . . .?'

'Yes, sort of, only she wants to stay a virgin, and then it's not very easy when my parents assume I'm going to be marrying Lottie.'

'I can imagine, and although we're under no obligation to recognise a Christian ceremony, I can see certain legal problems arising. Still, that's a thought . . .'

Charlotte was feeling more than a little apprehensive as she stepped from the train, wishing somebody had come with her. Father Dawson had provided a map, showing how to get to the church. It was too far to walk, and she took a cab from the rank outside the station. Ten minutes later she'd been dropped off, beside a huge structure, built in Victorian red brick with a high, square tower and tall stained glass windows. The only other building nearby was the priest's house, which she approached as instructed, along a short avenue of yews growing between clustered tombstones.

Doing her best to ignore the stifling atmosphere of Christian sanctity, she walked quickly to the door. All that was in her mind was to get through the ordeal with a minimum of fuss. Whatever Father Somner said, she would listen with polite attendance, adopting an attitude of meek stupidity and agreeing with everything he said as if in awe of his wisdom. With luck her attitude would bolster his vanity and convince him that she was genuine.

There was no bell, only a large iron door knocker, which she lifted and let drop, hesitantly at first, and then more firmly. A moment later a movement caught her eye beyond the diamond-paned window to one side of the door, before it swung open, revealing a thin, wiry man in clerical robes, his eyes oddly large and lustrous in a pinched face beneath a fringe of sandy hair. She gave a little curtsey.

'Father Somner?'

'I am Father Somner, yes, and I suppose you are Charlotte Dowling?' he answered.

She nodded and entered the house at a gesture. There was no warmth in his voice, in fact barely any emotion at all, beyond a hint of distaste, and even that she felt might have been her imagination. He didn't speak as he led her down the corridor, and they passed an open door leading into a drawing room of austere comfort, arriving instead in what was evidently a study. The walls were panelled wood, the carpet plain brown, the curtains a dull buff, all of it very neat, creating an atmosphere of prim severity she immediately hated.

He sat down, leaving her standing across the desk, feeling somewhat awkward and not daring to take either of the plain, straight-backed chairs in which she might also have sat. Looking at her with a gaze of disturbing intensity, he steepled his fingers and spoke, his voice both severe and tired, as if he was already at the verge of exasperation.

'I am given to understand by Father Dawson that you have fallen under the influence of Nicholas Mordaunt?'

Charlotte opened her mouth to reply, but he continued to talk without waiting for either admission or denial.

'Mordaunt is an extremely stupid and dangerous young man. He is also what is called a megalomaniac, that is, a person with an uncontrollable passion for self-exaltation and therefore an inability to respect others. To this end he denies the Church, and for years has been spreading his poison to anybody who will listen, especially young and impressionable women, the motive for which I trust I do not need to explain, given your unfortunate condition. No doubt he cozened you with his lies, casting doubt on aspects of theology you are far too young to understand in any case, and it saddens me greatly to think that you listened to him, you, a girl with a good education and from a respectable home. Can you imagine the distress you will have caused your parents, Charlotte?'

She responded with a weak nod.

'And this the result of listening to Mordaunt,' he went on. 'Do you not recognise the authority of the priesthood, Charlotte? Do you have no inkling of how foolish you have been? How is it that you listened to Mordaunt in preference to your own parents, to Father Dawson, to the sisters at St Cecilia's? Surely you have been taught to recognise temptation when it comes? Surely you know, in your heart, that his words are lies and that the path of earthly pleasure he espouses leads straight to hell, to hell, Charlotte . . .'

His voice was rising and taking on an angry tone, but Charlotte had switched off, her head hung in apparent contrition as if unable to meet the priest's eyes but in fact only half focused as she remembered how good it had felt to have maybe a thousand people looking on as Nich proclaimed her as chosen for the cycle. It had felt wonderful, and it was not something she wanted to put aside, not even for Rowena, and certainly not for the lifestyle which Father Somner was advocating to her, of cold piety and self-denial, of guilt for every pleasure taken.

Finally the lecture came to an end, with Charlotte still feigning contrition. Father Somner rose and, without troubling to ask if she had recently been to confession, walked her across to the church to do so. She stayed a respectful two steps behind him, looking at the ground with her hands folded in her lap as she wondered what it was best to say. Too little and he might not believe her, too much and she might end up being subjected to further harassment. By the time the opening ritual was complete she had made up her mind, to reflect the tone of his lecture as accurately as possible, and to keep it short.

'. . . for I have sinned. I have been foolish, and listened to the lies of an ungodly man. I have allowed him to put carnal thoughts into my head, and – and acted on these. I now realise my sin, and beg forgiveness.'

She stopped, and to her immense relief he made no demands for further details. It was over, with no doubt just some silly penance she could ignore, or so she assumed until he gave it.

'. . . to thoroughly scour the tiles of the church floor, for which my housekeeper will provide the necessary equipment. You may come to me when it is ready to be inspected.'

Annoyance immediately welled up inside her, but she held her peace, telling herself that once it was over and done with she need never see him again. Outside in the body of the church she was told to wait, and presently a heavy-set woman arrived carrying a large bucket full of cold water, a huge pot of scouring cream, two sponges and an assortment of clothes. She was given curt instructions and the woman left.

With no mop, she had no choice but to get down on her hands and knees in the pretty dress she'd chosen in the hope of softening Father Somner's attitude, her mind burning with resentment as she scrubbed at the dull brown tiles. It was hard work too, with ingrained dirt dried into the cracks in such a way that when she scrubbed it came up, leaving the tile dirtier than it had been before once the water had dried off.

After half an hour her arms and knees had begun to get sore, while the area she had scrubbed looked much the same as the area she hadn't, save where the tiles were wet. It was obviously a hopeless task, almost Sisyphean, the nave alone needing more time than she could possibly spare to do it properly, never mind the aisles or the areas beneath the pews. Yet still she persevered, sure that if she failed, let alone failed to fetch Father Somner to make his inspection, it would only lead to further trouble.

By the time a full hour had passed she was feeling thoroughly fed up, and had decided to cheat. Save for removing a few patches of mud where worshippers had failed to wipe their feet properly, there seemed to be little point in the task. It was better to wait a while, then wet a last corner and go to fetch Father Somner. If he wasn't impressed she could point out that she had to catch a train at ten past four in order to get home.

Standing guiltily in the middle of the church, she spent a long moment listening for the approaching footsteps of either Father Somner or the big housekeeper. Nothing happened. Bored and still resentful, she began to explore the church. The pulpit was the best feature, a wonderful piece of Victorian, neo-Gothic folly set ten feet above the congregation in the brick and stone of the dividing wall, and reached by a steep spiral stair.

Unable to resist, she climbed up, to find herself looking down from on high over the ranks of pews. For a moment she amused herself with an attempt to imitate Father Somner's pompous manner, only to abandon it as hopeless. A much better idea was to carry out some minor act of revenge. It was petty, perhaps, but also immensely satisfying. Plenty of options presented themselves, all safe. From her perch she could see the path leading to the church through the lower part of a high stained-glass representation of St Francis feeding the birds. Nobody could approach without her knowing.

For a moment she considered carving one or another of the symbols representing the Goddess into the soft stone, only to reject it as too risky. A profane act was better, and she set herself giggling at the thought of peeing in the font or on the floor of the pulpit. Unfortunately, Father Somner was sure to notice, and too rapidly to leave him in any doubt as to the culprit.

A better idea, a far better idea, was simply to masturbate, right there in the pulpit, where he stood so often to deliver his sermons. It would leave no trace, save perhaps a lingering hint of femininity, with luck just far enough below the conscious level to disturb him without being obvious. Even if he didn't realise at all, it was delightful to think of him pouring out his words where she had come, while she knew that Rowena, Nich and the others would delight in her rebellion.

To think was to act, and with a last anxious glance under St Francis' feet she pulled her dress up, first to show off her tummy, now gently bulging with the first flush of pregnancy, and then higher, over her full breasts. Her bra came up and they were showing, heavy and fecund, her distended nipples ready to give milk in just a few months. Her knickers came down, and off, pushed hurriedly into her bag. Leaning back against the pulpit wall, she pushed out her belly, flaunting her sex. It felt good, an act of defiance, and all the better for her trembling apprehension.

Ever so gently, she began to stroke her skin, first over her lightly swollen belly, then higher, to her chest, tickling her breasts, teasing her nipples until they had begun to ache with need, cupping them in her hands as if offering herself as Mother, to be suckled. It was a nice thought, and she closed her eyes as she caressed her breasts, enjoying their weight and the firmness of her flesh. Just possibly she'd be able to do it for real, offering the milk from her breasts as part of some fine pagan ritual, with the girls, and maybe men, taking her teats in their mouths one by one in a maternal sacrament of exquisite intensity – no dry wafers and poor wine, but warm girl's milk . . .

She paused, delighted by the idea but wanting something stronger to come over. It had to be in celebration of everything Somner and his church so hated and feared, open, joyful sexuality, pussy and cock, and the more immoral – by his standards – the better. Fucking on the altar was good, with her spread nude to take Nich into her arms and the priest chained to a pillar, forced to watch. Better still, she would go on her knees, taking Nich into her sex from behind, a thoroughly lewd position that would be sure to outrage the prudish Somner.

He'd be furious, screaming impotent threats as the two of them copulated in a wild frenzy, right in front of him. Better still, she could have Rowena on her face as Nich fucked her, her tongue lapping at her lover's pussy and bumhole too, in full view. If not both of them, why not others, enough to send Somner berserk with fury? There would be Rowena, Nich, Horst, Poppy, all the other girls, men too, in a tangle of flesh, slippery with their fluids, cocks in pussies and mouths, tongues on nipples and up bumholes, in an orgiastic welter and with her at the bottom. Rowena would be on her face, Charlotte's tongue well up her bumhole. Nich would be in her pussy, and Horst – Horst would be up her bottom, adding a final touch of wild, Rabelaisian farce to their sacrilegious orgy . . .

Charlotte screamed as she came, completely unable to hold it back. The orgasm was so strong her legs gave way, depositing her face down on the pulpit floor, still masturbating furiously as she imagined being spread on the altar with cocks in her anus and pussy at the same time while she licked and probed at Rowena's bottom hole. It was too intense even to let her rise quickly when the realisation hit her that she'd hadn't checked out of the window since exposing herself to the empty church.

When she did manage to look the path was as empty as before. St Francis' glass eyes seemed to be a touch less mild than before, but she merely stuck her tongue out at him as she scrambled into her panties. Content, she carried out her plan of wetting one corner of the church and went to report to Father Somner, entirely failing to spot the security camera installed high up among the eaves.

Six

Tucking her dress beneath her, Juliana sat down on the stile beside Rowena. From halfway up Stonebarrow their view extended out across a jumble of hills and valleys, woods and fields, set out in a patchwork among which the houses and roads were minor details. Berne Woods showed as an irregular blotch of varicoloured green.

'What are you planning for Lughnasadh?' Juliana asked.

'I'm not sure,' Rowena answered. 'It should be something joyful, of course, to celebrate the start of harvest. A feast perhaps?'

'Good idea,' Juliana agreed, and paused to pick a stem of long grass before going on. 'Perhaps we could use it to bring people closer together?'

'How do you mean?'

'Solstice was a great success, wasn't it, for us? So why don't we try and build on that for Lughnasadh, with a celebration for everybody? I think it's time we put our differences aside in any case.'

Rowena made a sour face.

'It's gone too far for that, after what Horst did.'

'I'm sorry to have to say this, Rowena,' Juliana stated, 'but if we go down that path everything will quickly fall apart. We need everyone together, male and female, especially as we now have a chance to come together as the core of a group.'

'How could it possibly work!?' Rowena protested. 'With that arrogant bastard around!'

'Horst will always follow Nich's lead,' Juliana pointed out, 'but we do need him as a figurehead, if only to represent the Horned God for this year.'

'I tell you what,' Rowena laughed, 'I'll be just as helpful as I possibly can, on the condition we sacrifice the bastard at Samhain.'

Juliana merely smiled and went on.

'I very much doubt we'd get away with that. But seriously, in the nature of worship a new male must represent the Horned God every year, so Horst's role is purely temporary. Why not agree to accept him for the time being? Next year it'll be somebody else, but you'll still be there.'

'That's true,' Rowena mused, 'but what about this marriage? Everybody seems to assume it'll just happen, and I know Lottie won't be able to defy her parents, or the church.'

'Do you recognise the Christian marriage, then?'

'No, of course not! The law does though.'

'So what? If Charlotte and Horst are married and living in Rockbeare, with his parents back in Austria, we'll have an excellent base. Our relationships can carry on as before. After all, he's sleeping with Poppy.'

'I know,' Rowena answered sourly. 'Still, perhaps you're right, we could become the focus of a larger group, a group based on belief.'

'It's worth doing, if only to challenge Ariesian's gross commercialism.'

'There is that. I'm still not sure it would be possible to organise. For one thing, if men are to be involved, they'd have to recognise the supremacy of the Goddess. We'd need levels of initiation too, with an inner circle open only to women ...'

She continued, with gradually increasing enthusiasm and Juliana hid a quiet smile by pretending to look up towards the long crest of Stonebarrow.

Ariesian gave Alice's bottom a firm slap as she passed, to make her squeak and set her cheeks jiggling. She was near naked, save for emerald green high heels and a ridiculous little satin skirt in the same bright colour, so short that it failed to cover her bottom even when she was standing upright. Underneath she wore nothing, quite bare, while her matching bra could scarcely contain her big breasts. A little maid's cap of the same bright green satin edged with lace decorated her jet black hair. She bent, to sweep the mess of ice cream he'd dropped into a dustpan, and in doing so exposing the rear lips of her cunt and rounded black bulb of her anal plug.

'Stay like that,' he ordered, and as always she obeyed.

He extended a finger, first to tickle between her cheeks and manipulate the plug in her anus, then to probe the hole between her sex lips. She was wet, as always, and the finger went in easily, until his knuckles were digging into her cunt flesh. Her only response was a low moan, repeated as he began to finger fuck her. Ariesian chuckled, enjoying his power over her nearly as much as the feel of velvet soft cunt flesh and thoroughly rude view. Casually, he thumbed down the front of his shorts, freeing his cock into his hand. As he continued to finger her he began to stroke it, wondering if he could be bothered to fuck her, or whether it would be more fun to see if he could find some new way to make her degrade herself. The second option seemed more fun.

'Let's see how your arsehole's doing,' he remarked. 'Pull the plug out.'

She reached back, grimacing as she extracted the thick plug, to leave her anus agape, showing the bright red interior of her rectum for a moment before it closed with a soft fart.

'Put it in your mouth,' he ordered, and laughed to see her expression change to disgust as she did it, then resentment with the bulb now protruding from between her painted lips. 'How can I inspect you like that, you stupid slut? Hold your cheeks apart.'

The now closed wrinkle of her anal flesh already showed between her slim cheeks, but it had amused him to give the rude order, while he wanted to make her hold her cheeks wide. She obeyed instantly, spreading herself to stretch her ring wide. Ariesian pulled his finger free of the lower hole, to wipe a little cunt cream on her anus, leaving her slippery and vulnerable. He pushed and his finger went in easily, meeting only a little resistance. Already she was getting slack, and he was only using the smallest of the butt plugs he'd made her buy in a gay sex shop in Reading.

The inside of her bottom felt very hot, and slimy, and his knuckles were pressed to the firm meat of her cheeks, helping his cock to erection as he masturbated. Alice stayed as she was, her head hanging down in a cascade of night-black hair, her heavy breasts lolling beneath her body. Her breathing was growing slowly deeper as he opened her anus, and when he pushed a second finger in she began to whimper softly. Ariesian's cock grew suddenly harder. He was going to have to bugger her.

'Turn around, and come here,' he ordered, easing his fingers from her now moist and open anus. 'Keep the plug in your mouth . . . no, on second thoughts, you can take it out. Suck on this instead.'

Alice nodded meekly and turned, her bright green eyes wide and full of trepidation as she got down into a kneeling position without having to be asked. Removing the butt plug from her mouth, she kept it open.

'Good,' he chuckled, popping both the fingers he'd had up her bottom into her mouth. 'What a little whore you are!'

Only the expression in her eyes betrayed her feelings as she sucked on his fingers – self-disgust at her own inability to resist her need for domination. He laughed, delighting in his power, his cock now a solid rod in his hand.

'Sit on it,' he ordered. 'Cunt first so I can see your tits, then up your arse, backwards.'

Alice nodded as he pulled his fingers from her mouth. She threw one elegant leg across his body and, as he held his cock upright, slid herself down onto his erection. With his cock engulfed in warm, slippery cunt flesh, Ariesian put his hands behind his head, relaxing as Alice began to work herself on his cock, wriggling and bouncing, to make her big breasts jump and jiggle in the ridiculous little bra. One popped free, then the other, making him laugh as she got down to a proper fucking motion. He beckoned, and she leant forward as he reached out, to take hold of both fat globes, one in each hand, to squeeze and pinch at her nipples until her mouth had come wide in mingled pain and pleasure. Again Ariesian laughed, and began to slap them together, watching the ripples in her breast meat and chuckling to himself.

She seemed to enjoy it, panting and wriggling her cunt onto his erection, so he let go, making a circular motion with one finger to indicate that she should turn around. Her obedience was immediate, lifting from his cock and swivelling her body to present her neatly rounded bottom to him, pushed out to show off the wet cavity of her cunt hole and her slightly pouted anal ring. Reaching down, she took his cock, guiding it to her bumhole. He was grinning as he saw the head go in, her once-tight ring now spreading easily to the pressure. With his knob up her bottom she sat slowly down, taking his full, fat length, with her bottom pushed out to make sure he could see her straining, buggered ring.

'Come on my cock, whore,' he ordered, and Alice nodded.

Ariesian lay back in comfort again, his hands once more folded behind his head as he watched Alice bugger herself. She had taken her breasts in her hands and was easing her bottom up and down on his erection, making her punctured anus pull in and out to the motion. A few hard thrusts and he'd have come, but he held back, enjoying the view. Soon she'd begun to wriggle, making her bottom cheeks shiver as she struggled to get as much of him in as possible, until he could feel her wet cunt pressed to his balls.

Her hand went down and she began to lift herself at the same time, taking hold of his cock as it came free of her bumhole. He could only stare as she began to use him to bugger herself, pushing the swollen head of his cock into the glistening hole of her anal ring, popping it free, and putting it in again. Four times she repeated the dirty routine, before once more settling herself down, his cock as deep as it would go, her bumhole a straining pink ring and her cunt pressed firmly to his ball sack, which she took in her hand.

Ariesian gasped as Alice began to rub his balls on her cunt, sliding them up and down in her wet slit and bumping them over her clitoris. It was almost too much to take, leaving his teeth gritted and his cock jerking in her rectum. She began to gasp, and to rub harder, her whole body shivering as she brought herself up towards orgasm. Her anus began to pulse, tightening on his cock, at first slowly, then faster, as if determined to milk his spunk into her rectum as she came.

She succeeded, Ariesian clutching hard onto the sun lounger with his eyes locked to the junction of his cock and Alice's bumhole as spurt after spurt erupted into her guts. She took it all, still coming herself long after he'd finished, and when he was done she rose, turned, and got down on her knees to suck his cock clean without even having to be told. As she walked away, her hips swaying in what he'd have thought was impertinence if it wasn't for what had just happened, he could only wonder at the sheer depth of her submission.

Her frequent buggerings had made no difference whatsoever to Alice's behaviour. She remained as languid and casual in her manner as before, and no less obedient to his sexual demands. Everything he had demanded of her she had done, no matter how dirty. She dressed as he ordered, in ever more revealing outfits, or went nude, even in front of other people. Twice he had invited guests round and had her go bare as they ate by the pool, and though it had driven his friends to distraction she hadn't turned a hair.

Aside from the occasional flicker of pain or disgust it seemed impossible to move her, which only made him keener to break her. Also, her acquiescence raised some interesting possibilities. The idea of being able to give a woman to another man and yet be assured she would still belong to him had always intrigued him. For one thing there was the pleasure of thinking how humiliated she would feel at being obliged to serve another, lesser man according to his orders. For a second there was the pleasure of the man's reaction, because he would know that the desirable, willing slut he was enjoying was only doing it because she'd been told to, and that ultimately she still belonged to him, Ariesian.

Despite the appeal of the idea, he had never dared try it. With every woman he'd had it had either been plain that she would refuse to co-operate, or that he risked losing her to the other man. With Alice, he had begun to wonder if it might not actually be possible. After all, no other woman he had ever known would have accepted not only being buggered and given a Champagne enema in front of his servants, but have cleaned the pool afterwards. Assuming he'd ever managed to get to the enema stage, or even the buggering stage, there would always have been storming rage or floods of tears. Not so Alice.

There was another reason, a more practical one. Local Christian groups were using the minor riot at the Solstice Festival as an excuse to put pressure on the police to have it banned. He and the Chief Constable had come to an understanding years before, and were now on good terms, occasionally playing golf or dining together. With leverage to ban him now coming from so many sources, the link he had forged was being stretched to breaking point. Possibly Alice's absolute submission to his will might be employed to forge new ones, this time unbreakable.

'No,' Poppy insisted, 'that has to be special. Here, let me suck you off.'

With considerable effort Horst restrained himself from driving his erection up her virgin pussy. She lay face down on the lawn, stark naked in the angle of two hedges, where she could catch the sun and not risk being seen. He'd come into her garden hoping to find her, but not lying naked on the lawn with a magazine and a cold drink. Her greeting had been a mischievous smile, and she'd made no protest when he'd begun to stroke her back and neck.

Instead, she'd simply closed her eyes and put her chin on her hands, sighing in contentment as his caresses became more intimate, moving to her thighs and then her bottom. She'd even allowed him to ease her legs open, providing a display of neatly tucked pussy and tight little bumhole which had set his already hard cock aching for her body. He'd imagined he could even see her hymen, a glossy bulge of bright pink flesh blocking the mouth of her vagina, and the temptation had been just too much.

He'd pulled out his cock, sure she was ready, only to be turned down. Not that she'd left him frustrated, turning to take his cock in her mouth before he'd even had a chance to reply. There was still a touch of frustration as her mouth began to work on his aching erection, but it didn't last long. Her position allowed him to touch her easily, and he explored the sweet curves of her petite body as she sucked him, enjoying the slender lines of her hips and legs, the pert firmness of her bottom and breasts, the soft swell of her belly.

As he rose towards orgasm he dared a little more, allowing his fingers to slip between the round little bum cheeks and between, to tickle the mouth of her anus and touch the virgin hole he so badly wanted to thrust his cock inside. He could feel her hymen, a barrier of wet flesh, oddly loose. Charlotte had felt the same, wet and open, then abruptly tense, before her flesh tore and his cock slid in, just as one day it would go into Poppy, his beautiful virgin ...

It was too much. He came, his teeth gritted in ecstasy as she sucked down his come, swallowing her mouthful, and a second time before he was released, to fall back onto the lawn in blissful satisfaction. Poppy rolled onto her back, her hands behind her head. Her thighs came up and open, showing off her virgin pussy. She nodded to him.

'Come on, fair's fair.'

Horst hesitated only for a moment, before crawling round to bury his face between her thighs, licking up the tart, hormonal cream from her sex before applying his tongue to her clitoris. She gave a happy purr, closing her thighs around his head and stroking his hair. Her legs locked behind his head, trapping him, and he licked all the harder, slipping his hands under her petite bottom to hold her cheeks as he worked.

Just seconds later her muscles began to tighten on his head. She moaned in ecstasy, her hands going to her breasts, teasing her nipples, and her legs locked hard on his head. He licked harder still as she went into orgasm, the muscles of her thighs and bottom in urgent spasm against his face, her pussy too, as she let go a cry of irrepressible delight. Only when her body went limp did he stop licking, and she was purring, catlike, as she released his head.

'Now that,' she stated, 'is how to worship the Goddess.'

Horst nodded and wiped the pussy cream from his face. For a long moment Poppy stayed as she was, her hands still on her little breasts, her head back and her eyes closed. Horst adjusted himself, his eyes lingering between her still open thighs, picturing the hymen where it nestled in the hole of her sex.

'When you say special,' he asked, 'do you mean special as in Lottie Dowling special?'

Poppy nodded.

'Something like that. Why, you didn't think I was saving myself for my wedding night, did you?'

'No, of course not, not in –'

'I don't know though. Not a Christian ceremony, of course, but perhaps as the peak of some wild, Pagan orgy, with lots of other people fucking, and our own union as the climax of the night.'

'Excellent!'

'Excellent, yes, but completely impractical unless you make up with Ro.'

'That's hardly my fault. She's the one . . .'

'You did shag her girlfriend.'

'Maybe, but –'

'Never mind that anyway. If we're going to do anything worthwhile, we need to stop squabbling. Juliana and –'

'No argument there, but try telling Rowena that.'

'Listen to me, and don't interrupt. Juliana and Nich are trying to persuade Rowena to join us for a Lughnasadh feast. There are a lot of conditions, but basically she's agreed.'

'What conditions?' Horst asked suspiciously.

'Just technical stuff,' Poppy answered with a dismissive gesture. 'Mainly, she wants you to acknowledge her status as Priestess. Nothing heavy, just a gesture.'

'I'll kiss her ring, happily.'

'What ring? She doesn't – you're a dirty pig, Horst! Then again . . .'

'I was joking.'

'I wasn't, but knowing Ro it's more likely to be her foot. How about that?'

'Kiss her feet!? No way!'

'But you'd kiss her bum, on the hole?'

'I suppose so, yes. On her cheeks, sure, but . . .'

'Okay, never mind the details, what matters is that you're prepared to offer some form of obeisance.'

'Yes,' Horst sighed, 'if only for the sake of peace.'

'Good. We're also trying to persuade her that it makes sense to let the rents have their way, and for you to marry Lottie.'

'Yes, but what about us?'

'It's a Christian marriage, no big deal, but the result is you get your place at Rockbeare, which would make the perfect temple.'

Horst nodded thoughtfully.

Alice watched from beneath half-lowered eyelids as the Chief Constable sipped his Champagne. He was a big man, not so much fat as solid, but with a peculiar ugliness brought on by bright, pig-like eyes beneath extraordinarily hairy brows and a gin-blossom nose. In manner he was brusque, assertive and very much aware of his status. To him, it was evident that she was nothing more than a pretty toy, a trophy, albeit the property of another man. He'd been admiring her since he'd arrived, particularly her breasts, which was hardly surprising considering the outfit Ariesian had made her wear.

It was rubber, black and tight, tiny shorts which left most of her bottom on show and kept her plug wedged deep up her bottom, a bra which provided support for her breasts but failed even to conceal her nipples properly, and a headpiece. Each of the three items was decorated with pink fur fabric, a trim on the bra, tall rabbit ears that dropped at the tips on the headpiece, and a round, fluffy tail on her shorts. Five-inch heels joined by a slender chain at the ankles forced her to walk with tiny, tottering steps. It marked her as a sexual plaything, which was precisely how she'd been treated.

She'd been made to serve, while the Chinese sisters dealt with the cooking. Initially respectful, both Yi and Xiu Mei had slowly changed their attitude to her as they came to realise how meek she was beneath her cool exterior. Both now gave her orders with confidence, and watched her degradations with a giggling blend of shock and delight. Now, after making her put her hands on her head and do a slow turn to show off her ridiculous costume, they had sent her out to the sound of high-pitched, mocking laughter.

Alice ignored them, walking cautiously out to the pool side where she put down her tray. The starter was tiger prawns served with a hot Jamaican sauce, each portion neatly arranged on a plastic scallop shell with a tiny silver spoon tucked in among the bed of salad. Serving first Ariesian, with downcast eyes and a whispered 'My Lord', then the Chief Constable, she took her own dish last and seated herself as she'd been ordered, cross-legged on the ground at Ariesian's side.

'I must say, you've got her well trained,' the Chief Constable chuckled.

'She's a good little dog, yes,' Ariesian replied. 'Watch.'

He reached down, to take Alice's scallop shell, from which she'd been about to take a mouthful, and casually pushed it into her face. She shut her eyes quickly as the mixture of prawns and spicy sauce was rubbed in over her features. Ariesian was laughing as he did it, and the Chief Constable added a slightly nervous chuckle.

'You see?' Ariesian stated as he let go, to leave the mess dripping slowly down Alice's face and into her up-thrust cleavage. 'She loves it, and she'll do anything I tell her to as well, anything. Get your boobs out, slut.'

Alice obeyed, her fingers slipping in the sauce as she scooped her breasts out together, holding them up for the men to admire. The Chief Constable gave an appreciative grunt and Ariesian pinched her nipples, first one, then the other, to leave both stiff in erection. Not daring to open her eyes for fear of the stinging sauce, Alice could only stay as she was, kneeling meekly with the remains of her first course running slowly down her body.

Ariesian and the Chief Constable had begun to discuss the difficulties caused by the Solstice Festival riot as they ate, and both men ignored her completely until they had finished their dishes. Only then did Ariesian attend to her, with a none too gentle kick to the turn of her thigh.

'Go on, fetch the main course, you stupid tart, what are you waiting for?'

Alice hastened to rise, groping out for the serviettes she knew were on the table. Ariesian laughed and took hold of her breasts, rubbing the sauce in to leave the surfaces of both fat globes smeared and shiny with grease. Her nipples already stung in reaction to the hot sauce, and stayed stiff as he casually fondled her, then spoke.

'Have a feel, Charles,' Ariesian stated, 'go on.'

His hands left her breasts and she moved forward a little more, letting them hang as they were taken again, now by the Chief Constable. His grip was firmer, his hands bigger, groping roughly at her slippery boobs as he chuckled to himself. She let him feel, but her groping hand had found a serviette, enabling her to wipe the sauce from her face and cautiously open her eyes.

Ariesian was sat back in his chair, gloating as he watched the Chief Constable molest her breasts. She gave both men meek, downcast looks, trying to ignore her rising feelings as rough thumbs began to brush over her aching nipples. At last it stopped, and she was able to totter away to fetch the main course. Back in the kitchen, Xiu Mei, who'd been watching, called her a slut and flicked the exposed part of her bottom with a tea towel. Yi giggled.

Alice returned to the men with the main course, big sirloin steaks covered in peppercorn sauce and served with chips and salad. Yi followed with wine and glasses. Once again Alice served the men first before adopting her kneeling position by Ariesian's side, still with her breasts out. This time they began to eat without abusing her. It was hard to know what to do with her plate, so she put it down on the ground and was just picking up her knife and fork when Ariesian spoke.

'No, no, that won't do at all, will it? That's not how dogs eat, or rabbits for that matter.'

He reached down, taking the knife and fork from Alice's fingers as the Chief Constable watched.

'Go on, eat up, good girl!'

The Chief Constable laughed as Alice shuffled back, to go down on all fours with her mouth to her plate. Ariesian reached down as she took a chip between her lips, stroking her hair for a moment before once more pushing her head firmly into her food. For a moment she was held down, the pile of chips and her sauce-laden steak squashed against her face, before being released. Meekly, she began to eat her dinner, and Ariesian and the Chief Constable returned to their previous conversation.

'So what can we do about this little shit Mordaunt?' Ariesian asked. 'Couldn't you just arrest him?'

'I doubt even a charge of breach of the peace would stick,' the Chief Constable replied. 'He's already banned from holding events anywhere in the country, but it's hard to stop him influencing people from behind the scenes. You might be better off trying to discredit him.'

'Maybe,' Ariesian admitted, 'but the trouble is, he's the real article. I mean, he actually believes his own bullshit. After what he did at Stanton Rocks, who's going to question his credentials?'

'Perhaps if he were to do something unacceptable?'

'What, with that bunch of loonies? Anything short of human sacrifice and they'll just lap it up. As it goes, I'm not too sure about human sacrifice.'

He laughed, and paused briefly to look down at Alice as she pulled at her steak with her teeth. She glanced up, half expecting her face to be rubbed in her food again, but he went back to his conversation.

'You see, Charles, you've got to be clever with these pagan types. What they're really into isn't religion at all. It's rebellion. Ninety per cent of the time it starts with a resentment of authority, and you'd be amazed at the number who were brought up as strict Catholics, or in some crank sect, anywhere they've been under pressure to conform. That's what they hate, authority, so unless you set Nich up as a police stooge or something ...'

'Could make a good rumour,' the Chief Constable agreed, 'but would they believe it?'

'Not many, no.'

'I've got a better idea anyway. The photos of that pair on the mound. They're both very blonde.'

'Yes. It's probably supposed to represent ripe corn. Nice bit of skirt that girl, shame she didn't get her kit off too.'

The Chief Constable nodded, took a large mouthful of steak and chewed on it reflectively for a moment before going on.

'How about you make out they're into Aryan supremacy and all that stuff? I bet that's not too popular with your little rebels.'

'Nice idea,' Ariesian admitted. 'The boy, Horst he's called, so he's probably a Kraut anyway.'

The Chief Constable gave a low laugh and went back to his steak. Ariesian continued to talk, expounding his theories as to why people abandoned the traditional religions in favour of paganism, while Alice continued to eat from her plate on the ground. The men had quickly finished the first bottle of wine, and she was sent in to fetch a second. She returned to find Ariesian still in full flow as she filled their glasses.

'. . . I had the TV contacts, of course, but evangelism's a pain. If you want any fun, you have to live a double life, and there's nothing the press boys like better than a bit of hypocrisy to get their readers going. Four, maybe five years, and some nosy bastard would have been sure to do a big exposé on me, and bang, that'd be the end of my audience. That's why I decided on paganism instead. This way, all I have to do is spout a bit of guff about Christian repression and Pagan sexual freedom, and everyone expects me to be a dirty bastard. Sure, the press boys still come and take photos over my wall and all that shit, but if they see me getting a blowjob off some dirty bitch, so what? The readers love it, and my followers love it, so everybody's happy, except maybe the bitch with a spunk facial!'

He laughed, loud and a touch drunkenly, the Chief Constable responding with a dirty chuckle. Alice went back to her plate, licking up the sauce and wondering what would happen to her after the meal when they were alone. At the least she could expect to be buggered and made to take him in her mouth, which seemed to be his favourite game. Possibly he'd think up some new and yet more demeaning refinement.

Her plate clear, she waited patiently while the men finished their wine, then rose to take the plates. Ariesian immediately pulled her close, to fondle her rubber-clad bottom, still drinking and talking to the Chief Constable even as he wormed a finger in under the taut hem. Alice gave a little squeak as her sex was penetrated, and another as a second finger was applied to the base of her butt plug, working it in her anus.

The Chief Constable could see what was happening, and was staring in fascination as Ariesian stimulated her holes. Her mouth had come open in a show of pleasure and she pushed her bottom out to take the finger in her sex deeper.

'You dirty, dirty bitch!' Ariesian drawled in satisfaction, sticking his finger deeper still, to make her gasp and clutch at the table. 'Watch this, Charles. Open wide, slut.'

Alice obeyed, although she knew what was coming. Ariesian chuckled as he pulled his fingers free, and they were pushed into her mouth. She sucked, tasting herself on his skin, and quickly swallowing. The Chief Constable swore under his breath and Ariesian's drunken laughter grew more boisterous still. He kept his fingers in too, making sure she'd sucked them clean before withdrawing.

'Can't get enough of it, can you, you filthy little whore?' he laughed. 'She's got a plug in at the moment, but she wouldn't care even if I'd been up her arse, she's that filthy.'

Alice shook her head in response and quickly picked up the dish, moving away as fast as she could with her hobbled ankles, but not fast enough to avoid another hard slap on her rump. With her smacked cheek stinging and acutely conscious of the ridiculous little rabbit tail bobbing behind her, she hurried for the kitchen, to find Xiu Mei and Yi waiting and a large chocolate gateau set out on a table, along with bowls, spoons and cream in a silver jug.

Both watched her with amusement as she picked up the tray and returned outside. Ariesian was sprawled in his chair, talking in a loud voice, the Chief Constable listening, relaxed and easy. Alice put the tray down and began to serve, half expecting to have her face pushed into the cake as she went through the ritual of cutting pieces, putting them into bowls and topping each with cream.

Neither man paid any attention to her, and as soon as she'd put her own bowl on the floor she began to gobble down the thick, sweet cake, eager to eat as much as possible before Ariesian decided to use it to add to her humiliation. She'd nearly finished when he turned to look down at her.

'Greedy bitch, aren't you?'

Alice nodded and he went on, now addressing the Chief Constable.

'You know, Charles, this one eats like a pig, I swear it, especially sweet things, but she never puts on an ounce of weight.'

'I expect you keep her well exercised,' the Chief Constable answered, and directed a meaningful leer at Alice's half-naked body.

'I do, Charles, I do,' Ariesian responded and once again looked down on Alice. 'This is a laugh, watch this. Stand up, you, and turn around.'

Alice obeyed, standing to her full height, close to the table, and putting her hands on top of her head as she turned slowly around, allowing them to admire her soiled, near-naked body.

'Not like that, you silly tart,' Ariesian scolded. 'So your arse is to the table.'

142

Alice adjusted her position, turning her bottom to the table and looking back over her shoulder, apprehensive in case Ariesian had at last decided to beat her. He hadn't, but his face was split into an ugly grin as he pushed one hand down into the tight rubber waistband of her shorts and pulled the rear pouch wide. The Chief Constable laughed as Ariesian scooped up what remained of the gateau, and Alice shut her eyes as the full, sticky handful was deposited down her shorts.

The heavy lump of cake felt cold and slimy against her skin as it rolled slowly down the back of her shorts. She shut her eyes, the men's cruel laughter ringing in her head, and a weak sob escaped her lips as Ariesian spoke again.

'A little cream, I think.'

Alice's buttocks tensed by reflex at his words, even before she felt the cool metal of the cream jug touch her lower back. He began to pour, and both men began laughing uproariously as the entire contents of the jug were deposited into the rear pouch of her rubber shorts. Only when the last few drops had gone in did he let go, releasing her waistband to allow the rubber to snap back against her flesh. Even as he did so she felt the cake squash against her bottom and the cold cream squeeze between her cheeks, wetting her penetrated anus.

'Classic!' Ariesian laughed. 'It looks as if she's crapped herself!'

Both men dissolved in laughter and Alice hung her head. With the tight shorts holding the cake in, it had stayed where it was, making a fat bulge in the seat of her shorts, while the cream had run down into the groove of her sex, cool against her hot flesh. Ariesian laughed again.

'Oh dear, that is comic! Go in and show the girls, Alice, and then you'd better wash up. When you're clean, bring some brandy out, and don't bother to get dressed, but leave that plug in.'

Alice nodded meekly and shuffled off. Yi and Xiu Mei were already watching from the kitchen door, in giggling delight, with a good view of the obscene bulge in her shorts. The moment she was out of sight of the men they had grabbed her, Yi holding her arms while Xiu Mei applied a big wooden spoon to her bottom, jamming the cake deeper into her crease and her pussy hole. A dozen firm swats were applied before she was released, to scamper for the bathroom with cake oozing from the hem of her shorts and squashing around her sex.

In the shower she stripped and washed her filthy body clean before bringing out a bottle of brandy as ordered, in the nude and painfully conscious that the stem of her butt plug showed between her bottom cheeks. She poured glasses for both men, the Chief Constable's eyes now feasting on her naked body, and Ariesian spoke out almost as soon as she'd knelt down.

'Willing little bitch, isn't she?'

The Chief Constable nodded, his gaze still lingering on Alice where she knelt with her hands folded in her lap and her breasts pushed well out, the way Ariesian enjoyed her.

'Like I said,' Ariesian went on, 'she'll do anything I say, anything at all.'

'Very nice, and she's a looker too,' the Chief Constable responded, struggling a little to imitate Ariesian's tone of casual contempt.

'Have her,' Ariesian offered with an easy gesture. 'Take her into the bedroom. Do whatever you like to her. If she complains call me, or just give her a slap.'

Alice threw Ariesian a pleading glance, but he merely laughed. The Chief Constable hesitated, glancing to Alice and then back to Ariesian.

'I mean it,' Ariesian assured him. 'Fuck her, if you like. Fuck her up the arse even, she loves that.'

The Chief Constable swallowed hard, glancing once more to Alice. Again she looked to Ariesian, who nodded across the pool towards the door of a spare bedroom.

'Go on, you little fuck pig, do as you're told. Get in there.'

Still Alice hesitated, but the Chief Constable had stood up, his face red with booze and lust. He took her hand, and with a last backward glance she allowed herself to be led around the side of the pool to the bedroom. Within was a simple double bed, spread with a white coverlet. He released her hand and she sat down, watching as he began to undress, never taking his eyes from her naked body.

'What – what do you want to do to me?'

His answer came out as a croak, thick with passion, but without malice.

'Nothing bad. Maybe, to have you between your lovely big tits?'

Alice nodded, watching as he removed his jacket and tie, then his shoes and his trousers. At that he stopped, coming towards her in just his shirt, socks, and a pair of voluminous blue-grey boxer shorts. She came to the edge of the bed, watching wry-faced as he pushed down the front of his boxer shorts over a fat, hairy set of genitals, his scrotum thick and heavily wrinkled, his cock hooded within a fleshy, dark brown foreskin.

Without waiting to be told, she bent forward to take him in her mouth, tickling his balls as she sucked. He'd quickly begun to grow, and a sour taste filled her mouth as his foreskin rolled back to release a bulbous helmet. She swallowed, her face wrinkled in disgust, of which he took not the slightest notice, merely grunting and mumbling about the size and shape of her breasts as his erection grew. As soon as he was properly stiff she pulled back. He gave a pleased sigh and looked down to take his big, crooked erection in hand.

'Come on then, love, time for that titty fuck. Hold them together for me.'

Alice obeyed, taking her breasts in hand and pushing them up, round and heavy in her hands. Already he looked fit to explode; his face was red and bubbles were starting from the tip of his cock. Moving a little forward on the bed, she pushed her breasts out, to fold them around his erection. He immediately began to fuck in her cleavage, his cock head bobbing up and down between the plump pink pillows of flesh, faster and faster, until she was sure he would explode at any moment. He stopped, puffing as he stood back.

'So you like it up the bum, yeah?'

A single, miserable nod was all Alice could manage. He reached down, to take her by her ankles, and the next moment she'd been rolled up, squeaking in surprise as her sex and her well filled anus were put on show in a position as blatant as it was vulnerable. Holding her ankles in one hand, he put the other to her body, pressing a knuckle between the lips of her sex, to rub in her hole and on her clitoris.

'Wet, eh?' he said happily.

Alice responded with a weak sob, then another, louder, as he took hold of her butt plug and began to pull. Her mouth came wide as her anus stretched to release the thick plug, and with it gone her hole stayed open. The air was cool on the inside of her gaping ring, but only for a moment, and then the round, hot knob of his cock had been pressed to her hole. He went up easily, her spoiled bumhole accom-

146

modating the full width of his penis, and she was being buggered.

She'd soon begun to pant, unable to hold back from the ecstasy of having his cock move in her slippery bottom hole. Her legs were still held, then released and she'd spread them, his hands taking her firmly by the thighs as hers went to her sex. She began to masturbate, her sex spread between two fingers, two more rubbing at her clitoris.

'You dirty bitch!' he grunted, jamming his cock deeper still into her rectum. 'You really are, you dirty bitch, I'll – I know what to do with you . . .'

Alice barely heard, gasping as she started to come, with her anus in firm contraction on his cock, an exquisite orgasm that broke only when he unexpectedly pulled out. Taken by surprise, and too high to stop him anyway, she found herself pulled back into a sitting position, his hands on her breasts and his cock between them, once more titty fucking her, as fast and furious as before, but now in a slimy, brown channel between her breasts. She managed a grunt of disgust and tried to push him back, too late, as his cock exploded and thick white spunk erupted full in her face and across her chest.

He stepped back almost immediately, to milk the last of his come into Alice's filthy cleavage. Contenting herself with a resentful look, she waited patiently until he had finished, and then rose, intending to clean herself up. He merely tugged the waistband of his boxer shorts up over his rapidly deflating cock, sat down on the bed and jerked a thumb towards the door.

'Go on, better clean yourself up, then run to your Master.'

Alice went, sent on her way with a firm slap to her bottom, her mouth set in a resentful pout as she scurried for the bathroom, with the Chief Constable's come dribbling slowly down her face and in the dirty brown channel between her fucked breasts. Ariesian, still sitting by the pool, saw what had been done to her and laughed.

Seven

'What's Ariesian doing?' Poppy asked, inspecting a large loaf of granary bread.

'Nothing like this,' Nich responded with a grin, 'just a straightforward celebration of first harvest. I think he's playing it down a bit after Solstice. That's perfect, take four.'

'Five. No, six,' Poppy answered as she began to load herself with loaves. 'It's always best to have too much rather than too little.'

'Fair enough,' Nich said, 'six it is. The butcher's next then, and we're done.'

He waited as Poppy paid for the bread, and they stepped out together into the High Street. The day was absolutely still, the sun a hot ball in a cloudless sky, creating a drowsy atmosphere. Even the cars seemed to be going more slowly than usual, and those few people who were around were gossiping or moving about their business with unhurried steps, save one, a lone figure striding towards them, black robes fluttering around his skinny body. He'd seen them, and the expression on his face, already angry, changed to fury. Nich stopped, recognising Father Somner.

'Good afternoon, Father, and a joyful Lughnasadh to you,' Nich said cheerfully.

Father Somner stopped, flourishing a video cassette at them, so close to Nich's face he was forced to step back.

'I thought I'd find you here, you vile abuser! What do have to say to this!?'

'I'm sorry,' Nich answered in a bemused tone. 'I think you may have the wrong person here.'

'No I do not have the wrong person!' Somner shouted. 'It's you I want, Mordaunt. How dare you, how dare you do this, and all for the sake of your selfish, carnal greed! Damn you, Mordaunt, it's one thing if you've lost your own faith, but why must you seek to corrupt the innocent!?'

'To which innocent do you refer? And on the issue of losing my faith, I feel I should point out that –'

'Charlotte Dowling, as you know very well!' Somner interrupted. 'You with your foul, libidinous practices and –'

'Do calm down,' Nich advised. 'You're starting to foam. I'd understood you'd absolved Lottie, after explaining my inherent wickedness and making her scrub the church floor?'

'Yes,' Somner rasped, 'I did, precisely that, and if I was taken in by her act, then I'd like to know how any decent man could be expected to conceive of the level of your corruption, of the depravity to which . . .'

He stopped, and drew in his breath before going on, once more flourishing the tape.

'This,' he spat, 'is a tape made from CCTV footage of the interior of my church.'

'A little dull, I'd have thought. Not much action –'

'Shut up! On it are recorded a sequence of images the details of which I cannot bring myself to describe.'

'What?' Poppy broke in. 'You mean you filmed

Lottie having a frig in the pulpit? You dirty bastard!'

Father Somner turned on her, his rat trap mouth working but no sound coming out. Poppy carried on blithely.

'Imagine doing something like that, you dirty Peeping Tom! You should be ashamed of yourself, and I hope you get a heavy penance.'

She was trying to sound serious, but unable to keep the laughter from her voice, allowing Father Somner to find his own.

'This is not a matter for levity!' he shouted. 'It is extremely serious, as you will find out!'

'Er . . . what do you intend to do with it?' Nich asked.

'I'll tell you what I intend to do,' Somner answered, suddenly triumphant. 'I intend to take it to Father Dawson, and lay the entire matter before the church, with the intention of securing Charlotte Dowling's immediate excommunication.'

'Hang on a minute,' Poppy answered him. 'She's getting married in two weeks, and if you do that, all hell will break loose.'

Somner's reply was smug, his anger fading in response to Poppy's obvious concern.

'If she wished to remain secure within the bosom of the church,' he stated, 'then she should have given thought to the consequences of her actions in advance, well in advance.'

As he finished he threw Nich a meaningful glance. Nich ignored him, wondering if it was worth making a grab for the video, only to realise it could only delay the inevitable. There was the original, and undoubtedly copies. Poppy carried on, now sounding seriously worried.

'Please, Father, don't do this! It's not worth it, for all the upset you'll cause!'

'Absolutely,' Nich agreed, 'and this is hardly the attitude of Christian forgiveness you always speak of so eloquently, is it?'

Father Somner gave a harsh laugh and pushed between them, moving up the street. Both followed, hurrying to keep up and both talking at once. The priest took no notice, but turned into Monmouth Road, stopping beside a black Ford. Nich was still talking, but stopped as Father Somner raised a finger.

'Yes,' the priest stated, 'there will be consequences, and yes, I fear that distress will be caused to innocent parties, not least Mr and Mrs Dowling. However, I will not be swayed from my duty, while the responsibility for all rests squarely on your shoulders, Mr Mordaunt. Think on that, the consequences of your idiotic rebellion against what I am sure you know in your heart of hearts is the truth. Furthermore –'

He'd opened the back door of the car, and his voice became indistinct as he lent in to place the video on the seat. Poppy glanced at Nich.

'We can't let this happen.'

Even as she spoke she gave the priest's meagre haunches a firm push, sending him sprawling into the car. Just his legs remained outside, bare above socks held up with garters. Nich hesitated as Poppy tried to slam the door closed. Somner gave a yelp of surprise and pain, but his legs withdrew.

'Get his keys!' Poppy urged, snatching open the driver's door.

With little choice, Nich acted, pushing in beside Father Somner and grappling for the keys where they'd fallen on the floor. For a brief moment he was wrestling with the furious priest, before the keys were free. He threw them to Poppy, despite cursing her in his mind as he threw his weight onto Father Somner's back, forcing him to stay down as the car started.

'Okay, so what are we supposed to do with him?' Nich demanded as they swung out into the road.

'How the fuck should I know!' Poppy yelled back.

'Where the hell have Poppy and Nich got to?' Rowena demanded.

'They're in town, picking up the food,' Charlotte explained.

'I know that,' Rowena answered her, 'but they're taking their time about it. And where are the men with the barbecue?'

Charlotte didn't answer. Rowena's mood had been tense all morning, for precisely the same reason Charlotte was so pleased with herself, so pleased that her mouth was set in a constant, happy smile. After a great deal of bargaining, with Juliana, Nich and Poppy acting as intermediaries, Rowena and Horst had been persuaded to set aside their differences and bring the two groups together in a celebration of Lughnasadh which it was hoped would mark the beginning of great things.

Better still, while she was to be denied the pleasure of actually taking a cock inside her, there was at least a male element to the ritual they'd agreed upon, a very male element. As she continued to set up the stone circle she was humming happily to herself, and thinking of the smell and feel of excited male bodies.

Father Somner lay on his side, his wrists and ankles securely tied with baling twine, his mouth slightly open around the cord from his own robe, with a few puffs of pink cotton showing at the sides where Poppy had forced her panties into his mouth to shut him up. She and Nich stood over him, he frowning in concentration, she looking doubtful, with her digital camera hanging limp from one wrist.

'It has to be convincing,' Nich remarked. 'Nobody's going to believe he's molesting you when he's tied up, never mind the look on his face.'

'Maybe if we strung him up from a tree and I whipped him?' Poppy suggested. 'I think most people would take my word for it if I claimed he'd paid me.'

'Perhaps,' Nich answered her, 'but hopefully it'll never get to that stage. We need something that'll make sure he'll never even dare to risk the pictures coming to light.'

'True,' Poppy admitted. 'Shame.'

There was a pause, both of them looking down at the priest, who'd stopped thrashing about, but whose face still registered a fury nearly as intense as when they'd forced Poppy's knickers into his mouth.

'I think he should have an erection for one thing,' Nich stated.

'Yeuch!' Poppy responded. 'I'm not touching that!'

'It would definitely add verisimilitude, and you could use a handkerchief or something.'

'True,' Poppy admitted, 'true. But still – Hang on, I think I've got it. Take this.'

She passed Nich the camera and squatted down, quickly lifting Father Somner's robes to expose long, bony legs and a pair of plain, grey Y-fronts. He'd begun to struggle again, and to make angry mumbling noises through his gag, but Poppy ignored him, leaning on his thighs in an effort to keep him still as she tugged the front of his underpants down. A skinny pink cock and a somewhat ropy scrotum tumbled out.

With her face flickering between amusement and disgust, Poppy wrapped her hand in a fold of the priest's black robe and began to masturbate him. His struggles abruptly became more furious still, until with a sigh of resignation she put her other hand to his balls, speaking as she dug her nails into his flesh.

'Calm down, will you? Or we'll have to do this the hard way.'

Somner's face had gone abruptly red, his eyes popping as she tightened her grip still more, and abruptly he'd gone limp.

'Good boy,' Poppy stated. 'Now just relax and enjoy yourself. After all, I don't suppose you've ever had a girl toss you before, have you? Nice isn't it?'

He didn't answer, his eyes now closed, possibly in a futile attempt to fight down the responses of his body, because his cock had already begun to stiffen in her hand. Poppy laughed as she rolled his foreskin between her fingers and an involuntary spasm of pleasure shot through his thighs. Nich began to take pictures.

Soon he was hard, his cock a stiff little pointer of bright pink flesh sticking up rudely from between his underpants and the hem of his robe. Poppy's disgust had vanished, to be replaced by an impish delight, and she was giggling as she gave his erection a final polish and rose to her feet. Nich stood back a little to make sure he had the entire scene visible in the viewfinder. Poppy straddled Somner's body, her pretty face twisted into a grin of evil delight as she tugged her skirt up to lay bare her richly furred pussy.

'Try not to look so happy about it,' Nich advised. 'Do that again.'

Poppy nodded in response, let her skirt drop and lifted it once more, this time with her face set in a resentful scowl, as if what she was doing brought her only misery and shame. Nich gave a pleased nod and began to reel off pictures, one after another. On the ground, Father Somner had begun to thrash again and, despite his rigid erection, his face registered only anger, until Poppy reached down, pushed out her belly and spread her sex lips, to show not just the

155

entrance to her virgin sex, but the tiny arch of flesh where her pee-hole came out.

'Ready?' she asked, glancing at Nich.

'Hang on,' he answered, and reached down to tug out a little more of her panties from the priest's mouth, with just enough of the frill showing to make it plain what they were. Poppy giggled as Nich stood back.

'Ready,' he stated, 'and keep that sorrowful look.'

Poppy nodded and looked down, her expression changing to concentration, then back to misery. Father Somner at last realised what she was going to do to him, and went pop-eyed in horror for one instant, before shutting his eyes as tight as they would go as a gush of bright golden urine erupted from Poppy's sex, to catch him full in the face. Nich took picture after picture as her urine splashed onto him, the stream aimed at his mouth despite his best efforts to turn his head aside.

His expression no longer mattered – the look of a man tied up and pissed on in order to satisfy a perverse desire being no different from that of one tied up and pissed on for any other reason – while his erect cock told its own story, or appeared to. Poppy was enjoying herself too, struggling to hold her abused expression as she moved to spray his cock.

The effect was almost instantaneous. No sooner had her pee begun to splash on his genitals than his cock simply exploded, spraying jet after jet of come over his robes, so high some went in his face. Poppy gave a shriek of mingled delight and disgust as she saw, and was laughing as the last of her pee dribbled out, with Father Somner's cock still jerking and oozing beneath her. She climbed off, leaving him soaked in piddle from his head to his thighs.

'I imagine that should do the job,' Nich said

happily as he extracted the memory card from the camera. 'What do you think, Father?'

Somner didn't respond, still trying to shake the pee out of his hair, although the mixture of shame and fury on his face was something to see. Nich went on.

'As a man of moderate intelligence, for all your misguided beliefs, I assume you appreciate the situation? Yes? I'll run over it anyway. You have just been photographed, easily recognisable and in your cassock, tied up, gagged with a pair of pink panties, and with an erect cock while a young and apparently very upset woman urinates over you. You came too, which makes any denial sound rather false. Should a third party, your Bishop for example, see these pictures, what conclusion do you suppose he'll come to? The truth? I suspect not. More likely, especially backed up by Poppy's tear-stained confession, will be the assumption that you set up the scene in order to indulge a singularly perverse fantasy, and that you forced Poppy, and some putative photographer, to comply with your wishes, by blackmail, bribery, threat of violence, perhaps all three. Should you not wish this to happen, you need merely refrain from handing over the video of Lottie Dowling masturbating in your pulpit, while the fact that you still have the original should guarantee our good faith. Is that clear?'

Father Somner opened one eye, glaring for a moment before giving a single nod of his head.

'Excellent,' Nich said happily. 'I suppose we'd better untie you, then.'

It took a while for them to release his arms and legs, and they let him do the gag himself, spitting the now sodden panties out onto the ground and spluttering pee and saliva for a moment before he could find his voice.

'I – I'll – both of you, you –'

'Spawn of Beelzebub?' Nich suggested. 'I've always wanted to be called that, not that it's strictly accurate, of course, because while I recognise Satanism as a valid –'

'Shut up!' Somner snarled, and turned on Nich, as if contemplating assault, only to think better of it.

Nich favoured him with a benign smile. Somner drew in his breath and turned towards where they'd parked his car, his voice coming out in an angry hiss.

'You may think you're clever, Mordaunt, and you, you little witch, but I'll make sure you regret this, for the rest of your lives, and after!'

Charlotte's stomach was tight with excitement as she watched the sun sink slowly towards the horizon through the trees of Berne Woods. The heat of the day had barely faded and the air had remained still, as if in anticipation of the evening to come. Everything was ready: each of the thirteen squat standing stones was topped with a cloth, a knife and an onyx goblet, the last a contribution from Coralie's shop. To one side a barbecue had been set up by Horst's friends, along with lights, filtered golden-green and powered by a generator set well back in the woods. All that remained was the food, for which Nich and Poppy had taken responsibility.

Just to watch the sunset was bringing her mingled sense of the sacred and erotic pleasure up to a delicious high, with the prospect of going nude with the men there enough to set her trembling. Even Rowena's mood had softened with the men doing as they were told and even Horst was treating her with deference, while the proposed details of the ritual were enough to set her nipples stiff just at the thought.

The distant sound of a car made her jump, as the prospect of their being interrupted, especially by the old man who owned the wood, was the only obvious thing that could go wrong. As the car stopped she was biting her lip, but it was Poppy and Nich who emerged from the path, each carrying a pair of obviously heavy bags.

'What kept you?' Horst asked as Nich dropped his bags by the barbecue.

'We ran into Father Somner in town,' Nich answered, grinning more malevolently than ever. 'He was a little cross, but we managed to sort it out.'

'What did he want?' Charlotte asked, stepping forward in alarm.

'Don't worry,' Poppy assured her. 'Let's just say he had some doubts about your repentance, but we convinced him you were genuine.'

'Thanks,' Charlotte answered, somewhat puzzled. 'I thought he hated you, Nich?'

'Yes,' Nich admitted, 'but he proved open to reason. Right, we have bread, good thick brown loaves as requested, and chicken, and pork, and lamb, and peppers.'

He was unloading the bags as he spoke, while Horst's friends Rob and Dan piled the food on a table to the side. They, along with Troll, who was responsible for the lighting and sound system, were to be servants for the evening, just one of Rowena's many conditions for their presence. Other conditions included the girls remaining clothed, and in bright colours appropriate to high summer, with Rowena herself in a beautiful yellow robe. With the exception of Nich and Horst, the men were obliged to dress simply, in plain colours, although they had resisted Rowena's demand for hessian tunics on the grounds of practicality.

Charlotte and Horst alone were to go nude, and then not until the height of the feast, a prospect that gave her the same blend of fear and excitement as the night she'd lost her virginity, and almost as strong. First, though, she had to change, and she moved a little to the side, out of the full glare of the lights, to do it.

Seated in his computer chair, the doors locked, the curtains drawn and the phone off the hook, Mr Pedlow stared at the Lughnasadh preparations with a mixture of rapidly rising excitement and envy. For the first time there were men present, and men could mean only one thing, given how dirty the girls were – cocks, cocks pushed into the juicy young cunts he'd so often longed to fill himself.

His equipment was full on, the images from all eight cameras showing in windows on his monitor, to allow him to flick between viewpoints at the click of a mouse. He was all set to record as well, both stills and video, with an automatic programme ready to capture the entire event and a manual override for when he needed more detail from some particularly juicy moment.

Not for years had he felt so alive, the adrenaline positively throbbing through his veins as he waited for the action. As the delectable Charlotte moved into position almost directly above one of the cameras and put her hands straight to the button of her jeans his tension grew greater still. One hand went to his cock, squeezing gently as he watched her begin to undress.

Even in jeans she looked glorious, the seat tight over her full bottom, but as they came down he was licking his lips in delight. Underneath, she wore plain white panties, full-cut, spanking panties as he'd come to call them, and the sort he liked best. They really brought out the shape of her chubby moon of a bottom, despite the uncertain light and the odd angle, and as she peeled her top off he was already getting hard.

To his deep disappointment she pulled on some other garment, a robe of sorts, before taking off her bra beneath it. She did turn though, briefly affording him an excellent view of her belly, now distinctly swollen in pregnancy, a sight which gave him a deliciously intrusive thrill. Her panties came off too, but under the robe, providing no more than a tantalising glimpse of opulent, bare bottom and plump pink cunt before she had let the robe fall and the view became abruptly less interesting.

The little clearing was already rich with the smell of grilled meat and vegetables, with both Rob and Dan busily attending to the cooking. Rowena took her place at the largest of the stones, sitting cross-legged on the grass. Nich gave her a mischievous grin as he sat down beyond Charlotte to her right. He was in black silk, adding to the somewhat Satanic air that always accompanied him despite his protestations of pure paganism. She returned the smile, telling herself that for all her ill feeling about letting men join them it was the right thing to do.

Horst came towards her, his muscular body well defined beneath a golden robe Charlotte knew to be Nich's. He too smiled, and gave a slight inclination of his head, which might have been genuine, or might have been mockery. Poppy was with him, and sat down one stone beyond, with the other girls quickly taking the remaining places, Melanie and Louisa careful to position themselves to either side of the two positions reserved for the three male servants. Both sisters were clearly happy to have the men there, and

Poppy was also full of nervous energy, as was Coralie, with only Eve and Andrea a little reserved. Juliana remained cool as always.

As Rob and Dan began to serve out thick pieces of bread, Rowena stood up, facing towards the west, where the last rays of sunlight just penetrated between the tree trunks, and began to chant the grace for First Harvest.

Juliana closed her eyes as she listened to Rowena's chant. It was new, Pagan, and yet clearly moulded by a Roman Catholic upbringing. Yet it was also evocative, and spoken with real passion, allowing her mind to drift back to other times, other ceremonies. Even as Rob reached her, to pile a mix of grilled lamb, pepper and onions onto her bread, she had taken hold of the edge of the yellow dress she'd chosen as a robe. Peeling it high, she laid herself bare, a condition vastly more appropriate for the ceremony.

Rob swallowed, his eyes fixing briefly on her chest, but he moved on without saying anything. As Rowena reached the end of her chant, Juliana took up her knife and began to eat, sawing off a corner of the thickly buttered bread and loading it with the rich, hot food. It tasted good, and as she crammed it into her mouth a little butter escaped, to trickle down her chin and into the deep valley between her breasts.

All five men were watching her, either openly or from the sides of their eyes. Rowena did too, with a touch of irritation, and Melanie, who, after an instant of hesitation, rose to peel off her own top and bra, baring her breasts but keeping her yellow slacks on. A minute later her sister had followed suit, leaving the three male servants rapt in their attention as they took their places.

* * *

Nich ate with gusto, enjoying both the food and the atmosphere, with Juliana now properly naked and at least two of the girls bare from the waist up. It was working, and would undoubtedly get better, especially once the more reserved of the girls had taken a little of the white powder Andrea was currently preparing in a chafing dish.

Rowena was offered the dish first, and Nich watched in amusement as she took a large pinch, then a second, a dose doubtless intended to make it easier to overcome her inhibitions. Charlotte was more cautious, but Horst was both greedy and casual, using a finger to push a considerable proportion of the remaining powder onto the blade of his knife. It came to Nich next, and he politely declined, intent on enjoying the evening with a clear head. Poppy showed no such reservations, and the powder was almost finished by the time Andrea got to the male servants.

Nich was left smiling, and already the conversation had taken on a new buzz as Rob and Dan once more began to serve out portions of food. Rowena looked imperious and confident, Charlotte and Poppy full of nervous excitement. A moment later Coralie had stood up, to step in among the stones, make a circular gesture with her hand to Rowena and pull off her dress and pants, standing naked for all to see before returning to her stone.

Melanie and Louisa followed suit, together, a double strip made slightly awkward by having to pull off shoes, slacks and panties while standing up, but clearly to the deep delight of the men. As Louisa returned to her place, she sat a little to one side, speaking in a low voice to Troll before laying her head against his chest. After a moment he put his arm around her and began to fondle a breast. With his other hand he adjusted something beside him, and soft music swelled up around them.

Horst's cock was hard beneath his robe. Poppy stood at the centre of the stone circle, her petite body swaying gently to the music. Her top was already off, her small breasts bare in rich green light, her nipples stiff, and an expression on her face of sleepy bliss. There was nothing of the striptease in her dance, no concealing and revealing, no jiggling breasts and wiggling bottom. She was lithe, slow, undressing because her clothes were no longer needed, because it was right for her to be nude.

The sight filled Horst with both pride and longing, pride to have a girl so full of life as his partner, longing to make her fully his own by filling her virgin quim with his erection. She had offered it too, so long as the moment was right, a prospect which had set his stomach in a hard knot and his balls aching. When she stood to let her knickers fall to the ground and stepped casually free he had to close his eyes or risk coming on the spot. The action left her completely, gloriously naked, from her dense black curls to her neatly painted toes, the firm, supple curves of her body an incitement to take her then and there, at the centre of the circle.

She was his, and the moment would come, but later. With Poppy nude, only four of the girls retained their clothes, and Horst knew that both Rowena and Charlotte were naked beneath their robes. Andrea had set a chafing dish of incense to smoulder, adding its scent to that of their feast, and the distinctly female musk that tugged at the edge of his senses. He glanced towards Rowena, but she was looking at Eve with a light smile of encouragement.

Eve rose, shy and uncertain, her trembling visible as she began to undress. Horst watched, enjoying her uncertainty almost as much as the exposure of her abundant curves. If Charlotte was motherly in modern terms, then Eve might have been the model for the ancient stone Goddess carvings so often found in Stone Age digs. Her breasts were huge, great heavy melons of flesh, her belly an ample double bulge, her bottom a heavy, deeply cleft ball of girl flesh.

Her confidence grew a little as she came to realise that Dan was squeezing his cock as he watched her. With a shy smile in his direction she reached back to unfasten her bra and pulled the cups up over her breasts. Her knickers came down, off, and she was nude, to a murmur of appreciation from the others. Horst made a surreptitious adjustment to his own erection, wishing he had the stamina, and the chance, to fuck all eight girls, to fill all eight pussies with hot come, first Rowena, and lastly his own Poppy.

Rowena signalled to Andrea, who stood, just a touch of resentment showing in her face as she began to undress, without fuss, and sitting down again as soon as she was nude. Again Horst glanced at Rowena, and this time she nodded and he climbed to his feet. It was impossible not to feel piqued as he returned her nod with a polite inclination of his head, and he was fighting his pride down as he stepped to the middle of the stone circle.

He stood, at the exact centre of the stones, his erect cock making a conspicuous bulge in his robe. Rowena's face flickered as she saw, in surprise and shock that quickly faded to amusement. Knowing he could not afford to break the moment, Horst held back the urge to tell her he was hard because of watching the girls strip, and not because of what he had agreed to do. Instead he shrugged his robe from his shoulders, to stand naked in a puddle of golden cloth lit bright with green highlights, his erection now towering up from his belly.

Charlotte's tongue flicked out to moisten her lips, while behind him another girl giggled. Rowena held her poise and stepped around her stone, to seat herself on the flat top. Her face was frozen as she lifted her robe and set her thighs apart, exposing the soft purse of her sex. Horst bowed his head and got slowly down to his knees, his pride still threatening to rebel as he moved forward. A slight twitch in the muscle of one of Rowena's thighs was all that betrayed her nervousness as he came close, perhaps because she realised he only needed to stand up, take her under her bottom and around her back, and he could drive his erection into her very wet and very virgin sex.

It was hard to resist, but the thought of how it would be to rape her held him back. Instead he leant forward, his hands folded in his lap, to plant a single, gentle kiss on her sex, a token of his esteem for her as his Priestess and in the image of the Goddess herself. Only as his lips actually touched the gently bulging flesh of her labia did he give in at all to the impish urges within. Pushing out his tongue, he began to lick, full on her clitoris.

Rowena immediately stiffened, and he caught the gasps and giggles behind him. Her hand found the top of his head, clutching in the short stubble of his hair. Triumph welled up inside him at the realisation that she was going to pull him off and so make herself seem insecure, but the pressure of her arm went the other way, pulling his face into her sex. The tables turned, he had no choice but to continue licking, full of chagrin, yet still enjoying the feel and flavour of Rowena's sex.

Kneeling, his cock still painfully erect against his belly, he lapped at her, knowing full well that all eleven of his watchers knew exactly what he was doing, and the state of his erection. None would even know that he'd started to lick in an effort to make her lose her cool, and he couldn't back out. Soon it was too late anyway. Her eyes had closed, the muscles of her belly and thighs were beginning to tighten, and he realised she was going to come under his tongue, although no doubt with images of Charlotte in her head – that, or sheer sadistic joy at his subservience.

Rowena's body tightened, her sex in contraction, her grip painfully hard in his hair, and she was coming, full in his face, but without so much as a whimper to express her ecstasy. Horst waited until it was over and she had let go, then rocked back on his heels, looking up. Rowena gave him a regal smile.

'A fuller obeisance than I had expected,' she remarked lightly, 'but entirely appropriate. Thank you.'

Horst responded with his best imitation of Nich's malevolent grin, despite cursing both what had happened, and that his cock had remained rigidly erect throughout.

Charlotte's whole body was shaking as she watched Horst return to his stone. It was her turn, and if Rowena could make Horst take her to orgasm beneath his tongue, it was hard to see her holding back now. As Poppy snuggled into Horst's side across the stones, Charlotte rose, to step into the centre, acutely aware of the ring of eyes on her body. As Horst had done, she let her robe drop away, on top of his, and stepped naked towards Rowena.

Rowena's chin came up, her face calm and beautiful as Charlotte dropped down to her knees. Her feelings as she moved forward were little short of worship, and grew stronger still as she leant forward to press her puckered lips to Rowena's sex. Not to lick would have been impossible, with her senses already reeling to the taste and smell of her lover's body. Her tongue came out, lapping firmly, and Rowena's hand touched her hair, taking a gentle grip of the golden locks.

As she licked, Charlotte was intensely aware of her naked body, of the weight of her breasts as they swung gently to her motions, of how open she was behind, her cheeks parted to show the mouth of her sex, but most of all, of the way her now distended belly hung beneath her, heavy in pregnancy. She already wanted to come, just from the exquisite sensation of kneeling naked and pregnant with her face between her lover's thighs and a dozen people watching her.

Rowena came, her sex going into contraction against Charlotte's face, her thighs locked tight to either side. She cried out too, hiding nothing, her head thrown back, one hand locked in Charlotte's hair, the other on her own breasts as she let out her feelings in full view of everybody. The act left both men and women completely silent. Every face was rapt in attention, full of excitement. As Charlotte rocked back on her heels she saw that Poppy had her head in Horst's lap, licking at his erect penis even as she watched.

She rose and turned, stepping once more to the centre of the circle, to glance around her before laying herself down. To her side, Juliana and Nich were twinned together. Louisa was sat next to Troll, his erection poking up into her hand as she masturbated him. Dan was laid out on the ground, his head in Eve's lap, suckling on one big nipple. Melanie was leant close to Rob, looking pleased with herself as she teased his cock to erection.

Behind her she heard Rowena's voice, raised to offer the chance to make obeisance to Charlotte. Looking back, she could see her lover, now naked, standing tall and beautiful in the green light, her arms folded lightly across her chest. For a moment nobody responded, until Nich moved forward, to kneel beside Charlotte's prone body, his erect cock rearing up above her belly. Juliana had come behind him, her hand curling around his body, to take his cock and begin to tug.

Horst and Poppy moved in to the other side of her, in the same position, his erection thrust out over her pregnant belly, his girl's hand wrapped around the shaft as she masturbated him. The other three couples moved in too, pressing close, Troll and Louisa to one side, Rob and Melanie to the other, Dan and Eve between her open thighs, five cocks held out over her, five cocks any one of which she would gladly have taken inside her, or all of them.

She took her breasts in hand, eager to masturbate herself to an ecstatic climax as much religious as physical. Her nipples were achingly hard and sensitive, the skin of her breasts taut and tender to the touch. She began to play, drawing in the thick cock scent from around her and thinking of how it would be if all five men were to fuck her in turn, leaving her masturbating in their sperm as it ran from her sex.

What was going to happen was nearly as good. Dan grunted, his cock jerked in Eve's hand and a spray of hot sperm erupted over Charlotte's belly and sex. A second eruption splashed down into her pubic hair, at the same instant Horst also came, with Poppy's hand working furiously fast on his shaft, to spatter come across Charlotte's body from her breasts to her belly button.

She closed her eyes in bliss, feeling the hot sperm on her taut skin, and more as Troll came in a gasping, grunting passion, Louisa giggling in delight as she milked him onto Charlotte's flesh. Melanie got the same result a moment later, Rob's erection sending a fountain of white high up to land plumb on top of Charlotte's belly. Last was Nich, leaning forward a little to allow Juliana to tug him neatly off into the already wide pool of sperm crowning the pregnant bulge of Charlotte's belly.

All five moved back a little as Charlotte's hands went to her sex. Some of Dan's sperm had landed between her lips and she began to rub it over herself. Her back was arched, her muscles already beginning to contract. She could see Rowena standing over her, and her mouth came open in need. Rowena hesitated only an instant, before squatting down, her bottom in Charlotte's face, pussy to mouth.

Charlotte was licking immediately, and wriggling her nose in Rowena's bottom hole, lost to everything but her pleasure as she started to come. Her bottom cheeks tensed, her thighs went tight and she was there, rubbing sperm into the slippery crease of her sex, her whole body jerking in ecstasy as she licked Rowena, on a long plateau of ethereal bliss that didn't break until the warm, wet pussy was finally lifted from her mouth.

Slowly she came down, her body still twitching, her fingers still moving slowly between her sex lips. A long sigh escaped her mouth, then a giggle as she raised her head to find the spunk running down over her lightly swollen belly like icing on a Dickensian Christmas cake.

Poppy had watched Charlotte come with her own excitement rising, until by the end her need was close to desperation. She wasn't the only one. The five men, Rowena and Charlotte might have come, but the others hadn't, and with Charlotte spread naked and dripping mingled sperm down her pregnant belly, inhibitions had fled.

Juliana had mounted Nich on the ground, head to tail, doing her best to suck some life back into his cock as she rubbed herself in his face. He was responding too, licking her sex with one thumb pushed well up her hole, and his long, black-painted nails scratching at the alabaster skin of her bottom.

Snuggling close to Horst, Poppy eased him back against one of the stones. She knew she could have him ready again within just a few minutes, his cock always stiffening to the feel of her mouth or hand. Laying her head in his lap, she took it in her mouth, sucking lazily as she teased his balls and watched the others at play.

Eve was with Dan, just outside the stones, kissing, her arms around him, his hands working clumsily to excite her, fondling one huge breast and rubbing between her thighs. Just feet away were Melanie and Rob, in a delightfully rude position, she on all fours, her bottom stuck high, sucking and licking at his cock and balls as she masturbated. Troll and Louisa were to one side, closely entwined, she giggling and sighing as he licked at her breasts and masturbated her.

Andrea and Coralie had disappeared, but a new thrill came to Poppy as she realised that they were in the grass at the very edge of the circle of light, pale limbs tangled together, Coralie's neat bottom lifted, thighs wide, with Andrea's fingers working between wet pink pussy lips.

Her time had come. Horst's cock was already beginning to stiffen in her mouth, while his gentle caresses to her bottom and back grew more urgent. She put her hand between her thighs to find her pussy wet and ready, save for the tense bulge of her hymen where it held her closed. To touch it sent her thrill of anticipation soaring, and to think if it being broached by the big cock now swelling in her mouth raised it higher still.

There was just a touch of fear as she pulled her head up from Horst's cock. He was already stiff, wonderfully virile. She looked up into his eyes and nodded, before planting a last kiss on the head of his cock, the head that was about to be pushed in up her sex, breaking her hymen.

Rowena and Charlotte had moved aside, cuddling together with their mouths open in a kiss. Poppy scrambled close, to shake Rowena by the shoulder, demanding that an announcement be made. Rowena understood and rose to climb onto her stone at the west of the circle even as Poppy rolled over onto her back at its centre.

Horst stood tall, his erect cock in his hand, towering up between Poppy's open thighs. Rowena raised her hands, calling out, to announce that Poppy had chosen the night to become fully a woman. The couples turned, staying together but watching, as Horst got to his knees, pushing his cock to Poppy's open sex. She closed her eyes, clutching at the grass, her bottom cheeks, her anus, her sex, all twitching. His cock head pressed to her hole, stretching out her hymen, only to move higher, rubbing between her lips.

Just moments later her mounting rapture had tipped over into full orgasm. She cried out as her whole body went tense, loose, and tense again as she went into violent contractions, gasping and squirming under his cock. He pushed lower once more, quickly, and forward, hard. Poppy was still coming as her hymen tore open, and the scream that split the night air was more of ecstasy than pain.

* * *

172

Mr Pedlow lay slumped in his chair, gasping for breath, come running slowly down his fingers.

Eight

Ariesian lay back in comfort, occasionally sucking at a straw as he drank a reflective martini. Alice was on her knees between his open thighs, naked, her lips and tongue working on his balls as she masturbated him. He was already rock hard, and wondering whether to take the session further or to simply spunk up on her head, but in no hurry. He chuckled as a new thought occurred to him, and cocked his legs wider still.

'That's good. Now lick my arsehole.'

She looked up, for once hesitant, her eyes full of doubt, then down, at the hairy knot of flesh she'd been ordered to lick.

'Lick it, you little whore,' he ordered. 'What, d'you think you're too good to lick my arse?'

She shook her head, but still she hesitated, her big green eyes now moist with unshed tears. Ariesian reached out, intending to take her by the hair and force her to do it whether she liked it or not, only for her to suddenly overcome her reservations and lean forward, with her pretty pink tongue poked out between her lips. He chuckled in amusement, then gave a pleased sigh as the wet tip of her tongue found its target, full on his anus, and she set to work, licking.

He settled back, enjoying his drink as she once more began to masturbate him, only now with her face pressed between his open buttocks. It felt good, very good indeed, and she was jerking hard on his cock, no doubt hoping he'd come quickly and put an end to her ordeal. Smiling in malign satisfaction, he promised himself he would do exactly the opposite.

Reaching out for the vermouth bottle, he positioned it over her head, making sure she realised what was going to happen before he began to pour. She quickly closed her eyes, adding fresh misery to her expression as the pungent liquid began to run down over her head, wetting her hair and her face, splashing his cock and balls and trickling down over her breasts. It felt cool on his anus, making the sensation of being licked more intense, which added to his pleasure, both physical and in knowing where she had her tongue.

He lay back, watching in satisfaction as she licked between his cheeks, not daring to do otherwise without an order. She didn't dare open her eyes either, for fear of the stinging liquid still dripping from her fringe, and she was still wanking fervently at his cock. He laughed.

'You really are pathetic, Alice, you know that, don't you? Now get your tongue right up, and you can taste my arse while I spunk on you.'

She nodded and pushed her face close in, her tongue tip delving into his anus, to send a shiver of pleasure the length of his spine. He took his cock from her, holding it up as he wanked, determined to make the spunk go in her face and hair. Her licking and probing grew more intense, his anus open on her tongue, which was simply too much. The come erupted from his cock, a white fountain rising high, to splash down on Alice's head, and in one eye just as she opened it.

'Fucking bull's eye!' he crowed the moment he'd caught his breath. 'Will you look at that, right in the peeper!'

Alice had sat back, and was desperately trying to get the spunk out of her eye while more of it ran down her sodden hair and across her face. Her wet chest was quivering with emotion, a sight that made him wish he could come again, immediately, all over her tits, and in her cunt, and up her bottom. Unfortunately he needed time to recharge, but that didn't mean her humiliation had to end there. He stood up and took hold of his rapidly deflating cock.

'Here, let me help you . . .'

She looked up, just in time to catch the full force of his urine stream right in her face. Her mouth came wide in shock, just for an instant, but an instant too long, as it filled with golden, bubbling piss. Struggling not to swallow, she went into a coughing fit, a mixture of pee and mucus exploding from her nose as she sicked up the rest. Blinded, coughing, and utterly helpless, she could only grovel down on the ground as he emptied the rest of his bladder over her head and breasts. From the kitchen doorway Xiu Mei and Yi watched, giggling hysterically as he shook the last few drops of piddle loose into Alice's hair.

'Suck this,' he instructed, holding out his cock with the last drop of golden fluid hanging from the tip.

Alice obeyed, leaning meekly forward to take him in her mouth, and sucked until he told her to stop. She was left kneeling in a puddle of pee, her body glistening wet, her hair a mess of bedraggled rats' tails.

'Take a shower,' he instructed, 'then mop your mess up and take another one.'

'Yes, my Lord,' Alice replied, and scampered off.

Ariesian went back to his lounger, considering his position as he sipped the martini. Between giving

Alice to the Chief Constable and holding a very reserved festival for the first harvest, he was now back in favour with the authorities. He had even allowed a local priest to attend, and give a brief speech on brotherhood among worshippers and the ties between Christian Lammastide and Pagan Lughnasadh. It had been received with only muted applause, but then the price of the tickets and a little careful selection had ensured that he would have a reasonably polite audience. Nich Mordaunt hadn't applied for admission, nor even troubled to put in an appearance outside.

Nevertheless, there was a problem. His reputation relied on the respect of those who wanted an alternative to Christianity, and more often than not that went hand in hand with a distaste for authority. Too many toned-down events and he would quickly lose his following, while he was all too aware of Nich Mordaunt's rebellious appeal.

Mabon he could probably get away with, perhaps with a solemn ritual at Stonehenge, celebrating the equinox at sunrise. Not that many people would turn up anyway, and he could use police and local authority restrictions as an excuse for limiting numbers, perhaps even gain a little credit by pretending to fight the decision. He'd be losing money, but there were still the TV rights.

Samhain was a different matter. He'd have to do something big, something designed to draw in a good-sized, paying crowd. It would have to be at a sacred site, but somewhere other than Hampshire, Wiltshire or the neighbouring counties. Then there was Nich, who was sure to have some rival event in mind, and after Solstice, might well pull a good crowd. The thought set his face in an angry frown.

A squeak of pain from the house interrupted his thoughts and he turned, looking into the kitchen, where Alice was touching her toes as the two laughing Chinese girls flicked at her naked bottom with wet dish clothes. He shook his head, amused at the way the girls had begun to inflict little cruelties on Alice, who took it without complaint, save for her squeals. Presently she came out, still stark naked, as he had instructed her to remain, and holding a mop and bucket.

'Do you know what your ex-boyfriend is doing for Samhain?' he demanded as she began to mop up the pool of urine.

'Yes,' Alice admitted.

'What?'

'He – he's planning a big event, something spectacular. I don't know the details. I'm sorry.'

'Where?'

'On Cape Cornwall.'

'Cape Cornwall? I didn't know there was a pagan site there?'

'Yes. There is. There was. It was in use long before Stonehenge, but specifically for Samhain, as the setting sun appears to fall directly into the sea. There were stones, but when the tin mining began there they were used for buildings, so . . .'

She went on, but Ariesian was no longer listening. If Nich Mordaunt was planning a big festival it would undoubtedly be illegal, and it would undoubtedly draw a crowd. It was quite obvious what to do.

Looking out over the assembled guests, each group neatly spaced around a white-clothed table, with white napkins and white flowers, all set against the backdrop of the white marquee, Charlotte's principal emotion was guilt. The day had been perfect, her dress magnificent, the weather bright sunshine but cool enough to be bearable, each little detail just as it had been planned. The service had been held at the chapel attached to St Cecilia's, complete with the school choir, many members of which she could remember as younger girls from her own time there. Father Dawson had conducted the entire affair like the benign patriarch he liked to be thought of, and was clearly well pleased with his actions in having, as he jokingly put it, brought her back from the brink.

He was wrong, and yet his bonhomie, along with the very genuine pleasure so many people took in her marriage, was part of her guilt, albeit a minor part. Her strong feeling that in submitting to a Catholic marriage she was betraying her principles and the Goddess herself also contributed something, but again, a minor part. The major part was reserved for Rowena, and what was going to happen with Horst just as soon as he and Charlotte had been packed off to their honeymoon cottage beside the Neusiedler See.

To deny it was pointless, because she knew she could no more resist him than she could Rowena. If it didn't happen during the journey, perhaps in the lavatories at Exeter Airport or somewhere equally sordid, the moment they were safely alone, up would come her dress and down would come her knickers. She might even protest, half-heartedly, to save a little pride, but it would make no difference. Up would go his cock, and she'd get the good, long fucking she so desperately craved.

She was already wet, just thinking about it, making her panties distinctly uncomfortable. Now, with the wedding feast over, she was going to have to get up, and dance, and mingle, and inspect her presents. Somehow she was certain that Rowena, now sitting rather stiffly in her pale blue bridesmaid's dress talking to old Mr Pedlow, who owned Berne Woods and was the nearest thing the village had to a Squire, would smell her sex, and know.

For all her misgivings, everyone else seemed blissfully happy, smiling and chattering merrily as the reception continued. There was one slightly embarrassing moment when Nich and Juliana, who had not been at the church, presented their gift, an ebony-handled athame with the silver guard worked to form stag's antlers and the blade an elongated and highly stylised deer face. It was a work of art, and inevitably everybody wanted to see it, but fortunately only her fellow pagans seemed to realise what it was. Not wishing to leave it with the other presents where Father Dawson might see, she gave it into Rowena's keeping as soon as was decently possible.

'Could you drop me here?' Rowena asked as the cab drew level with the trees of Berne Woods. 'The lay-by there will do.'

The driver pulled over, letting her out. None of the others made to follow, doubtless realising that she wanted to be alone. Throughout the day the tight feeling in the pit of her stomach had been growing worse. Walking behind Charlotte up the aisle and being forced to listen to the slow, inevitable progress of the wedding service had been bad enough. With Charlotte in her gigantic meringue of a dress, Rowena's mind had been crowded with images of the grinning Horst flipping up the layers of satin and lace to bare her lover's bottom and take her roughly from behind. Seeing them driven away towards the airport had been worse still.

As she walked down the narrow, dusty path with her dress held up around her calves, her feelings only grew stronger, and the stone circle, where she'd hoped to find refuge, brought only memories. So much had happened there, so many moments of intimacy and of affirmation, both alone and with the other girls present. Knowing that Charlotte would at that moment be waiting for her flight to Austria, and would inevitably succumb to Horst's coarse, masculine embraces, filled her with pain. She had agreed to it. In theory it made no difference, but it was impossible not to feel that she had lost.

Taking a seat on the western stone, she spent a moment in contemplation before deciding she was in fact sulking and that it was hardly a worthy emotion. Reaching into her bag, she brought out the athame, fingering the smooth silver of the guard and blade as she let her thoughts drift. As Juliana had explained, and also Alice before she went to Ariesian, the neo-pagan assertion that an athame should only be used for casting the circle and not for cutting were laughably timid.

It was a sacrificial knife, plain and simple, and in those few cults which had indulged in the sacrifice of the man chosen to represent the Horned God, it would have been a not dissimilar black-handled knife that the priestess plunged into his chest. At the thought her fist tightened on the handle and her lips compressed into a savage grimace as she imagined how it would feel to have Horst spread-eagled on a stone altar, drowsy with drugs and religious ecstasy, and to drive the beautiful athame to the hilt in his heart . . .

She gave a low chuckle at her own overactive imagination. It was hardly practical, when even the sacrifice of a ram was so hedged around with restrictions that what was being planned for Samhain breached a dozen petty laws, regulations and guidelines. Not that it mattered, when the entire event was illegal anyway.

The sound of a car caught her attention, and as it stopped she clicked her tongue in annoyance, sure that somebody was about to invade her privacy. Sure enough, a minute later she heard the rustle of foliage along the path and caught a glimpse of blue identical to her bridesmaid's dress.

'Poppy?'

'Hi,' Poppy replied, slightly uncertainly. 'Sorry, Ro, if you want . . .'

'No, that's alright. You must understand, if anyone does.'

Poppy nodded and came to sit on the next stone. For a moment neither spoke, then Poppy finally broke the silence.

'Do – do you suppose they'll –'

'Yes,' Rowena sighed. 'Of course. You know what Lottie's like. She promised not to, but . . .'

Poppy nodded.

'And Horst.'

'And Horst,' Rowena agreed. 'I was just thinking how nice it would be to sacrifice him at Samhain. Sorry.'

Poppy laughed.

'Don't be. I understand, and it's not as if it's for real. How about poor Mac? Are you going to do it, or is he?'

'It really ought to be me, but I'm not sure I want to. We're going to meet up with Nich when Horst and Lottie get back to sort out the details.'

'It's definitely Cape Cornwall then?'

'Definitely.'

'And this friend of Nich's, Thomazina, she's up for it?'

'Apparently. I think she's Juliana's sister.'

'Oh. Right. I must admit, I would like to see that. There's something very special about a woman giving up her virginity like that, and I suppose, after Lughnasadh . . .'

Rowena nodded, trying to understand, although the thought of surrendering herself to a man, let alone publicly, filled her with outrage. Poppy went on.

'Would you?'

'No, never. I – I could never submit myself to a man.'

'It doesn't have to be an act of submission, more one of sharing.'

Rowena shook her head firmly.

'Men hold nothing for me.'

'I suppose it's a chemical thing?'

'Maybe, but no, it's not that so much. I'd feel I was losing part of myself, like taking somebody else's name, as if to imply I've become no more than his property.'

'You don't have to do that.'

'It would feel that way. When I was first at St Cecilia's I wanted to become a nun.'

'No! Really? But then you'd be a bride of Christ anyway.'

'I could manage giving myself to a God, only not that one. Lottie has this fantasy about being taken by the Horned God in the image of a Green Man.'

'I know, chased through the trees and ravished with his huge wooden cock. Not you too, surely?'

'Not like that, no. For me it would be mutual, giving something of myself as a gift, but then there would be no repercussions. I'd still be me, not somebody's girlfriend.'

'But you are. You're Lottie's girlfriend.'

'It's not the same.'

Poppy shrugged, obviously not understanding.

'Lottie's mine. I'd be his.'

'I think of Horst as mine, and just now he's probably in the air, with your girlfriend.'

Rowena made a sour face, and again both fell silent. After a long while Poppy extended a hand, rather cautiously.

'Do you – I mean, because they're together, and – Well, why shouldn't we?'

Poppy's hand was on Rowena's leg, her intentions quite clear. Rowena hesitated, a little taken aback, until the thought of enjoying Horst's girlfriend rose up clear in her mind. She smiled and reached out, helping Poppy across to her lap. Their mouths touched, a little clumsily, Poppy giggling as they tried to get comfortable, then silent as their lips came open against each other. Rowena closed her eyes, enjoying Poppy's taste and smell, also the feel of the firm, vital body in her hands.

Nothing more was said. They went down together, onto the grass, heedless of their pretty dresses as they clung together, kissing and exploring each other's bodies. Poppy seemed shy at first, but soon both had their dresses undone, then off, laughing together in their underwear as they rolled on the grass. Inconvenient bras and knickers had soon been removed and shoes kicked off, leaving them in just their pale blue stay-up stockings.

At last Rowena took charge, rolling Poppy onto her back and straddling her head. Poppy made no protest, burying her face in Rowena's sex, then both were licking firmly, mouths to pussies, hands cupping sweetly rounded bottoms. Soon Poppy's legs had come up, around Rowena's neck to pull her in, and a moment later she'd come. The moment it was over Rowena sat up, pressing her bottom into Poppy's face. There was a moment of resistance as Rowena wriggled her bottom hole into place on Poppy's nose, but no more. Once Poppy's tongue had begun to work on Rowena's clitoris once more, it took just moments to orgasm.

Mr Pedlow extracted a tissue from the super-size box that stood permanently ready by his computer and with a series of fastidious gestures wiped the spunk from his fingers. He had guessed that one or more of the girls might go to the stone circle after the wedding, and he'd been right. When he'd seen Rowena his hopes that she might masturbate had been dashed by her troubled expression, and Poppy's arrival had raised his hopes only slightly.

When they'd got off he'd been surprised and delighted, their reason for having sex confirming his theory that every one of them was a dirty little bitch at heart. Their sixty-nine had been heaven, bringing him right to the edge of orgasm, and seeing Rowena queen Poppy's face had been too much. He'd come.

What he hadn't expected was the news about their next event. It was annoying, as he'd hoped for a replay of the August one, which had ended in such a delightful orgy. Cape Cornwall was a long way, and yet the thought of knowing that a girl was to be publicly deflowered was simply too much for him. When Horst Sachs had fucked Poppy he'd had a good view, but not a perfect one. Also, the petite, girlish Poppy was a poor substitute for the voluptuous Charlotte. Perhaps Juliana's sister was better? Juliana certainly had glorious tits, and she was tall too. There had to be at least a chance the sister had a good fat bottom to match.

There was really no question. He had to go, and he had to go quickly if there was to be any hope at all of getting his equipment set up.

* * *

Alice made for her dressing room, wondering what she could use to cover her nakedness until Ariesian got back. He'd been generous, in the sense of spending plenty of money on her, but everything had been chosen by him, and was either designed to show off her body or make her feel humiliated, often both. Colourful heels, tiny bikinis, little shorts and halter tops, flounced or ultratight microskirts, thong panties, fishnet stockings – not one item would she have chosen herself, and yet being naked suddenly felt vulnerable.

Before he left she had seen the Chinese girls giggling together, and as her degradations from him grew ever more extreme, so their attitude had become ever more disrespectful and cruel. Only that morning they had told her to clean the lavatory, normally their own task, and when she protested he had taken their side and told her to strip. They'd watched while she did it, arms folded, faces set in haughty contempt as she'd got down on her knees in the nude to scrub and polish the bowl.

Now the best bet seemed to be to get some at least half decent clothes on and go out into the garden where she could hide, but as she pushed open the door she froze. Both girls were in her bedroom, Xiu Mei seated on the bed, Yi standing by the window, holding in one hand a long-handled hairbrush that Ariesian had more than once applied to Alice's naked bottom. Xiu Mei spoke.

'On the bed, big bitch!'

Alice made to retreat, but Yi nipped smartly behind her, pushing the door closed and twisting the key in the lock. Xiu Mei grinned.

'You go when we finish with you. On the bed. Bottom up.'

Swallowing the huge lump in her throat, Alice hesitated, not wanting to go forward, not daring to back out. Really there was no choice, and with a sigh she did as she'd been told, climbing onto the bed on all fours with her bottom lifted. Both girls laughed.

'Good,' Yi said. 'Very good. You obey, and it won't be so bad.'

'Bottom up, right up!' Xiu Mei added.

Reluctantly, Alice obeyed, lifting her haunches to allow her cheeks to spread and show off her anus and the rear view of her sex. Both girls burst into laughter at the sight, sending a hot flush to Alice's face. Slowly, methodically, Yi began to beat her, smacking the hairbrush down on Alice's upturned bottom with firm deliberation. Alice hung her head, trying to block out the pain, but failing. Soon she was whimpering and gasping to the smacks, drawing more delighted laughter from both her persecutors.

Alice took it, shaking with pain and humiliation as her bottom quickly grew hot and her body underwent the inevitable reaction, her sex growing swollen and wet, her nipples stiff. Yi responded by using the hairbrush harder still, and calling Alice a slut and a whore, along with many of the other choice words Ariesian used to describe her. Still she stayed down, until her bottom was a hot ball of pain, when Yi finally reversed the brush in her hand, to slide the handle deep up into Alice's sopping, ready hole.

Xiu Mei gave a peal of laughter to see the big hairbrush sticking out so obscenely from between Alice's bottom cheeks, and bounced onto the bed, her back to the wall and her thighs up, to show taut white panties stretched over her softly bulging sex. She pointed at Alice.

'Now you, you do as we say. You lick cunt, or we beat you good, yes?'

Alice gave a single, sorrowful nod of her head.

'Good,' Xiu Mei crowed. 'You understand. You lick when you are told, or you get beaten. Yes?'

Again Alice nodded.

'Good. Now you lick my cunt. Then you lick my sister's cunt.'

Lifting her bottom, Xiu Mei quickly bunched up her dress to the level of her waist. Pushing the full white panties down and off, she spread the hairless pink mound of her sex in Alice's face. Alice crawled forward, the hairbrush wobbling in her hole, to press her face to Xiu Mei's sex and lick up the pungent, feminine taste. Yi gave a squeal of high-pitched laughter, pointing.

'See! No resistance! You are a slut, Alice, a big, clumsy, stupid slut! What are you!?'

'A slut,' Alice managed through her mouthful of pussy flesh.

'Properly, say it!' Yi demanded, and smacked her hand down on Alice's upraised bottom.

'A slut,' Alice gasped. 'I'm a big, stupid, clumsy slut!'

Yi gave a chuckle and withdrew, watching as Alice worked on her sister's sex. Xiu Mei had her eyes shut and had tugged her dress right up, so that she could play with her breasts. Alice licked diligently, working on the tiny pink clitoris peeping out from between Xiu Mei's sex lips, and soon she could feel the first slow contractions of the approaching orgasm.

'You will be a good slave, Alice,' she sighed, 'a good, good slave. We will beat you anyway, to keep you good, but not so hard, maybe. You will obey too, and not speak to his pigship, not a word. If you speak, do you know what we will do?'

'This,' Yi supplied. 'We take you to the lavatory. We piss and shit in the bowl, both of us. When we finish, in goes your head. We flush the lavatory. After that you stay quiet.'

Alice nodded urgently and redoubled her efforts to make Xiu Mei come. Yi laughed, then went quiet,

188

watching bright-eyed as Xiu Mei's body began to tighten. Clutching her breasts, the Chinese girl came with a long sigh that broke to a little choking sound, with Alice licking for all she was worth. Yi crowed in delight to see, and immediately took her sister's place on the bed, only facing the wall, with her creamy white bottom pushed out towards Alice's face.

'Like this,' she ordered. 'In my arsehole, like you do his pigship, then my cunt when I say.'

Alice swallowed hard, her eyes fixed on the tight pink dimple of Yi's anus, where tiny rolls of green loo paper had caught in the star-shaped crevices leading to her hole. Already the taste of Xiu Mei's sex was thick in her mouth, but she crawled obediently forward, to press her face between Yi's bottom cheeks, poke out her tongue, and lick.

'Dirty bitch!' Xiu Mei laughed in delight as Alice began to lap at Yi's tightly puckered hole. 'Taste it, big bitch, taste her shitty arse!'

Xiu Mei finished with a peal of near hysterical laughter and reached out to slap at Alice's bottom, making the hairbrush wobble, then squeeze slowly out to drop on the bed. Immediately Xiu Mei had picked it up, wiping the handle on Alice's bottom before laying in, harder than before, a frenzied, irregular spanking. Alice fought to ignore the pain, her licking now clumsy as she struggled to get Yi's bottom hole properly clean so that she'd be made to lick pussy instead.

Yi was laughing, and craning around to watch Alice beaten, in no hurry, and quite content to have their victim's tongue at work on her bumhole. Not daring to stop, Alice licked at the fleshy little knot, which had begun to soften and spread, inviting her to probe deeper. In went her tongue, pushed up into the hot, tight hole, and Yi gave a sudden gasp of delight.

189

'Deep in, deep in, like that, big slut!' Yi demanded. 'Beat her, Xiu Mei, beat her hard!'

Alice gasped in pain as Xiu Mei laid in with the hairbrush. Every smack was sending a shock wave through her body, and for all her shame and misery she was reacting, her sex already twitching in helpless ecstasy. Yi began to wiggle her bottom, then lifted abruptly, to press her swollen sex against Alice's mouth. Alice gave in, her face smothered in meaty, female bottom, the girls' taste strong in her mouth, her own rear hot with spanking.

As Yi began to come, Alice's hand had gone back, clutching at her own sex and licking just as hard as she possible could. The pain of her beating vanished, blending to a glorious sexual heat, and she was there, gasping out her ecstasy into Yi's spread bottom and sopping cunt to the sound of peal after peal of delighted laughter from Xiu Mei.

From one window marshland stretched to the edge of the lake, from the other, a wooded hillside rose above high-gabled houses. Charlotte felt tired after the long journey, and her guilt had only grown stronger as the moment drew nearer. Now it had arrived and her need, and Horst's, were not going to be denied. As she lay back on the double bed she was telling herself that he would fuck her anyway, and all she had to do was not to fight.

They'd had a cup of coffee and she'd gone straight into the shower. Now fresh and clean, all that covered her body was a towel, and it was no defence at all. Horst was taking his turn to shower, and would soon be out, and ready. All the way from Rockbeare he'd taken every opportunity he could to tease her, kissing and nuzzling her neck, even stroking her thighs and breasts to fill her with longing and embarrassment, often applying gentle pats to her bottom, every one of which made her want to stick it out and have her pussy filled. Now it was going to happen, but she was determined to at the least make a show of resistance.

Horst emerged from the bathroom, the blond stubble of his hair still wet, his lean, muscular body stark naked, his cock already half hard, and with a large blue and white tube in one hand. He was grinning.

'What's that for?' she asked, suppressing a nervous giggle.

'So we can keep our promise to Rowena,' he answered, his voice sweet and gentle, although with the orange light striking his face from one side and his Nich-like grin he looked positively demonic.

'How?' Charlotte answered, then realised with a little shock that set her stomach tight, also her bottom cheeks.

'Pop this in your mouth and I'll show you,' Horst answered and lay down on the bed, his head propped up on the bolster, his cock held up in his free hand.

'That's not keeping my promise,' Charlotte answered weakly, but she was already wriggling around to get her head in his lap.

Horst didn't bother to answer her, but as she leant across his body he twitched her towel away, leaving her nude. His cock was right in front of her face, and she let him feed it into her mouth, the smell and taste of man mixing with a hint of soap. She closed her eyes as she began to suck, telling herself it was just her mouth, although she knew full well it would be more, far more. Her bottom was turned to him, and as his hand settled on one heavy cheek and lifted it to inspect her anus, her worst fears were realised. He was going to bugger her.

'No, Horst, please,' she managed, pulling her head up from his cock.

'Sh,' he urged. 'I promised Rowena I wouldn't fuck you, and I mean to keep my promise.'

'Yes, Horst, but what you said – what you said was that you wouldn't have sex with me, not –'

'Have sex, fuck, shag, bonk, why split hairs?'

'Yes, but it's still sex if you – you go up my bum, and besides – ow! That's cold! Ow!'

He had squeezed a blob of jelly onto his finger as they spoke, jelly which proved to be extremely cold when applied to her anus. The second complaint had come because he'd no sooner wiped one finger onto her bumhole than he'd slid another in, as deep as it would go. Her mouth came a little open as he began to ease it in and out of her ring. It hurt, a little, with an odd, hot sensation, but that had quickly faded, to be replaced by pleasure and an undeniably delicious sensation of being dirty. With a little whimper she went back to sucking his cock.

'That's my girl,' Horst chuckled, and began to make little circular motions inside her rectum with his finger, distending her ring.

Charlotte closed her eyes, telling herself that it didn't matter what she did, or said. He would bugger her anyway. She knew it was a lie, but it helped the dirty feeling overcome her shame and guilt as her anus was opened for the insertion of the big cock growing in her mouth. After a while he introduced a second finger, then a third, splaying them to hold her open behind, her tiny virgin ring now stretched taut. By then he was rock hard in her mouth. Her jaw was wide on his girth, and she was wondering if she really could take it up her bottom.

'On your knees,' he ordered suddenly. 'I want to see this.'

Her breathing already deep, Charlotte came off his cock and scrambled around on the bed, presenting him with her naked bottom, on all fours. The jelly still felt cold around her bumhole, and where some was dribbling down over her pussy lips, keeping her acutely conscious of her lewd rear view and her open, slippery anus.

'Gorgeous!' Horst mumbled, kneeling up. 'Just gorgeous!'

'Do – do I have to be buggered every time?' Charlotte asked as he got behind her.

'Only if you want to keep your promise to Rowena,' Horst answered happily, and put the head of his cock to her anus.

Charlotte gave a little whimper, genuinely resentful despite the lovely sensation of having the fat tip of his cock rubbed on her bottom hole. She could feel herself opening, her slippery ring responding to the gentle pressure, just a little, then growing wider as he pushed. Her teeth gritted as her bumhole began to open properly, for just an instant before her eyes popped and her mouth came wide in a heartfelt gasp as her ring gave way and a good three inches of cock were jammed roughly inside her rectum.

'Whoops! Sorry,' Horst laughed. 'Just relax, yeah?'

She didn't answer, her mouth agape and drooling onto the bed as he began to force the rest of his cock into her rectum, withdrawing a little to grease his shaft, pushing an inch or so up, withdrawing again, and pushing again. Long before it was all in she was clutching the bed cover and gasping, with water running from her eyes and spittle from her open mouth. Her rectum felt impossibly bloated, creating a desperate need to visit the loo despite the knowledge that she was well and truly plugged.

By the time he'd wedged the whole thick mass of his cock into her protesting gut, her entire body was prickling with sweat, her eyes unfocused and her toes wiggling in reaction. It felt awful, but it also felt glorious, as if her whole body was full of cock, right up to the top of her head. His pubic hair was tickling between her cheeks too, making them twitch, and she could feel the thick, rough skin of his ball sack against her empty sex, all of it enough to set her whimpering and shivering. Last of all, there was the knowledge of how she'd look, her meaty bottom flaring from her waist, her big, pale cheeks wide open, and his cock stuck deep in the taut, pink ring between. It was almost too much, and as he began to rock back and forth, pulling her buggered ring in and out on his cock, she was wondering whether she would faint or come first.

'Rub off,' Horst grunted, his voice thick with passion. 'Rub off while I'm up you.'

Charlotte's answer was a broken whimper, but she reached back to find her sex puffy and swollen, slippery with her juice and with the jelly he'd used to bugger her. Supported on one arm, she felt her tits swinging under her chest to the motion of his cock in her gut, her nipples rubbing on the woollen bed-spread. It was almost too much to bear, and she was sobbing out her emotions as she began to masturbate.

'Good girl,' Horst sighed as Charlotte felt her ring tighten on the intruding cock. 'That's nice, really nice.'

She shut her eyes and reached back, to touch the junction of rock-solid cock and straining bumhole, her bumhole. The feel of it brought what she was doing home harder still, kneeling naked on a bed with a man's penis up her bottom, her husband's penis. He was going to spunk in her too, a final, delicious degradation, and why not? She was his, to do with as he pleased, at least for the two weeks of their honeymoon, and if what pleased him was to bugger her nightly and spunk up her bottom, then it was only right she let him.

Horst began to move faster, pushing himself deep in up her rectum with his hands locked in the flesh of her bottom and her cheeks pulled wide to show off her penetrated bumhole. Thinking how she'd look, she began to masturbate in earnest, rubbing at her bump with her bum cheeks twitching in his grip and her holes in slow, steady contraction, both empty pussy and bloated anus.

It took just moments, her contractions growing faster and harder, her body more and more out of control, with her legs kicking on the bed, her head hung to spatter her dangling breasts with flecks of spittle, every muscle hot and tight. She collapsed as it started, her buggered anus pulsing on his cock, her teeth locked in the sodden bedcover. Her head was full of images as she came, of her bottom hole leaking jelly, of her cheeks spread with a fat cock shaft in the straining ring, of her shamefully empty pussy from below and, as he came up her bottom with a strangled grunt, of her well used anus bubbling sperm down between her sex lips and into the empty hole between.

Nine

Alice considered her options. On the whole, the best choice seemed to be to tell Ariesian the full extent of the degradations Xiu Mei and Yi had taken to inflicting on her whenever his back was turned. True, both girls were quite happy to pinch or slap her bottom when he was around, also to make her perform the dirtier or more demeaning household tasks, but they were clearly scared of him, and reserved the worst of their excesses for his absence. With the big Samhain festival at Cape Cornwall coming up, his absences had been becoming more frequent, and despite her obedience she knew it was only a matter of time before they chose to flush her head in the lavatory through simple spite.

Just possibly, if she told, he would decide that he preferred her to remain under his control and so take both sisters with him when he went out. More likely he'd simply laugh at her, while it seemed hard to believe that he hadn't noticed the bruises they'd not infrequently inflicted on her bottom. Nevertheless, if she told him, there was a chance of escape, perhaps even a chance that he would punish them in turn, while to say nothing could only result in the slow escalation of her punishments, continuing until they decided to flush her head, or worse.

She was on her knees in the big waterbed, sucking his cock, which had become a normal part of her morning routine, her sole item of clothing the upper part of a see-through pink baby-doll with a fur-trimmed edge. It came with matching knickers, but they'd been removed the night before so that she could be buggered more conveniently, and still lay on the floor by the bed, leaving her with her bare bottom stuck in the air as she sucked. The base of her large butt plug protruded from her anus, a larger size than before, so that her rectum constantly felt heavy and swollen, and something she was now obliged to wear as she slept.

Not infrequently one of the Chinese girls would bring in his morning coffee while Alice was still giving her blowjob, and so she was doing her best to make him come quickly, working hard on his cock and occasionally dipping down to lick at his balls and anus. They knew she sucked him off on most mornings, they knew she wore a butt plug, but that didn't make the humiliation any less intense when they came in.

Ariesian came, snatching his cock just as she took his balls in her mouth, to jerk himself rapidly off into her hair and across her face. Alice merely closed her eyes, still rolling his balls over her tongue as he shook in ecstasy and the spunk pattered down on her head. Only when he'd definitely finished did she sit back, watching him with one eye because the other was closed with a heavy blob of come. He gave a contented sigh, then a chuckle.

'Eat it up, it's good for you,' he stated.

Alice obeyed, using a finger so scrape the thick clots of spunk from her face and popping it into her mouth for cleaning. He watched, his face set in a faintly amused smile, occasionally pointing out stray blobs in her hair until she'd reduced the mess he'd made to a few dirty smears.

'May I shower, please, my Lord?' she asked.

He was about to answer when a tap sounded at the door. Xiu Mei appeared in response to his call, carrying a tray with coffee, hot buttered toast and the morning paper. She gave a polite bow to Ariesian, a sneer to Alice, and left. Alice stayed as she was, not wanting to risk punishment by repeating her request. Ariesian ignored her, his cock still slowly deflating against his leg as he ate. Only when he put the paper down did she venture to speak.

'There is a matter, my Lord, which I would like to discuss.'

He answered casually, around a mouthful of toast. 'Yes?'

'The girls, my Lord,' Alice went on, determined and trying not to pout too much. 'Xiu Mei and Yi, they – they beat me, on my bottom, and – and make me lick them.'

'I know,' Ariesian answered. 'So?'

'I – I just thought ...' Alice began to stammer as her hopes faded. 'I thought, you – you might wish them to – to, perhaps, show me a little respect?'

'Why?'

'Because – because I am your willing slave, my Lord, but – but they're only servants. Is it right that they should punish me?'

Ariesian shrugged.

'You're just a slut, Alice, why shouldn't they have their fun with you too?'

'I – I don't know. Because I'm yours?'

'Mine to have, Alice, and mine to give away, to Charles, or whoever I wish. I'm sure a good beating now and then does you good, and besides, it keeps them happy. Still, I suppose I had better make things clear.'

With a faintly exasperated sigh he reached out to press a tiny button on one bedpost. Just moments later both Yi and Xiu Mei appeared, bowing politely to him and ignoring Alice.

'Alice here tells me you've been beating her,' he stated.

Both girls bowed their heads a second time, a little lower. Xiu Mei then cast Alice a single, poisonous look from the corner of her eye. Ariesian went on.

'It's not a problem, so long as it doesn't inconvenience me. I don't like her bottom too badly bruised, it's not pretty, and I like her cunt and anus in good working condition. Otherwise, you can do as you like with her. Got that?'

'Yes, my Lord,' both girls answered in unison and bowed once more before retreating out of the door.

Alice bit her lip and looked up as he took another piece of toast.

'But, my Lord –'

'Shut up.'

Alice hung her head in defeat, trying not to imagine how it would feel to have her head pushed into a well used lavatory and flushed.

Charlotte's smile was only slightly nervous and slightly guilty as she saw Rowena standing near the baggage collection belt. Poppy was there too, and both smiled and waved as they saw her. Nobody else she knew was about, and she went straight to Rowena's arms, even risking a brief touch of their tongues as they kissed. Horst had gone to Poppy, greeting her with no less enthusiasm, and lifting her in his arms with their mouths open together.

Having collected their bags, they piled everything onto a trolley and left the terminal. Arm in arm with Rowena, Charlotte felt far better about the situation than she had expected to. Most importantly, she could honestly say she had not allowed Horst to fuck her. Not that she was entirely happy, because she was waddling slightly, her bottom hole sore and bruised from repeated use, but when the inevitable question came, she'd be able to answer with at least some truthfulness. It was Poppy who broached the subject, as they were still walking towards the car park, where her red 4 × 4 was clearly visible.

'So, did you?'

'No,' Horst answered immediately, his voice firm and level. 'I gave my word, and I kept it.'

'Seriously?' Rowena queried. 'Not once?'

'I can honestly swear,' Horst went on, 'that my penis has not entered Charlotte Sachs' vagina once, not since Beltane.'

Charlotte found herself blushing, but also nodding vigorous agreement.

'You've done better than us then,' Poppy laughed. 'We've been at it like rabbits since the day of your wedding.'

'Poppy!' Rowena protested.

'Ro!' Charlotte exclaimed.

Horst laughed.

'I might have known it! Anyway, do you get lesbian rabbits?'

'How are the Samhain preparations going?' Charlotte put in quickly.

'Really well,' Rowena answered. 'All the arrangements have been sorted out. It's technically illegal, but there's nothing to stop people going there, so as long as the Devon and Cornwall police don't get really bolshie about it we should be fine. I don't think they will, because even if they have found out about it there's no reason they should think it's anything more than an outsize barbecue.'

'How many people are we expecting?'

'I don't know. Hundreds, maybe over a thousand. Nich managed to get hold of Ariesian's mailing lists, snail mail and email, and that's nearly ten thousand names alone. He's done a flyer too, under our names, of course, both electronic and printed. They don't say too much, just what's needed to get there, but everyone who's handing them out has been spreading the rumour that there'll be a sacrifice, and that any man who partakes will be eligible to prove himself the most virile –'

'– and fuck Juliana's little sister,' Poppy finished with a trace of awe. 'That's Thomazina. She's cute.'

Charlotte bit her lip, thinking of how many times she'd fantasised about being in Thomazina's place, with dozens, even hundreds of virile young men all chasing her, and every one intent on the prize of her virginity.

'You've met her?' Horst asked.

'She's lovely,' Rowena began, 'beautiful, very easy-going and –'

'Don't even think about it,' Poppy answered Horst. 'You've had Lottie, and me, so don't be a greedy bastard!'

'I think I ought to run,' Horst protested, 'after all, technically, shouldn't I be the one to impregnate –'

'I'll do you a deal,' Poppy cut in. 'You can run, but if you succeed, Ro gets to sacrifice you.'

'Very funny. Seriously though –'

'Seriously,' Rowena interrupted, 'as Nich and Juliana and Alice have pointed out, there were dozens of different rituals across the years, both Celtic and pre-Celtic, so there's no such thing as an orthodox version. Anyway, Nich wants you and I to officiate, Horst.'

'Fair enough,' Horst sighed, 'but it would have been nice to go for a hat-trick.'

They'd reached the car, and Poppy gave him a friendly kick as she unlocked the door, dodging the hand aimed at her bottom in retaliation and climbing in. The others followed, Rowena getting into the front.

'If you've sent flyers to Ariesian's list, surely he's bound to find out?' Horst queried.

'I think he's supposed to,' Poppy answered. 'So seriously, you two spent a fortnight alone in a cottage and didn't even shag once? What did you do, jigsaws?'

'No, no . . .'

He broke off as Rowena gave him a sharp look. For a moment his face held a look of plainly artificial innocence, before he shrugged and spoke again.

'Okay, okay, so we weren't completely innocent.'

'But we didn't actually have sex, not sex sex!' Charlotte said hurriedly as Rowena's stinging glance moved to her.

'Sex sex? What's sex sex, Lottie?'

Charlotte turned her face to the window, blushing hot, her guilt welling up stronger than before. Horst carried on, his voice defensive as Poppy steered the car towards the exit.

'What do you expect, Rowena? I promised we wouldn't fuck, and I stuck to that, but we were on our honeymoon, for fuck's sake! Anyway, by the sound of things you and Poppy . . .'

He trailed off as Rowena made to speak, but she thought better of it. They'd reached the gate, and the silence held as Poppy sorted herself out with the attendant, speaking rapidly as she drove on.

'Can we call it quits, please? So Lottie's been taking it up the bum, or whatever.'

Poppy was obviously just being crude, but that didn't stop Charlotte's cheeks from flaring from rose pink to blazing scarlet. Rowena's mouth came open in shock, her head twisting back to stare accusingly at Charlotte, who hung her head, unable to speak, her well buggered ring twitching in her knickers. It was Poppy who spoke again, correctly interpreting the silence.

'You didn't!? Up your bumhole!? You dirty bitch! And as for you, Horst Sachs . . .'

Poppy was forced to pause as she pulled out onto the main road. Horst folded his arms.

'Pussy licker.'

'You bastard!'

'Pussy licker.'

'Sodomite!'

'Maybe I ought to spank you, like Ro does to Lottie?'

'You can just try it, Mr Sachs! See what you get in return.'

'Maybe I will.'

'She's not the one who deserves to be punished!' Rowena cut in.

'Why me, again!?' Charlotte protested automatically, but at the same time as Horst, with Poppy and Rowena also trying to speak, and as they gathered speed on the A303 towards Rockbeare the conversation had dissolved into a babble of voices.

Mr Pedlow looked back from the peak of Cape Cornwall with both irritation and perplexity. There were several ruined buildings visible, and it wasn't at all obvious which Nich Mordaunt might have meant. The nearest, on the col of land that joined the bulk of the Cape to the mainland, was clearly a chapel, with a stone cross still standing above one gable. That presumably made it a sacred site, but not a pagan one, unless of course the chapel had been built on an old pagan site. Further away, not really on the Cape at all but in one of the steep valleys leading down to either side, was a whole cluster of buildings. A half-collapsed chimney suggested an old mine, yet it was perfectly possible that the mine was on an ancient site.

The mine buildings were at least remote, well hidden from view and apparently not at all easy to get to. By contrast the chapel was beside a major path to the Cape and in full view of the car park and quite a few buildings. He nodded to himself, sure that nobody, let alone Rowena, would risk doing anything rude somewhere so public. It had to be the mine buildings, but which one?

Puffing somewhat, and grumbling under his breath, he set off back down the narrow spine of the Cape, presently reaching the old mine. It had been hard going, along tracks half overgrown with bracken and cut into the side of dizzyingly steep slopes running just yards above a hundred foot cliff. He felt hot and sweaty, making even the rocky, wave-torn cove below him seem inviting.

He wasn't the only one, and his gristly little mouth curved up into a smile as he realised the petite woman pulling herself onto the rocks below was not merely topless, but nude. Ducking quickly down among the bracken he fumbled for his binoculars, bringing her into focus.

A stab of shame and self-condemnation struck him as he realised how small she was, then fear at the prospect of her parents being nearby, only for both emotions to fade as she turned, revealing a richly grown bush of jet black pubic hair. There was nothing of the child in her face either, for all her petite figure. As she turned again he was presented with a tiny but well rounded bottom. She stretched in the warm sunlight, apparently as oblivious to her nudity as she was to the Atlantic breakers crashing among the rocks just feet away from her, and from which she'd emerged with no more concern than had the sea been a swimming pool.

She didn't seem to be in any hurry either, standing to let her body dry in the sun and running her fingers through wet black hair that fell to the small of her back. He was wishing she'd been a little more voluptuous, or at least had a decent pair of tits, but it was still arousing to watch her. When she bent to pick a piece of seaweed from between her toes he was briefly rewarded with a flash of cunt, neatly pursed between slim thighs. Wondering if he dared risk a quick toss, he glanced around him. A group of hikers was visible, a long way off, but coming towards him. He cursed softly and swung his binoculars back towards the cove, but the girl was no longer in view.

After a moment of puzzlement he continued on his way, happy that he had at least enjoyed one voyeuristic thrill to make his trip worthwhile. Five minutes later he had reached the first of the old mine buildings, a squat structure with no roof, but otherwise showing little damage. A high, square door led inside, to an open chamber with no obvious function. He nodded thoughtfully, thinking of what an excellent place it would be for the sort of dirty rituals the girls got up to. It was also an excellent place in which to conceal his cameras, with plenty of nooks and crannies among the stones and along the ragged tops of the walls.

Wishing he was younger and fitter, he considered the task, only to pause, realising that he ought to investigate the other buildings as well. There were two that seemed worthwhile. A little way up the slope a pair of crumbling walls bordered a flat space, which had to be another possibility, while higher still was the engine house itself, with the half-collapsed chimney, which seemed less likely. He started up the steep incline, puffing and wheezing as he reached the first building, only to stop in a fluster of embarrassment.

The girl he had seen by the sea was there, and a companion. She was no longer naked, slightly to his relief, but had pulled on a red jumper, so big she'd had to roll the arms up, while it came down to her knees. Her companion was altogether different, her curves so magnificently luscious she made Charlotte look positively sparse. A tight top held in breasts like footballs, and they were clearly unfettered, with her nipples showing through the thin yellow cotton. Blue jeans struggled to contain a true peach of a bottom, fat – there was no other word for it – but perfectly formed and wonderfully firm. Between, her hourglass waist and teasingly chubby tummy were bare. The girls stood to either side of an iron hatch set in concrete. Both had the same long black hair, and as they turned to him he realised both had the same brilliant green eyes.

Mr Pedlow began to mumble apologies, smiling and backing away. There was something horribly unnerving about their gaze, particularly the smaller of the two. Up close, her face had an odd look, rather like the impish caste that put him off Poppy Melcombe, but stronger by far. The other girl was pure West Country, save for her green eyes. Juliana and the girl Alice both had the same green eyes and the same black hair.

Stepping quickly away from the building, Mr Pedlow was feeling more than a little frightened, despite telling himself that it was either coincidence, or all four girls were sisters, despite their physical differences. It made sense though, especially if the two he'd just met lived in Cornwall and had been asked to check over the site by Juliana. Yes, that would be it, plain and simple.

Now feeling rather foolish for his reaction, he continued up the hill. They'd seen him, which was a nuisance, but no more. Dressed as he was, and with his binoculars and rucksack, they would simply put him down as a birdwatcher. Nevertheless, with them around it would be impossible to install his apparatus, so he would have to wait until the coast was clear.

He'd soon reached the old engine house, and after a quick glance inside had dismissed it. Rubble from the ruined chimney choked one end, while the pit itself was a serious hazard. That left the other two buildings, and there seemed to be every chance that by careful observation of the two girls he could work out which one it would be. Choosing a section of low wall, he sat down, removed his rucksack from his back and extracted his lunch.

Nich extended his tongue, to lap gently at the softly swollen lips of Juliana's sex. She was on top of him, her neat, muscular bottom more or less in his face, so that as he licked her his view was of her moist, open sex, the tight dimple of her anus and the smooth curves of her bottom and thighs. His cock was in her mouth, as each treated the other to leisurely oral sex.

Outside the hotel window, a wide, cloudless sky extended out above green fields, grey stone, and the ruffled slate blue of the Atlantic. It was already early afternoon, but neither had bothered to dress, preferring the unhurried enjoyment of each other's bodies and, as Nich applied his tongue a little more firmly to Juliana's clitoris, he was only just beginning to be concerned about the time.

In response to his pressure she gave her bottom a delicate wiggle, signalling that she wanted more attention. Nich broke off, to adjust the pillow behind his head to make himself comfortable while keeping his mouth pressed firmly to her sex. She also moved, cocking her legs wide to spread herself fully to his caresses. Nich took hold of her bottom, using one long, black-painted fingernail to tickle her anus as he began to lick firmly between her pussy lips.

Juliana sighed, and took hold of his cock, the head still in her mouth, licking and sucking as she masturbated him, more for the enjoyment of his cock than his pleasure. As one sharp-talonned hand took a firm but gentle grip on his balls, Nich licked harder still. The muscles of Juliana's pussy began to twitch, her bottom cheeks squeezing together, her anus pulsing, and she was there, sucking firmly on his cock as her orgasm swept through her, with Nich concentrating everything on her pleasure.

Even when she'd finished he continued to lick, enjoying her pussy and bottom as she quickly turned her attention to his pleasure. Her sucking grew firmer, her lips began to work on the ultrasensitive flesh of his peeled-back foreskin, her grip on his balls tightened and her tugging became more purposeful. As his orgasm began to rise up in his head Nich buried his face in the warm wetness of her sex and eased a finger into the tight, slippery ring of her anus.

As he started to come he was acutely aware of her whole body, the exquisite feel of her mouth and hands on his cock and balls, the round bulges of her big breasts where they pressed to his flesh, the elegant, muscular yet utterly feminine lines of her legs and bottom, and most of all the scent and taste and feel of her pussy. Holding it all in his head, he came, Juliana milking his cock down her throat, to swallow every drop, and at last pull back with a quiet, satisfied purr.

'Delicious, thank you,' Nich sighed, lying back.

Juliana climbed off, smiling as she stretched languorously in the pale Cornish sunlight coming in through the window. Padding across to it, she pulled down the upper part and took a deep draught of sea air, indifferent to her nudity and the prime view of meaty breasts squashed against glass that anybody who happened to be in the hotel garden would get.

'Shall we get dressed and go down?' Nich asked after a moment.

'Presently,' she answered. 'Elune and Thomazina can cope.'

'And Thomazina's virgin?'

'So she says.'

'Good, and she does look the part, but don't you think she's likely to get caught rather quickly? Is she the right choice?'

'Yes,' Juliana answered emphatically. 'It's in her nature to want to be caught, and it ought to happen before the sun is fully set, so everyone can see. Besides, there are too many people who know Alice and I aren't virgin, Elune would just lead them on a while goose chase, and Lily's not really ready. Besides, you may find Thomazina can run faster than you think. Unless you had a genuine virgin in mind?'

'There is one,' Nich replied. 'Rowena.'

Juliana merely gave a deprecating shake of her head. Nich grinned, turning his head a little to admire the perfect roundness of Juliana's bottom, the tuck of her still-moist cheeks, her arms folded under her chin, an unselfconscious, careless display of sexuality which accorded perfectly with his desires. Grinning to himself at the thought of the day, and night, to come, he threw his legs off the bed and walked into the bathroom.

Mr Pedlow chuckled in satisfaction. It was perfect, the little nook in among the rocks providing shelter both from the weather and from prying eyes. As long as he got there well before dark there would be no danger, but once the sun had set there was no chance whatsoever of anyone attempting to negotiate the rocky path that led to his hideaway. A folding chair provided comfort, a sleeping bag somewhere to take his well earned rest once the festival was over, while thanks to an ingenious body harness contrived from several leather belts, he would be able to monitor the show on his laptop while keeping both his hands free, to make adjustments, and to masturbate. It was an achievement to be proud of.

So was the actual setup. Four cameras covered the building, set among the crevices of the walls at a fraction below average cunt height. Between them they were sure to provide a juicy view, while the dense bracken and thick, coarse grass on the slope between the building and his hidey-hole provided perfect concealment for the wires. Even the possibility of a sound or lighting rigger discovering his wires had been taken care of, with a single strand leaving the building below a stack of rubble. It simply could not fail.

A further four cameras were concealed among the bracken, where grassy patches provided good positions for intimate moments, either sexual or lavatorial. It was something of a risk, as he had no way of knowing how much lighting there would be, nor how it would be arranged. Yet there had to be some, or the steep hillside became a potential deathtrap.

He sat down, intent on making a final test before retiring to his boarding house in St Just. Flicking on the switch of his battery pack, he opened his laptop and powered it up. A few adjustments and he had all eight windows displayed on his screen, four showing rather aimless views of grass, bracken, rocks and sky, four showing the interior of the mine building. Each was clear, with no more than the occasional fuzzy edge where a stone or a blade of grass obstructed the side of a lens.

Chuckling to himself in mischievous delight, he activated the sound, flicking from one pick-up to another, to catch the same seagull cries and gentle smack and hiss of waves he could hear from his vantage point, both faint, then, loud and clear, voices, girlish voices.

'... do you think people will be able to see properly?'

'Juliana says there'll be a big screen above our heads.'

'Yes? Amazing what they can do.'

'I know. We always had that problem. Once there're more than a hundred or so people, half of them don't really get to see what's going on. That was the good thing about this valley, because the circle was at the bottom and everyone could see down into it.'

One of the speakers came into Mr Pedlow's view, then the other. It was the same two he had seen before, the tiny, impish girl and her gloriously voluptuous sister. The little one remained standing, but the bigger sat down on a great square rock, her wonderfully rounded, gloriously resilient bottom spreading only slightly in the taut seat of her blue jeans. Mr Pedlow blew out his breath at the sight as the two of them continued to talk.

'So all the stones are gone now?' the big girl asked.

'Yes and no. The miners used them. In fact, I suspect you're sitting on a piece of the original altar.'

'Oh. Should I bend over it to be taken, do you think?'

'They're supposed to catch you, silly. At least try and run and, if you want it from behind, pretend to trip and go down on your knees. I'm sure the God would be quite happy with your bum.'

'Probably. After all, deer do it like that, and sheep.'

'Most animals, really, except fish. And octopus of course, and snails.'

'We're having roast mutton, aren't we?'

'Yes, but Nich's promised to bring some ice cream, and fish and chips.'

'Mussels?'

'If you want mussels, just go down to the shore. There're limpets too, really big ones.'

The small woman was also in blue jeans, and extraordinarily restless, pacing to and fro and jumping on and off rocks with all the unselfconscious pleasure of a small child. Several times she presented him with fine views of her tiny but well tucked bottom, which was enjoyable, although he'd have far preferred the same performance from her more amply endowed sister. It was still worth watching, and he'd switched off from their rather bizarre conversation about seafood when the little one abruptly changed the subject.

'How's your hymen?'

It was the strangest of questions, but one that instantly had Mr Pedlow's fat pink tongue flicking out to moisten gristly lips.

'Good,' the big girl answered, and to Mr Pedlow's inexpressible joy she stood up and began to unfasten her jeans.

He watched wide-eyed as he tore at his fly and she, very casually, as if it were the most normal thing in the world, pushed down her trousers and panties as one, exposing quite simply the most glorious bottom he had ever seen; meaty, plump, yet perfectly firm, as pale and smooth as cream, deeply cleft to conceal the yet ruder secrets between the cheeks.

'What do you think?' she addressed her sister, pushing her belly out and spreading the lips of her sex to show what was quite obviously a virgin cunt hole.

Wanking frantically at his cock, Mr Pedlow struggled to get the right window open on his screen. It came, revealing another view of the girls, now with the small one squatting down to peer at her own sister's naked sex, held spread for inspection, the plump lips wide to show off the moist centre and the glistening, pinky-red bulge of flesh that blocked the hole.

'Neat,' the small woman commented approvingly. 'The boys'll love it.'

The bigger girl giggled. Mr Pedlow, now tugging furiously at a slightly moist erection, was praying she'd leave her trousers down long enough to let him come over the sight of her divine bottom. The smaller girl stepped away, to spring backwards in a sudden cartwheel. Her sister bent, to take hold of her panties, which had fallen right down, and for one perfect moment Mr Pedlow was presented with the full, naked moon of her bottom, the perfect cheeks spread to show a tightly puckered anal mouth, and the chubby lips of her virgin cunt peeping out from between fleshy thighs.

A fountain of spunk erupted from his cock, only missing the keyboard of his laptop because of a desperate last-second change of angle, and covering the front of his jumper instead. He gave a soft curse, but he was smiling as he came down from his orgasm with the girl still in the act of wriggling her now panty-clad bottom into the seat of her jeans.

The system worked perfectly, his harness worked perfectly, although he clearly needed to find some way to make the actual climax a little less messy. He had also been provided with a voyeuristic delight he would never forget, and which was likely to get better still. Beyond doubt, and even though it seemed extraordinary that a girl at once so abundantly sexual and so uninhibited remained a virgin, there was no doubt either that she was, or that she was the one who was going to be ritually deflowered the following night.

Wringing his hands in sheer glee, Mr Pedlow closed down his apparatus.

Alice watched Ariesian's sleek black Mercedes move off down the driveway with some trepidation. Her task was to follow in the lorry that held most of the equipment, to make sure it arrived at Cape Cornwall without mishap. The driver, a huge black man known only as Mac, had already been told he could make use of her mouth if he felt so inclined. Judging by the big, ugly grin with which he'd received the news, it seemed likely that he'd take full advantage of the offer. The lorry was now parked in a lay-by out on the main road, waiting for her after she had dealt with any late phone calls. She wore only the briefest of bikinis, in which she was supposed to travel, bringing only her abbreviated Samhain robe of dark blue cotton and a pair of black high heels Ariesian had chosen himself.

There was another reason she had been left to follow on. Walking back towards the house, she found just what she had been expecting: the two Chinese girls, leaning indolently against the sides of the door. Yi carried a painfully familiar hairbrush, Xiu Mei a detergent bottle. Reporting them for abusing her had been a calculated risk, but it had paid off. She faltered as she approached the door.

'Get in here,' Xiu Mei ordered, jerking her thumb towards the interior of the house.

Alice hesitated, glancing towards the garden. Yi laughed.

'You run,' Xiu Mei warned, 'we make it twice as bad for you when you are caught. Get in, bitch girl!'

Her head hung low, Alice obeyed. Both girls were giggling with glee as they took hold of her arms. She was frog-marched indoors and around the swimming pool, Yi urging her on with hard smacks of the hairbrush to her bottom and both talking in high-pitched excitement.

'We told you not to tell! Didn't we tell you?'

'Yes, we told you. So now you get it. Now your head goes down the lavatory.'

'Yes, down the lavatory, where it belongs.'

'Yes, right down, but not until we have used the lavatory.'

'Yes, big, stupid slut, used it well, piss and shit too, plenty, from both of us. We saved up for you. You like that, yes, with your head well in? I bet you will frig your dirty cunt.'

Xiu Mei finished with a laugh of gleeful anticipation at the thought. They'd reached the bathroom, and quickly pushed her inside, the Chinese girls twittering in delight at the prospect of flushing Alice's head. Both her arms were twisted behind her back, the girls holding her securely, until Yi let go, to scamper over to the lavatory and lift the seat, revealing the deep bowl and the pool of water at the bottom, currently crystal clear.

'On your knees, big, ugly slut!' Xiu Mei ordered in rising excitement as her sister sat down.

Alice began to squirm, and Xiu Mei's tone was growing manic as she snapped out her orders.

'Hold still, or good whipping! Good whipping and head in lavatory hole anyway! Head in lavatory hole, anyway, whatever, big, stupid slut!'

Alice was dragged forward and forced down, into position for flushing. Yi's thighs were open, and Alice watched as the golden stream of the Chinese girl's pee erupted with a hiss and a gurgle, quickly followed by a heavy plop. She relaxed, twisted hard, and threw herself to one side even as her fist locked in Xiu Mei's long dark hair. Xiu Mei screamed in shock and surprise, but her balance was gone and she tumbled forward and out of the door. Yi was shrieking orders and threats, which Alice ignored, following Xiu Mei, kicking the door shut behind her, and twisting the key in the lock. Xiu Mei rose, spitting curses in Chinese, her face red with anger, and threw herself at Alice.

Alice caught Xiu Mei's charge, ignoring the raking nails and kicking feet as she lifted the Chinese girl off the ground and hurled her away, into the swimming pool. Xiu Mei gave a final shriek of fury before her body disappeared under the water with an impressive splash. Behind, Yi had begun to pound on the locked door, but still Alice ignored her, bracing her legs wide and sticking her bottom out to ease the heavy butt plug from her anus. She blew her breath out as it came, her eyes watering slightly as she closed her well stretched hole to more reasonable proportions.

Tossing the butt plug into the pool, Alice watched as Xiu Mei hauled herself dripping from the water. Again the Chinese girl came at Alice, and again was simply hauled off her feet, this time to be tucked up under one arm and carried to the lounger.

'A little lesson for you, I think,' Alice hissed, and forced Xiu Mei down over her lap, twisting one arm hard up to keep her victim helpless in spanking position.

As she realised what was going to happen to her, Xiu Mei went wild, screaming abuse at the top of her voice, kicking and thrashing, raking Alice's legs with her free hand. It made no difference whatsoever, any more than Yi's threats of increasingly revolting vengeance from beyond the bathroom door. Alice maintained a small, cool smile as she tugged up the furious girl's sodden dress and took down the equally sodden white panties beneath.

With her wet pink bottom bare, Xiu Mei's struggles grew more furious still, but Alice held on tight and with firm deliberation began to spank. As the first impact sent a ripple through the fleshy little cheeks and spattered Alice's midriff with water, Xiu Mei let out an animal howl of raw fury and dug her nails in with all her strength. Alice merely laughed and carried on spanking, watching in amusement as the Chinese girl's buttocks bounced and quivered, showing off the neat pink anal star between and the split fig of cunt flesh below.

Still Xiu Mei writhed, screaming and cursing and scratching as her bottom began to take on a rich pink flush. Alice merely spanked harder, until the smacks of palm on beaten girl flesh had begun to ring out around the courtyard, and finally Xiu Mei broke, her howls of rage turning to distress and her curses to pleas. Alice took no notice, spanking merrily away at Xiu Mei's now red bottom.

Alice began to hum to herself, still spanking, as slowly but surely the cruel, haughty Xiu Mei was reduced to a squalling, spanked brat, her legs kicking pathetically in her lowered panties, her face set in misery and pain, the tears streaming down her cheeks. Only when she was quite satisfied did Alice stop, but rather than let the now snivelling Xiu Mei up, she maintained a firm hold on one twisted arm.

Xiu Mei was quickly frog-marched into the kitchen, where Alice found the ball of string used to tie the joints of stuffed belly pork of which Ariesian was particularly fond. When she saw what was to happen, Xiu Mei began to fight again, briefly, but Alice quickly had her pinned, applying a painful double armlock before lashing her victim's wrists together. Before Xiu Mei was secure she had begun to make threats again, so as soon as she'd tied off the string Alice took a medium-sized apple, forced it into the Chinese girl's mouth and knotted it in place. Still kicking, Xiu Mei's ankles were lashed securely together and fastened up to the bonds around her wrists, leaving her securely hogtied.

Alice paused briefly to inspect her scratched legs, clicking her tongue in irritation at the sight of her torn skin and the slowly welling blood where Xiu Mei's nails had dug in. Lifting her leg onto a kitchen chair, she quickly stroked each cut closed, and went to deal with Yi, who was still hammering on the bathroom door and screaming threats which were if anything filthier than before.

Using the string, the kitchen scissors and another apple, Alice made short work of Yi. A brief struggle and the Chinese girl was pinned down on the bathroom floor. Five minutes more, and she was as helpless as her sister, and also had her dress up and her panties pulled down for good measure. After applying three dozen firm swats with the hairbrush that had been intended for her own bottom, Alice left Yi red-bottomed and quivering.

A glance at the clock in Ariesian's bedroom showed that she still had the best part of an hour. Walking to the kitchen, she raided the fridge, creating for herself a magnificent sundae with Ariesian's best ice cream and an assortment of toppings. She ate it with her feet up on the table where the bound and gagged Xiu Mei lay wriggling and pleading with her eyes, evidently in desperate need of the toilet.

Alice took no notice, finishing her sundae and a couple of nectarines before going to her dressing room for her robe and a few other essentials; chocolate, Ariesian's collection of sovereigns and a few objects of genuinely sacred significance. When she finally returned to the kitchen she was just in time to watch Xiu Mei wet herself, pee first dribbling out from between tightly clenched thighs and then erupting in a gush, across the table and into the already sodden white panties.

Shaking her head, Alice watched until the girl had thoroughly wet herself, then filled a large jug with water and emptied it over Xiu Mei's bottom. Hefting the helpless girl onto her shoulder, she left the house. Yi came next, both girls carried down the drive and dumped in the bushes just out of sight of the gate. Briefly Alice returned indoors, to collect her bag and make a final check of the house.

By the time she returned a white van stood outside the gate, the side bearing a large and abstract picture of a smiling fish, in sea green, with the words TREMAYNE BROS – FISHMONGERS, ST JUST, CORNWALL beneath. A woman's head was visible, stuck out from the driver's window, her brilliant green eyes shining with a viscious amusement, her sharp, pixie face set in a toothy smile. Alice gave a friendly wave and activated the gate, watching as the van entered. The small woman climbed out of the cab and Alice stepped forward, greeting her with a hug and a long, open-mouthed kiss before speaking.

'Thank you, Elune, that was welcome.'

'Always my pleasure, Aileve. Who're they?'

'His handmaidens,' Alice replied. 'Could you take them?'

'My pleasure again,' Elune answered, eyeing Xiu Mei's wet pink bottom cheeks with open amusement.

'Let's get them in the van then,' Alice instructed. 'There's a lorry waiting for me.'

'I saw. Big, hairy driver, very dark,' Elune answered, pushing her key into the van's rear door lock.

Alice bent down to lift the still squirming Yi in her arms as the doors came open and a rich waft of fish swept over her. Disgust was added to the fear and anger of Yi's expression and her squirming became violent, so that Alice was forced to more or less hurl her into the interior of the van. Seeing what had happened to her sister, Xiu Mei put up even more of a fight, thrashing her body and kicking her bound legs, until in the end Elune had to help Alice. With both the Chinese girls safely locked in the van, Alice and Elune started back down the driveway.

'Spirited,' Elune remarked.

'Very,' Alice admitted, making a sour face.

The house seemed strangely quiet as they stepped in at the front door. Elune immediately made a symbol across her chest. Alice led the way around the swimming pool, glancing only briefly at the sun lounger on or beside which she had suffered so many degradations. She allowed herself a brief chuckle as they entered the kitchen.

'What was he like, for sex?' Elune asked.

'Fair,' Alice replied after a moment's consideration. 'He has a cruel streak, but lacks the courage of his convictions. In fact, he's a coward at heart, and it took him a while to work himself up. It was ages before he even buggered me, but yes, towards the end he was getting fairly depraved. The Chinese brats were fun too, but I couldn't resist my revenge.'

Elune responded with an understanding nod. Walking across to where a door opened onto the service yard, they began to carry in the brightly coloured gas cylinders, distributing them around the house, with two on Ariesian's dining room table. Alice then collected as many newspapers as she could find, and make a neat stack between the two cylinders. Elune produced a thick altar candle of dull yellow wax, which she placed carefully on the newspapers. After making a brief invocation, she lit it.

Ten

'Time for tea, love.'

Alice came awake with a shiver. It was warm in the lorry cab, but she felt oddly cold, while her cheek had somehow become glued to the plastic of the seat as she slept. Shaking herself and rubbing her eyes, she spent a moment staring out at the strip of grey-black tarmac that seemed to be being sucked in under the lorry as they moved.

'Tea? Please, yes, that would be lovely,' she answered, glancing at the dashboard clock. 'It's only two o'clock, but so what?'

'Not that sort of tea, love,' he answered, finishing with a dirty chuckle as he slowed the big lorry. 'This sort, you're the only one who gets a mouthful.'

Alice groaned as she realised what he meant. Outside her window, a bleak slope of rough grass and bracken led up to a jumble of grey rocks, too high to be anywhere beyond Bodmin Moor. Already he was pulling off the road, and she closed her eyes, considering the options of sucking Mac's cock or attempting to hitch the rest of the way to Cape Cornwall. It was a close thing, but Ariesian would be expecting her to arrive with the lorry.

'Okay,' she sighed, 'if I have to.'

'Oh, you do,' he drawled. 'That's what the man said, isn't it? I want it, you got to give it.'

Even as he spoke he had pushed his body back against his seat, to lift his hips for better access to his fly. Alice watched as he peeled it down, to flop out a thick, very dark cock, the little hole where his foreskin ended suspiciously moist. He turned, grinning.

'Tits out then, love. I like it tits out, me, and you've got a great pair!'

Again Alice sighed, but took hold of her bikini top, hauling it up to spill out her breasts, fat and round in the warm light of the cab, heavy in her hands as she lifted them for his inspection.

'Satisfied?'

'Fucking gorgeous!'

The sarcasm she'd injected into her voice was evidently lost on him, and she shook her head sadly before leaning her body into his lap, face to cock. He smelt of unwashed man and diesel, but she took hold anyway, closing her eyes as she popped him into her mouth. He gave a contented grunt, and one rough hand settled onto her left breast. She let him grope, sure he'd come sooner if he was allowed a good feel while she sucked him.

Sure enough, he was soon stiffening in her mouth, the thick taste growing stronger as his foreskin began to roll back, until she was struggling not to gag. Oblivious, he groped happily at her breasts, all the while complimenting her on how big and firm they were. He'd got her nipples erect before he'd come to full erection, and despite herself she was growing warm between her thighs.

Doing her best to ignore her own, involuntary, reactions, she continued to suck, taking the base of his cock in her hand as soon as he was hard enough to masturbate into her mouth. He called her a 'fancy little tart', in a tone which suggested it was meant to be a compliment, and began to jiggle her breasts and push his cock up and down. Alice held herself in place, still, making a slide of her lips as he began to fuck her mouth.

He grunted, his fingers dug into the soft flesh of one breast, and abruptly her mouth was full of slimy, salty come, making her eyes pop and her cheeks bulge. She fought to swallow, her stomach lurching in protest, and he'd taken a firm grip in her hair, forcing her to stay in place as he emptied the full contents of his balls down her reluctant throat.

When he finally let go, she came up coughing, with strands of sperm and mucus hanging from her nose and lower lip. Even as she sat up she realised that she couldn't hold it. A moment later her stomach gave another lurch and sick filled her throat. Clapping her hand to her mouth as her cheeks bulged with lumpy, foul-tasting fluid, she struggled to get the window down, only just succeeding in time to spew the contents of her stomach onto the ground outside the cab.

Retching and coughing, her head spinning with nausea, it took her a moment to realise that she was being watched, by a middle-aged woman in a car parked opposite, whose small eyes were fixed in deep disapproval on Alice's disarranged bikini top and the twin bulges of flesh where her breasts were pressed to the bottom of the cab window. She managed a weak smile and spat out the last of the lorry driver's spunk as his voice sounded from behind her.

'Nice blowjob, love. Right then, how about a cuppa?'

Ariesian glanced at his watch. It was going to take precise timing, to ensure that it was too late for Nich to move on elsewhere and take a significant number of people with him, but too early to make it difficult for him to set things up. In the valley below him, Nich and a dozen or so others, including the blond boy and the pregnant girl, were milling around in one of the roofless mine buildings. It was a foolish choice, because there was only room for a few dozen people, and several hundred were already scattered across the slopes, in small groups and ones and twos. If Nich wanted to make a proper display, he'd have to come out from the building.

A much better choice was a second, more ruinous structure a little way up the slope. The front had collapsed completely, leaving the interior open to most of the valley – an ideal spot to serve as the focus for the festival. Nich was evidently planning to use it for something, as a low structure, perhaps an altar, stood at the centre, spread with black cloth. At present it was empty. Ariesian nodded and turned to his group of riggers, security men and drivers who also served as general roustabouts, with Alice and the four exotic dancers he'd hired in Plymouth beyond.

'Okay, in we go,' he ordered. 'That building there, the one with the front wall gone. Try not to let 'em see you're coming, but once you're there, work fast.'

He was smiling to himself as the men set off down the slope. Of the people with Nich, most were women, with Horst and three others, only one of above average size, the only men present. If it came to force, there was no question at all who would win. For the moment, Nich hadn't even noticed, apparently busy helping Horst tether a large and irate black ram, presumably a sacrifice, into one corner of the building.

After a while he started down the slope himself, having realised that the takeover was going to be even easier than he had imagined. Nich's generator and sound system were woefully inadequate when compared with his own, while the police, who knew all about his own plans, were sure to take an interest in the sacrifice of the ram. Nich would be arrested and, while a few of the more rebellious spirits might make a fuss, the day would belong to him, Ariesian. After all, when it came down to it, official sanction, police backing, and the presence of TV crews weighed more than any amount of mere reputation.

One crew had already arrived, just a private production company but nevertheless worthwhile. They'd been filming the gathering crowd at the bottom of the valley, but started up towards him immediately as he entered the building where his crew were already setting up their equipment. Alice had followed, looking rather petulant in her abbreviated blue robe, beneath the hem of which the green triangle of bikini fabric covering her sex could just be seen.

'Do you know what he's up to here?' Ariesian asked, indicating the structure at the centre of the building.

'This is where the ancient circle was,' she answered. 'He must be planning to do something here.'

'I can see that,' he answered. 'What?'

'I don't know. Ask him.'

She nodded as she finished, and Ariesian turned to find Nich himself striding up the slope towards him, already in his black silk robes, his face set in anger, with the German boy and a pretty but rather hard-faced brunette tagging along behind. The TV crew were also drawing close, and as Alice quickly scuttled away into the background Ariesian was already pulling on his magnificent golden robe. As the two little groups approached, he stepped onto a convenient block of stone, giving himself enough extra height to ensure he'd be looking down on Nich's head.

The camera crew arrived first, but he raised a patient hand to silence them as the producer started on a question.

'I'll be with you in a moment, gentlemen. Meanwhile, by all means film.'

The crew didn't need prompting. The camera was already trained on Nich as he climbed the last few feet of slope with a face like thunder. Nich ignored them as if they weren't there, facing Ariesian instead.

'What are you doing here!?'

'A more appropriate question would be: what are you doing here?' Ariesian answered calmly.

'I suspect you know perfectly well,' Nich snapped. 'I am here to celebrate Samhain, in accordance with ancient tradition.'

'And I am here to celebrate Samhain with permission from the council and the support of the police,' Ariesian answered. 'I suggest you leave, or, if you wish to remain within the perimeter fence my people will shortly be setting up, that you pay your admission fee.'

Nich ignored him, folding his arms across his chest as he went on.

'Enough, Ariesian. Isn't it time you admitted the fraud you have inflicted on the Pagan community? Do you have no conscience? Leave the ground to me, Ariesian, but first, confess your crimes so that they can be recorded.'

'Crimes?' Ariesian laughed. 'What are you blathering about, Mordaunt? Everything I do is entirely above board, which is more than can be said for your own operation! What was it at Stanton Rocks, Nich? A Black Mass, wasn't it? Not to mention consorting with known prostitutes.'

'I acted as consultant to a group of Satanists, yes,' Nich admitted. 'They have the same right to worship as any others, and as to their priestess' profession –'

Ariesian interrupted with a rich, throaty laugh.

'Listen to you! Will you take a look at yourself, Nich? You really have no idea, do you? You're lost, an anachronism! Do you think you're Aleister Crowley, Francis Dashwood perhaps? That sort of behaviour won't be tolerated in modern Britain, Nich, oh no!'

A tiny black-haired woman had come up to stand beside Nich, her piercing eyes staring up at Ariesian. Nich held his hand up and spoke again.

'Do you deny the desecration of Wilsford Henge?'

'Wilsford Henge was a ring of rotting post holes,' Ariesian answered firmly. 'I bought the land, yes, and I built my house there, yes, in order to partake of the energy associated with the site. This is not desecration.'

'And do you also deny that your beliefs are false, your position a mere posture to extract money from those hoping for a resurgence of the old religion?'

'I deny it, absolutely.'

To his surprise Nich didn't press the point, but made a formal bow and withdrew. His companions followed, only the small woman lingering, to address him in a high-pitched voice full of laughter.

'You'd best see to your handmaidens.'

Ariesian looked about, puzzled, but Alice was nowhere to be seen and the four dancing girls were seated together on a patch of grass, smoking and sharing a bottle of vodka. Only when he looked a little further up the slope did he see Xiu Mei and Yi, and his mouth came open in surprise. Both were naked but for their panties and bras, along with shoes and the tattered remains of their beautiful silk dresses, cut to ribbons, but still on around their necks and waists. Both were walking, or rather stumbling, and he realised that their hands had been tied behind their backs. Both were gagged, their mouths straining on whatever had been stuffed inside and tied off with string. As he drew closer he realised that they did differ in one important aspect. Yi's plain white panties were only wet, while Xiu Mei's showed a round and suspiciously dark bulge hanging down beneath the tuck of her bottom.

'You didn't really expect him to confess and slink off with his tail between his legs did you?' Horst asked as they returned to their mine building.

'No,' Nich admitted. 'So then, if he's going to be here, we'd better do something to keep the attention on us.'

'We could prepare the sacrifice,' Rowena suggested.

'Good idea,' Nich agreed. 'That'll be better than anything he can manage.'

'It may also get us arrested,' Horst pointed out.

'The new exposure laws are ambiguous about female nudity,' Nich stated. 'Unless a deliberate display of genitals is made with the express purpose of causing distress, it's legal. Nobody could fairly claim we intend to cause distress. I asked that old fellow Pedlow after the wedding reception, and he ought to know. Thirty years as magistrate apparently.'

'Yes,' Horst objected, 'but they might arrest us anyway and make us prove our point. Maybe just in their panties?'

'Let the girls decide,' Nich said firmly.

'I'll be in robes, naturally,' Rowena put in.

'I'm going nude, sod the police,' Elune said happily as she ran up beside them.

Nich threw her a grin and stepped in under the door to the mine building. The ram was in the corner where they'd tethered him, tugging impatiently at his ropes and emitting bass, aggressive bleats. The girls were clustered around, except for Andrea and Coralie, who were rigging the sound and light systems with Horst's three friends. Poppy was with Charlotte and Eve, also a fifth black-haired, green-eyed girl, Lily. Juliana and Thomazina were sharing a huge tub of chocolate chip ice cream, one stark naked, the other in nothing but her knickers, both with glossy brown trickles running down over their chins and breasts. Melanie and Louisa were rather doubtfully inspecting the ram.

Against one wall a tripod held the largest of Rowena's chafing dishes, full to the brim with smouldering yellow incense that filled the air with sweet, heavy scent. Nich drew a little into his lungs, cautious of Rowena's skill at creating narcotic smoke, and almost at once felt himself lifted by a heady euphoria. Alice slid herself in through the single rear window, giggling as she embraced Nich.

'All set,' she said happily. 'It's good to be back. Oh, and by the morning Ramspound will be so much ash.'

'Elune told me,' Nich answered, kissed her and clapped his hands for attention. 'Listen, everybody, it's time to get ready. With Ariesian here we need to do what we can to keep the attention on ourselves, so if those girls who don't mind stripping off could set up the altar and everyone else do what they can to help.'

There was an immediate bustle of activity. Horst went outside, to find blocks for the base of the altar. Elune was already out there, her tiny, neatly proportioned body stark naked in the wan autumn sunlight, picking flowers. It was warm for October, but hardly balmy, yet for all her tiny size she appeared indifferent. So did Juliana and Lily, who quickly came out to join Elune, both stark naked, and showing the cold only in that their nipples were stiff.

Horst's cock was stirring in his pants as he watched the three girls work, happily nude and indifferent to the display of pussy they were making as they bent to pick the tiny yellow flowers. Nor was he the only one watching. Right across the valley there was a general movement in their direction, while up the slope Ariesian was alternately arguing with his dancers and calling for Alice in an increasingly loud and angry voice.

Alice stayed where she was, but Poppy came out, in nothing but a pair of diminutive black knickers, then Melanie and Louisa, naked. Coralie had seen, and abandoned the lighting rig to join them, stripping nude before teasing Poppy into removing her final garment. Eve appeared, nude and giggling, despite a flush of embarrassed pink on her cheeks, holding the altar clothes. Horst paused in his work, his cock now a rock-hard pole, wondering if they really were going to be allowed to go unmolested.

There had been two policemen in the car park, conspicuous in their brilliant yellow reflective jackets, but neither were visible. Up the slope, Ariesian's four girls were dancing, with slow, languid motions designed to show off their legs beneath their short blue tunics, but only a small minority of the rapidly swelling crowd were paying any attention.

A glance the other way showed the sun setting slowly towards the Atlantic Ocean, far too bright to look at, but casting a butter-yellow line across the tops of the gentle swells. It was nearly time, and unless things went very wrong very rapidly, it looked as if they would get away with it, and pull off an event that was sure to establish him as a legend.

Poppy's excitement was rising rapidly as she wove the little yellow flowers into a garland with trembling fingers. She was naked, stark naked, and outdoors, with several hundred people focused on her and her friends. It felt glorious, truly liberated, and a million miles from the stifling moral constraints from which she had worked so hard to break free. Soon, with the sacrifice and virgin's run completed, she would be making love with Horst, and she was more than happy for all the world to see.

With her first garland ready, she settled it neatly onto her thick black curls. Most of her friends were already similarly adorned, and right across the valley other girls, and men too, had begun to make garlands. Behind her, the altar was nearly ready, a low platform of stones spread with a black cloth and hung about with flowers. At the top of the slope, and across the valley, there seemed to be some difficulty with the fences Ariesian's people were trying to put up, but it made little difference.

Nich stepped out from the mine building, raising his hands, and as he spoke his voice boomed out across the valley from the speakers. A ragged cheer went up, and a second as Rowena emerged, svelte and elegant in pure black, her head crowned with flowers. Poppy hurried up the slope, to join the line of naked girls around their Priestess. Horst stepped out behind Nich, to stand with his well muscled arms folded across his chest and the light evening breeze tugging at the hem of his robe, and a third cheer rang out. In his hand he held the athame, the silver blade shining gold in the light of the setting sun.

232

Poppy could feel herself swelling with pride as maybe two thousand people focused on the tableau outside the old mine building. Her stomach was fluttering with excitement, but there was a touch of jealousy for Rowena, and more for Thomazina, although the thought of being given up to run naked among the crowd until some athletic and virile young man brought her down in the grass and simply fucked her brought more fear than thrill.

First came the sacrifice, and she turned as Troll and Rob appeared, hauling the reluctant ram between them. The great beast was starting to put up a fight, bleating and snorting, throwing his heavy shoulders from side to side. As the two men struggled to get the ram onto the altar, Horst reached out the athame, to let Rowena share his grip, their fingers entwined around the ebony handle.

Poppy watched, in mingled reverence and pity, as Troll finally forced the ram up onto the altar with a heave of his shoulders. Rowena and Horst began to chant the Samhain prayer, in perfect unison, his voice a rich boom, hers high and clear. Absolute silence had fallen over the valley, save for the furious, bass bleats of the ram and, as the chant rose to its peak and the athame came flashing down, Machiavelli gave a single, furious lunge, right towards Horst.

Horst went down like a bowling pin. Rowena shrieked as she hurled herself aside, a fraction too late. His horn caught in her robe, she went down with a scream even as the silk ripped, full on top of the beast. For one moment she was on his back, the tear in her robe wide to show her bottom, before tumbling off in a sprawl of limbs, to lie dazed and half naked on the ground.

Poppy shrieked, backing away as the ram gathered speed, straight at the line of girls. Lily screamed as she threw herself aside. Poppy tried to dodge, but struck against Eve, and the beast's shoulder smacked into her thigh, sending her tumbling backwards among the others. Coralie went down under her with a shriek of alarm, and for an instant the two of them were rolling on the ground in a tangle of limbs. She caught one final glimpse of the ram as he barrelled past, his huge leathery scrotum bouncing obscenely between his spindly black legs, and he was gone.

She got up, shaking and a little dizzy, her heart pounding, onto all fours. Above her, amplified a hundredfold by his powerful sound system, Ariesian's laughter rang out across the valley.

Father Somner stopped at the brow of the hill, to look down over Cape Cornwall, his mind burning with righteous indignation. There was a moment of surprise as he realised just how many people were there, just how far the rot had set in, but it did nothing to dampen his determination, just the opposite. Every word of the sermon he intended to deliver was etched clearly in his mind, and he had no doubt whatever that they would have the right effect. As always, all that was needed with those who had strayed from the path was a touch of gentle, but nonetheless firm, guidance.

Nich Mordaunt was another matter, and Father Somner's face set in a disapproving frown as he realised that some of the girls around one of the buildings were stark naked. Sure enough, Mordaunt was among them, easily distinguishable by his red hair and flapping black robes. He shook his head, wondering how anybody could possibly mistake Mordaunt for anything other than a Satanist, even for a moment.

There seemed to be some difficulty, although it was hard to see what, and he realised that a naked girl sprawled on the ground was the one who had helped Nich degrade him. He clicked his tongue in satisfaction, only for it to fade to annoyance as the memory came back, not only of his anger and shame, but the dreadful, irrepressible lust as she handled him and then exposed herself, before –

He shook his head, refusing to give way to temptation. Mordaunt's behaviour had been grossly immoral, hers no less so, and what they were doing in the valley seemed no less depraved. Nor was that all: the man Ariesian was also involved, with a separate installation a little way up the slope and, like Mordaunt, he had girls cavorting for the salacious pleasure of the crowd, only in this case in indecently short dresses rather than nude. Ignoring the abundant display of female flesh, he started down the slope.

At a crudely constructed fence a man tried to bar his way, demanding money. Several others were already arguing, and Father Somner merely sidestepped a clutching hand and strode past. Below him, Ariesian was performing some sort of heathen ritual, and the crowd were beginning to turn towards him, with Mordaunt's group in disorder. Father Somner hesitated, determined that his sermon should be delivered from the focal point of the event. Yet Ariesian had several burly men in attendance, while Mordaunt was largely surrounded by girls, and naked girls at that.

He continued, stoking his righteous anger with thoughts of the misguided ideas to which he intended to put a firm stop, and of Mordaunt's depravity. As he reached the top of the ground made rough by mine tailings, he saw that Mordaunt was struggling to regain control, his sound system blasting out in competition with Ariesian's, both men's words made nonsense by the other's.

Beside Mordaunt, two girls had climbed up onto the altar, one in a tattered black robe, the other stark naked and with the body of a succubus. The dressed girl raised her companion's arm as Mordaunt began to shout into the microphone in a redoubled effort to drown out Ariesian. Sure that some perverted pagan sex ritual was about to take place, and determined to nip it in the bud, Father Somner hurried on, stumbling over the rough ground. Coming close, he caught Mordaunt's words.

'. . . her virginity yours to take! Come then, all who think themselves worthy, to show your virility before the Goddess, to prove that you are worthy to take on the image of the Horned God!'

Father Somner's teeth ground in anger as he realised what was happening, a revival of one of the most indefensible of pagan customs, and just the sort of thing Mordaunt would do. The poor girl, undoubtedly coerced or brainwashed, was going to be made to run out into the ground, where she would be hunted down by men, like an animal, and raped. Fury spurred him on, jumping from rock to rock down the slope, feeling fit and sure footed as never before.

None of them had seen him, providing the perfect opportunity to slip through the window at the back of the building and come on them from behind, snatching the microphone from Mordaunt's hand. Reaching the rear wall, he peered within, to find it empty. An instant later he was through the window, where the air was thick with sweet-scented smoke that rose from a chafing dish to one side. Mordaunt was burning drugs, obviously, which explained the girl's acceptance of such gross immorality. He kicked out at the tripod in fury, knocking it over, to send up a burst of sparks and a cloud of choking smoke.

Mordaunt and others turned at the crash and Father Somner threw himself forward, grasping for the microphone, only to realise that the girl was already running, laughing in foolish, drug-induced glee as she dodged among the bracken. It had to be stopped, immediately, and his sermon could be preached to even better effect when she was safely rescued. Thrusting the celebrants aside, he leapt onto the altar, briefly catching a glimpse of Mordaunt's astonished face, lit red by the setting sun.

The girl was well ahead, and in the thick of the crowd, but as yet untouched. Still there was a chance to save her. The men were drunk, or high, and she seemed to have amazing energy, dodging their clutching hands and indifferent to the scratches of bracken and gorse. One huge, bear-like man tried to take her in his embrace but she wriggled free and darted off between a pair of gorse bushes. Another threw himself forward, trying to tackle her, but missed completely, and her laughter rang out like bells as he sprawled among the spiky foliage.

She was free, running up the far slope, but with at least two hundred men in pursuit, behind, and converging from the sides. Father Somner joined them, passing the drunken, the lazy, the fat, his legs burning but pushing him on with the strength and stamina of a thousand early morning runs. Again and again his robe caught on gorse or bracken or heather, but he forced himself on, up the steep slope, past one panting, exhausted man after another, until only he and a dozen of the fittest remained.

'Leave her!' he bawled. 'Rapists! Ungodly –'

He snatched at the tattooed arm of one half-naked runner, who went sprawling, buffeted another from the path and he was ahead. Spinning on his heel he turned to face them, gasping for breath. One came right at him, face set in a grotesque and idiotic leer, into which Father Somner drove his fist.

'Get back!' he yelled. 'Leave her alone! Can't you see she's been drugged!?'

Two stopped, more ran past. Again he turned. The girl was now fifty yards ahead with five men in pursuit. Snatching up the hem of his robe he followed, putting everything he had into the chase. She turned, heading along the ridge above the valley, inland. A man tripped in a rabbit scrape and went down with a gasp of pain, clutching at his ankle. Another gave up, falling to the ground. Father Somner passed the third, the second, pushed the last violently aside and he was alone, racing along a wide, grassy track with her flying hair, twinkling legs and bouncing bottom just yards ahead.

Again she turned, and glanced back, seeing him, that he was alone, and instantly slowing, to fall to her knees. He staggered the last few yards, trying to ignore the view he had of her bottom and the rear of her virgin sex. His head was spinning, his lungs on fire. He stopped, leaning on his knees as he fought for breath, but the words of comfort he'd intended died on his lips as she turned her head, and spoke.

'Take me, Lord.'

He stopped, his mouth falling open in shock at the raw lust in her face. Her great, green eyes were half-lidded, her scarlet mouth a little open, and beneath his robe his cock has started to grow. Lust hit him like a physical blow, the need to sheathe himself in her virgin sex so strong it hurt, and growing stronger.

'Oh, Lord, deliver me . . .' he began, but still she was looking at him, and the rich, thick cunt scent was invading his nostrils, and his cock had become a rigid pole, and his head was swimming with every image of lust he had ever fought down, sultry faces and thrusting breasts, soft-fleshed bellies and rounded bottoms, legs, and arms, and hair, and eyes, and lips, and cunts, a thousand cunts, cupped in tight blue denim or cotton panties, naked in the pages of a confiscated magazine, plump and wet and split and ready . . .

Father Somner screamed.

'No! Oh, Lord!'

The girl giggled.

It was impossible, his cock too hard, his lust too strong. Somehow he'd been bewitched, he knew, but that knowledge was no defence as he found himself clawing at the hem of his robe and falling to his knees behind the girl even as she gave her rump an inviting wiggle. One tug and his cock was free, in his hand, a burning rod, against her sex, moist and welcoming, pushing at the hole, her hymen taut, and in, up her, slippery with blood and juice as he rammed himself home with a final groan of despair.

He fucked her, unable to stop himself, surrendered himself to pagan ecstasy as he clutched at the soft flesh of her hips, slamming himself in again and again, to make her bottom bounce and shiver, to ring screams and gasps from her open lips. In just seconds he was coming, and as his eyes went wide he saw it in front of him, what he'd thought had been a twisted hawthorn tree, mere wood and leaf, now a great knotted figure, autumn green and brown as horn, great antlers sprouting from the laughing face, a monstrous penis projecting out . . .

. . . a simple dead branch, but he had already filled the girl's cunt with sperm, and there was no doubt whatever in his mind that he had seen the Horned God.

* * *

'Why's he praying to a tree?' Nich queried, slitting his eyes against the awkward light in an effort to make out exactly what was happening on the opposite hillside.

The sun had gone down, and the lights were on, along with a multitude of torches sold by Ariesian's followers. A thousand confusing shadows crowded the valley, but Thomazina's run, and her surrender, had been plain for all to see.

'As a Green Man?' Rowena suggested.

'That's Father Somner!' Charlotte answered.

Rowena shrugged. Across the valley, Thomazina had risen to her feet and waved before turning to the men who were rapidly surrounding her, losers in the race for the privilege of her virginity, but still hoping for a consolation prize. One, at least, was going to get it: Thomazina was going down on her knees, presumably to suck him, although she was blocked from view.

'Will she be okay?' Rowena queried.

'She'll be fine,' Juliana answered her, 'but look.'

Nich glanced up to where she was pointing. Three yellow-jacketed figures were clambering over Ariesian's makeshift fence, clearly intent on where Thomazina was now invisible in a ring of men. There were other hotspots, several couples also giving in to the what was rapidly becoming an atmosphere of unrestrained sexuality. Above them, Ariesian was standing on the black-covered structure, a microphone in one hand, the other raised high as he spoke.

'... celebrate, my friends, yes, celebrate, but be careful to keep your activities within the law of the land. Be restrained. Be considerate of other people's values, which may not be your own. My friends, we cannot behave like criminals, not if we are to spread our message far and wide ...'

'Now?' Nich queried.

'Now,' Alice answered him.

He took her hand, and Juliana's, and started up the path towards where Ariesian was preaching. Elune and Lily followed a little way behind, leaving the others to continue the celebration, the ritual complete. Ariesian continued to talk into the microphone as Nich approached, with several cameras trained on him as he urged the crowd to a peaceful and sober festival. Only when Nich and his companions were directly in front of him and the cameras had swivelled round to take both in did he turn, raising his chin as he faced them.

'Are you proud of your behaviour, Mordaunt?' he demanded. 'Is this your intention, to have the great resurgence of Pagan belief viewed as no more than a drunken, promiscuous rabble?'

Nich ignored the question.

'I grant you one final chance, Ariesian. Confess your falsity.'

'You!?' Ariesian laughed. 'You grant me nothing!'

'So be it,' Nich answered, and bowed deeply. 'As you refuse to yield, it seems I must do so. I accept you, Ariesian, as the manifestation of the Horned God, deity made flesh, to give seed to the Mother and bring bounty from the land, from Beltane dawn to Samhain dusk, when you return to the Earth.'

Fully amplified by his own system, his voice boomed out across the valley. Done, he stepped back, his head bowed, and Alice took his place, stepping forward, falling to her knees, a black object held out in her clasped hands.

Ariesian vanished in a flutter of golden robes and black cloth.

Nich leant forward, to peer down into the gaping black mine shaft where Ariesian had stood a moment before.

* * *

Charlotte sighed as she put her lips to Rowena's pouted sex. Outside the building she heard a sullen thump and the light grew suddenly dimmer, but she paid no attention. Naked on her knees, her hands were cupped around her heavy, distended belly, revelling in the feel of being pregnant as she gave tongue duty to her lover and Priestess. Rowena was standing, her upper body against a wall, her tattered robe lifted, her bare bottom pushed well out for Charlotte's attention.

Horst and Poppy were at the door, guarding against intrusion, and as Charlotte used her tongue tip to lap and tease at the creases and folds of soft flesh between Rowena's thighs and bottom cheeks her whole existence was focused on what she was doing. Even with the rising volume of shouts and shrieks from beyond the wall she continued, caressing her bulging belly and already milk-swollen breasts, wriggling her tongue into the tight dimple of Rowena's bumhole, probing the moist vagina until she could feel the tension of the skin that held it virgin, kissing at the tight bud of the clitoris ...

'Police, hundreds of the fuckers, run!' a male voice screamed, almost in her ear.

Charlotte jerked back as Rowena swore. For one instant Troll's bearded face was visible in the doorway, lit by torches, and he was gone. Beyond, flickering lights filled the valley, the yellow of Ariesian's torches and the white of police flashlights. Rowena swore again, already grappling among the discarded clothes that littered the floor. Sobbing in near panic, Charlotte snatched out, her hand finding the thin cotton of a pair of panties.

Clumsy in her desperation to get dressed, she jerked them up her legs, realising too late that they were far too small. Her foot was on wool, a jumper, and she grabbed for that instead, pulling it quickly on. It was male, huge, easily enveloping her nudity. White light stabbed in at the rear window, blinding her. A harsh, male voice called out, ordering her to stay put. It was met by a stream of abuse from Rowena, and Charlotte was already on her feet, wrenching the absurdly small panties up around her bottom as she staggered for the door.

She made it, rushing out into the night, not knowing where she was going, as long as it was away. A beam of light swept over her, and a second, from behind, where the slope was thick with police. Ahead were only yellow torches, and a confused rabble of people, some running, some apparently too dazed to react, some shouting abuse at their tormentors. Charlotte ran, the same way Thomazina had fled, down across the shallow valley floor and up the far side, only to find the slope too much for her. She slowed, gasping and clutching her belly. Fear and self-pity welled up as she realised she had no chance of escape, and she screamed in despair as a powerful male arm took hold of her, then another.

'Come on!' a voice urged and she was moving again, stumbling as she was pulled up the slope and into the welcome night.

Behind her all was chaos, in front, peace, near blackness with just the occasional shadow moving furtively up the slope among the gorse bushes and lonely hawthorns. She let the men guide her, on and up, until at last they released her arms. Exhausted, she slumped down and rolled over, vaguely wondering if they would expect blowjobs for their help and a touch guilty because the idea excited her so much.

'Thank you,' she panted, 'thank you . . .'

The response was a bass grunt as a massive body forced her thighs wide, and as she screamed in shock a rigid cock head pushed to the crotch of her minuscule panties. She began to struggle, instinctively, but a thick scent caught her nose, animal and intensely male, pushing her fear aside and replacing it with an urgent, heady lust. A great black figure loomed over her, blotting out the stars, his head a massive bulk, from the side of which great curled horns protruded and she realised it had come true, her deepest fantasy, to be caught and taken by the Horned God.

His huge, rock-hard cock was pushing to the crotch of her knickers, and even as she cried out in ecstasy at what was to be done to her the thin cotton ripped asunder. Her body filled, his massive cock plunged deep into her willing, cream-wet hole and she was being fucked. A single motion snatched her jumper up to bare her breasts to her God and her arms were around him, clinging tight as his penis drove into her in a frenzied, exalted pumping far beyond the human.

As she was taken, her ecstasy was far beyond anything she had experienced before. The full glory of having a powerful male on top of her and working his cock in her vagina, and so much more, brought utter rapture which in moments had tipped over into orgasm. Her pussy had spread, thick, curling pubic hair rubbing on her clitoris as she was fucking, to keep her up, in climax that went on and rising, rising and falling as she squirmed beneath him.

When his spunk exploded inside her she was brought higher still, and higher, as the thick rod of his cock slipped free of her hole, to jam hard into the groove of her sex, rubbing between her lips and full on her clitoris as gout after gout of burning come was ejaculated over her pregnant belly, to take her to a final, screaming, thrashing peak before she finally fainted.

* * *

Rowena ran through the flickering light. The police were coming down the slope, slowly but for a few who had gone ahead. None were focused on her, but the thought of arrest, semi-naked, was unbearable. They were sure to be looking for her, and to run barefoot across the valley, among gorse and tailings dumps, could only delay the inevitable. She had to hide.

Ducked low, she pushed on, up towards the upper mine buildings, intent on evading the search line. White beams were flicking to every side, illuminating greens and browns, people, and once a nightmare vision, of Mac, his brown haunches jerking on top of a gape-mouthed, wide-eyed Chinese girl as he fucked her doggy-style. More scared than ever, she quickened her pace, darting alongside a wall, to where Ariesian's generator stood silent, a hunched black shape, with a tarpaulin beside it.

Quickly, she pulled herself under, ignoring the oily smell, and curled into a ball against the rocky wall, making herself as shapeless as possible. No lights had caught her as she hid, and she was praying the men would pass as she stayed frozen, in absolute blackness, her heart jumping at every sound.

Voices came, close, and not the angry or frightened calls of the pagans, but level, confident talking, between individuals and into radios. She redoubled her prayers, the voices passed, and slowly, gradually the other noises grew faint, until at last all was silent. Finally, after an unknown amount of time, she risked peeping out from under the tarpaulin.

Nobody was visible. The only lights were where Ariesian had been, and across the valley. Stealthily, she extracted herself from under the tarpaulin and started back towards the mine building, wanting her clothes, and her car keys. It was absolutely dark, no lights within three, four hundred yards, and her hopes rose as she approached, only for her heart to leap wildly as a voice spoke just feet away, in an urgent whisper.

'Rowena! No, there are men in there, waiting for us.'

It was Nich's voice, and she ducked down next to him, her legs weak with relief. He took her arm, gently, and led her a little way up the slope, to an area of soft grass among the bracken, beneath a jut of rock. She put her arm around him, her body shivering. Together they watched the lights dance in the valley moving up and down as the last of the pagans were herded back towards the road. Finally, none remained, and Rowena had drifted into sleep.

She woke to orange light from one of Ariesian's torches, and cold air on her face, although her body was warm. Nich sat beside her, naked, his robe spread over her, his face serene. As he saw that she was awake he turned her his wicked smile. She smiled back, the events of the night before already marching through her head.

'Do you suppose everyone's alright?' she asked.

'They'll be fine,' he assured her. 'I helped Lottie get away, over the hill opposite.'

'Good, thank you. I think Ariesian called the police in, when he saw things weren't going his way, the bastard!'

Nich simply chuckled.

'We did it though, didn't we?' she sighed, and paused. 'Nich, tell me the truth? Thomazina . . . Thomazina, Juliana, Alice, their sisters. They're not quite . . . quite . . .'

'No,' Nich answered, 'they're not.'

'And you?'

Nich merely grinned, the orange light flickering across his features. Rowena lay back with a sigh, lifting her knees and letting her thighs come apart, to show and yield her virgin sex. Nothing needed to be said. Nich moved to her side, kissed her tenderly on her cheek, her forehead, her lips, and as he climbed between her welcoming thighs their mouths came open together.

High above them, Mr Pedlow sat gaping at his screen, his hand hammering at his cock. All night, frustration had followed frustration, his cameras catching plenty of bare flesh, but nothing really rude. No more. His eyes were starting from his head, fixed on his perfect view of Rowena's most intimate details, her legs rolled high, her bottom spread, her anus a perfect star of pink lines leading down to the central hole, her cunt a wet, pink oval of fleshy folds, but no gaping mouth. Instead, a glistening, ruddy pink hymen blocked all but a tiny part of the entrance, with Nich's hard cock poised above it, ready to deflower her, to take her, to fuck her, to spoil her . . .

Nich pushed, and Mr Pedlow's eyes bulged out as he saw Rowena's cunt open, her hymen pressed in, deeper, and split. He heard her cry. He saw the blood spatter Nich's erection as it was driven home. He came, gout after gout of spunk erupting from his cock as every muscle in his body seemed to lock as one, focused on his straining cock, his stomach, his chest as ecstasy turned to pain.

Nich clung tight to Rowena, his delight in her surrender as strong as the physical ecstasy of having his cock sheathed in the tightness of her body. She clung to him, shivering, her mouth hot against his. He took his time, not wanting to rush the moment, but keeping his cock easing slowly in and out of her pussy. It would sting, he knew, but she didn't seem to care, in a state of rapture beyond a simple physical response.

Only when he could barely hold himself back did he reach down, to withdraw his cock into his hand and press the head between her sex lips. She moaned, her body tightening and her kisses growing yet more passionate as he began to rub himself on her clitoris. Nich also was on the edge of orgasm, the flesh of his cock so sensitive his own muscles were twitching against hers as he fought to hold back. Rowena's thighs locked on his body, her arms clamped tight around his back and she was there, coming under his cock as he rubbed. Her whole body was in violent contraction, her mouth crushed to his, and even as his cock jerked in his hand he was pushing it deep up into her body.

They came together, locked tight in each other's arms, Nich's cock driven so deep into her sex he could feel the mixture of pussy juice and sperm and virgin blood squeezing out over his balls and into her twitching anus. More came out as he lifted, to treat himself to one last, deep penetration, the final thrust of her virgin fuck.

High on the slope, Mr Pedlow lay dead in his harness.

Epilogue

Aileve gave the sea a final glance to make sure no yachts were nearby, allowed a wave to carry her some way up the smooth stone slope and pulled herself from the water. A quick scramble and she was clear of the wash and stretching herself in the cool autumn sunlight. To the north and east the coast of Cornwall showed as a low, hazy bulk, while two container ships were moving along the Channel to the south, too far away to be a nuisance.

She paused to wring out her hair and to pluck a ribbon of green weed from one of her breasts, now once more a svelte rise rather than the fat balloons with which she had tempted Ariesian. Further up the rock, Elune and Juliana sat against the lighthouse wall, sunning themselves. Aileve raised a hand in lazy greeting and padded up the rock. She kissed both girls before seating herself where a few tufts of grass and thrift had managed to find purchase in the shelter of the lighthouse.

'So,' Juliana asked, 'will you miss being Dr Alice Chaswell?'

'Yes,' Aileve admitted, 'but it was beginning to get difficult. My female colleagues kept asking me for beauty tips, and I really couldn't be bothered with the whole ageing process, so she had to go. Why not do it in style?'

Juliana nodded her agreement.

'Were there any consequences?' Aileve asked.

'They've worked it all out,' Elune stated, 'the press, that is, and presumably the police.'

Aileve laughed.

'Any juicy details?'

'It depends which paper you read,' Elune went on. 'The tabloids are the best. There's lots about the marks of cloven hooves . . .'

'That would be Horst's ram.'

'Absolutely, though one paper has witnesses to say that Satan came to take Ariesian away in person.'

'I read a slightly less dramatic one,' Juliana put in. 'They claim that the naïve young archaeologist Dr Alice Chaswell was seduced by the Pagan leader and notorious Satanist known as Ariesian, who ritually abused her over a period of months. Finally his perverted demands grew too much, and she hatched an elaborate plot with her sisters, to kill him at a depraved satanic orgy called the Halloween Festival of the Dead.'

'The what?'

'Don't ask me, that's what it said. Apparently you were unable to endure the shame of what Ariesian had done to you, or face the consequences of your crime, and leapt to your death from the cliffs of Cape Cornwall, hand in hand with your sister. Neither body has been recovered, but a suicide note has been found, while the third sister has not been found and is assumed to have also committed suicide.'

'Fair enough. How about Lily and Thomazina, and Nich?'

'They all got taken in for questioning,' Elune answered, 'but as Juliana's note blames the three of us and there's no evidence, they were released.'

'Good. How did the fire go?'

'Burnt to the ground,' Elune said with satisfaction. 'Second time.'